THE SWEET SCENT OF DEATH

Lesley St. James

For Surya

CHAPTER 1

I was late again for work. I don't know if I slept through the alarm, if I hadn't set it, or if there had been a malfunction. The reason didn't matter. I was late again for the third time that week, and it really wasn't the day to be late. It was the day of the Eshellon Cosmetics fall fragrance event, an event I had been putting together for months and that was costing hundreds of thousands of dollars. On this day, being late probably meant being unemployed.

In a panic I stumbled around my minuscule studio apartment yanking clothes from the closet so fast I heard stitches pop. There was no time to shower and no time for makeup, a cardinal sin in the world of beauty public relations. I'd just have to throw some mascara on in the cab. That thought brought me up short. There wouldn't be a yellow cab in Astoria at this time of day, and an hour-long subway ride was not an option. I could Uber, but there was an even quicker solution.

I grabbed my Behemoth Black Bag, the bag that carried all my city-dweller essentials, and fished in it for my wallet, praying all the while that I had cash. A glance at my wallet revealed a crisp twenty-dollar bill and a fiver. I was flush. I dug out my cell phone, leaped four feet to the refrigerator, and grabbed the business card stuck to the door, more out of habit than necessity. The number was difficult to forget. I hastily dialed 718-MEXICAR.

"Guadala-Car-a. Where are you?" chirped the heavily accented voice.

"I need a pick up at…."

"Si, Señora Jill. Fi' minutes."

Click.

Yeah, they knew me. At the rate I was going, I was probably putting the dispatcher's kid through college.

Five minutes actually meant four and change to my favorite cabbie, Jorge, the proprietor and lead driver of the Guadala-Car-a gypsy cab service of Astoria, Queens. While the citizens of Manhattan have but to step out their doors and whistle to summon a metered cab, those big yellow taxis are few and far between in the outer boroughs. We bridge and tunnel trash had to make do with unmetered "car services" usually run by immigrants from Central and South America. Car-gentina, Van-ama, and Lima-Limo were all quality car services with an interesting and only marginally unsafe array of vehicles, but for my money, Guadala-Car-a was the fastest, cheapest, and most fascinating. Jorge and company had never let me down.

I was just putting on some socks when the blare of the *La Cucaracha* car horn announced his arrival. I shoved my feet into some loafers, grabbed my Behemoth Black Bag, checked to make sure I had everything I'd need for the day, and raced out the door.

A maroon Lincoln Town Car of an eighties vintage was parked at the curb in front of my building. My old pal Jorge was at the wheel. It was 8:56.

"Good morning, Señora Jill," sang Jorge, a lean, clean-shaven man with wavy black hair cut short on the sides but long and flowing on top, almost like a pompadour. His hair game was strong. If I ever scored a shampoo client, Jorge was going to be my model.

"Morning, Jorge," I replied. "And it's *Señorita* Jill." A mischievous smile flitted across the cabbie's face.

Once settled on the velour backseat, I made a mental checklist of the day's tasks. First on the list was to meet the client in Central Park for a walk-through of the space for the night's event. I was supposed to meet the head of Eshellon Cosmetics' internal PR department, Meredith Hopkins, at 9:00. It was 8:58. If Jorge really put on the gas, we might make it from Queens to Manhattan by 9:20. Might. I quickly texted Meredith to let her know I was running late.

Second on the list was the final dress fitting for the star of the show, actress and model Juliet Scott. The fitting would be followed by confirmation calls to all the vendors, follow-up calls to all the reporters who were supposed to attend, social media posts promoting the event, ferrying all the press materials to Central Park, a final walk-through of the event space with the inevitable trouble-shooting of last-minute problems, and, finally, a trip home to get ready for the event before another car ride back to Central Park. It was going to be a heck of a day.

You know why you're late.

Yes, I admitted to my subconscious. *I do.*

The real reason I was late had nothing to do with my alarm clock. I didn't want to go to work because I didn't want to face the pressure of knowing that if only one thing fell through the cracks, the whole PR campaign could be ruined. I didn't want to fail.

Jill Cooksey does not fail.

I had been high school valedictorian and Phi Beta Kappa in college. I had been offered jobs at every public relations firm I had applied to, but as soon as I went to work at the prestigious Waverly Communications, all my confidence in my abilities had evaporated. From day one, it seemed that my boss, Waverly vice president and resident task-master Pamela Van Princis, was just waiting for me to screw up. She rode me hard, even though she was rarely in the office, blowing up my cell phone with texts and calls at all hours. She was quick to pick apart my work, and I couldn't remember a single word of praise crossing her lips. After three years, I got promoted from account assistant to account executive, and that should have renewed my confidence. Instead it just added more pressure. Two years after that, I moved up to senior account executive—more clients, more criticism, even more pressure. Now, I was at a breaking point. If anything went wrong with the Eshellon event, I was going to quit and go home to Virginia.

"Doughnut?" asked Jorge as if he sensed my need for serotonin. He held a pink bakery box over the seat, and my stomach let loose with a leonine growl.

Cheeks hot with embarrassment, I thanked him and chose a chocolate frosted with sprinkles. Two more doughnuts and thirty-two minutes later, we pulled up to the entrance to Conservatory Garden, an exquisite formal garden within Central Park and the site for the Eshellon Cosmetics fall fragrance event. I paid Jorge and climbed out of the car. Several passersby were staring at it, and I think it had something to do with the row of air fresheners in the shape of luchador masks lining the rear window. Jorge wasted no time in speeding off to a chorus of *La Cucaracha*.

As I was thirty minutes late, Meredith Hopkins was already there tapping the toe of her tidy leather boot and looking pointedly at her Cartier Tank Américaine watch. Before I could come up with a suitable excuse, she held up a perfectly manicured hand.

"Save the excuses, Jill. In Dallas, being on time is part of being a professional, but this isn't Dallas, sadly."

Somewhere between forty and fifty, Meredith Hopkins

didn't look a day over thirty-five, a testament to the quality of Eshellon's product line. A native Texan, she was sun-kissed in a delicate way. A smattering of tiny freckles dusted her nose, and her face and hands were lightly bronzed without being tanned. Her frosted blonde shoulder-length hair served as a foil for her warm, healthy complexion, and she sported a fitted gray suit accented with an olive green scarf the exact shade of her eyes. She certainly knew how to put herself together. I suddenly felt a bit insufficient in my dress yoga pants, turtleneck sweater, and loafers, but I reminded myself that I had been dressing for warmth and hard work, not a limo ride.

"I'm very sorry, Meredith. Let's check out the space. Shall we?" I tried to sound chipper as I led the way into Conservatory Garden.

The morning was sunny, and the dew was evaporating from the late roses that grew in abundance. It was going to be a beautiful event providing everything fell into place. Conservatory Garden is a formal garden made up of many smaller gardens and terraces. I was glad to see that the nearly circus-sized tent and stage were just as I had left them the day before, set up on the immaculate lawn. Above the lawn on a u-shaped terrace was a space for dancing. I led a sulky, grunting Meredith through each of the event areas while explaining how the evening would go down. The food was coming from the restaurant of a trendy TV chef, the flowers from the hottest celebrity floral designer. But the crowning achievement was all my doing—well, mine and my mother's.

Juliet Scott, one of the stars of the most popular sitcom on television, *Singletons*, was the guest of honor for the evening. She was also the Eshellon Cosmetics spokeswoman, thanks to my negotiation skills—and the fact that her mother was my mother's best friend. To think a girl could be well-connected simply because she came from little Luthersburg, Virginia. Signing Juliet was a proud moment for me, and I half-expected some congratulations from my boss, Pamela. Luckily I was used to disappointment. Still, that accomplishment gave me some value in the eyes of my client, even if I was perpetually late.

Meredith must have been pleased with the arrangements in Central Park because she offered me a ride back to the office in her limo. Next on the to-do list—the dress fitting.

When we arrived at the office, I could hardly contain my laughter. Tanya, our Holly Golightly of an account assistant, was tottering around the office on her stilettos with a bottle of fancy European sparkling water in one hand and a lime in the other.

"Does anyone have a knife?" she asked.

I made a show of patting my pockets.

"Not on me."

Her work attire was one-part refugee chic, one-part Tokyo fashion week disaster—a short, shapeless, long-sleeved, and asymmetrical gray dress paradoxically slit open from the neck to the belly button. I was pretty certain a couple of strips of double-stick tape were the only things standing between Tanya's breasts and the rest of the world. The dress was entirely inappropriate for a place of business and entirely Tanya. As if in sympathy with the plight of the dress, her hair was also asymmetrically cut and very severe, as was the kohl eyeliner thickly framing her eyes. As she stumbled around the office on those stilts she called shoes, three words came to mind—Bride of Frankenstein. I made a mental note to sneak a snapshot before the day was over, for posterity or Instagram. It wouldn't be hard to do. Tanya rarely acknowledged my exis-tence even though she was only an account assistant while I was a senior account executive. Even when I outright asked her to do something for me, she had a way of acknowledging the task without ever recognizing me, as if she were receiving instructions from on high.

While Tanya was yanking open every drawer in the office in search of a knife, everyone else was standing around looking uptight, like some hidden bomb was about to explode. Jeannie, Pamela's middle-aged assistant, came bustling out of the conference room.

"Thank goodness! Get in there!"

I shot Meredith a perplexed look, but she just shrugged back at me.

"I'll do all I can," I replied, even though I had no idea what I was walking into. Meredith followed me into the conference room where my boss Pamela Van Princis, spokesmodel Juliet Scott, Eshellon Cosmetics President Hoss Buckworth, and a seamstress were all sitting at the conference table with varying expressions of misery on their faces. When I entered, everyone looked up at me expectantly, and I could have sworn that Juliet winked.

I hadn't seen her much in the last few years, since I was in college and then in New York and she was in L.A.—just the occasional Thanksgiving or Christmas meeting at the mall or market back in Luthersburg. She was at my father's funeral though, which I thought was sweet. The press was too. I think Dad must have been laughing in heaven at the fame he acquired after death with a television star attending his funeral. By then she was a movie star too, having just completed her first film role, a supporting part in a romantic comedy. Decent reviews. Her star was on the rise. Now with the Fall Fantasy campaign, we had rekindled our friendship.

"Juliet darling, I'm so sorry I wasn't here to greet you," I purred. "I've been setting up for your big event. Hoss, I haven't seen you since Dallas. How are you?"

"Right as rain, Miss Jill," said the gigantic, silver-haired Texan. He had been married to Shelley Buckworth, Eshellon's founder, for thirty years and had inherited the company several years before when she lost her battle with cancer. By all accounts, Shelley had been a classy lady—the salt of the earth, hardworking, and kind—and Hoss had been devastated. Then about a year later, so the rumor mill said, he discovered Viagra and that life was not yet over for him. He started chasing skirts and found the hobby suited him. I hadn't seen him since we pitched the business, but I remembered him as a loud but likable fellow. And I loved it when he called me Miss Jill. Somehow it took me home.

I turned to Pamela. "So where are we?"

"We're in a bit of a predicament," she replied evenly. "It's the dress." Her flushed face looked even pinker than usual against snowy white linen that I knew had never seen the subway. As always, Pamela's Barbie-blonde hair was perfectly highlighted, her eyebrows perfectly arched, her nails perfectly shellacked in vixen red. Working for a cosmetics company, you had to walk the walk, but there was something altogether too perfect about my boss.

"It's a lovely dress," smiled Juliet, "but I just don't know about it."

The seamstress sat in her chair and fumed.

"I don't know much about dresses," offered Hoss, "but I think you would look perfect in just about anything." I couldn't tell if the old charmer was flirting or just offering a sincere compliment.

Juliet gave him a smile of thanks and returned to her examination of the gown.

The garment in question was a gorgeous scarlet velvet creation cut on the bias with long, tight sleeves and a slit up to the hip. It was draped across the table, and I could tell that Juliet, with her black-brown hair and ivory complexion, would look like a million dollars in it and hopefully sell a million bottles of perfume.

"I believe Tanya has some refreshments in the other room."

I smiled. "Why don't we take a break and you all help your-selves to a glass while Juliet and I catch up?"

Pamela, Meredith, and Hoss immediately took that as their cue to let me "deal with the talent" and headed for the door followed by the seamstress.

"Don't forget me!" shouted a laptop that was lying open on the conference table, making me jump and bang my knee.

"Oh, Dustin! Sorry, son." Hoss picked up the laptop and held it out for me to see. "This is my son, Dustin Buckworth. He's holding down the fort in Dallas, but he's attending this meeting via Zoom."

"Pleased to meet you," I said to the face on the screen. I could make out brown hair and tortoiseshell glasses, but not much more. Wherever Dustin was, the lighting was terrible.

"Likewise," he responded. Then Hoss carried him, I mean the computer, from the room. I shut the door, and both Juliet and I started to giggle.

"I love these performances," she said between fits of laughter.

"You better watch it, or you'll develop a reputation for being difficult."

"Hey, somebody has to make you look like a super-publicist. You're completely under-appreciated around here, Jilly."

"Maybe," I replied lamely.

"Maybe, nothing!" Juliet looked me straight in the eye, but when she saw me start to flush, she relented and changed the subject to comfortable territory. As she started to peel out of her clothes and into the gown, we chatted about home. Her father's tomato crop had been glorious this year. Our mothers were taking a pottery class together.

"So how have you been?" I asked casually. To my surprise, Juliet avoided my gaze.

"I'm okay."

Now I don't like to pry, and it wasn't like Juliet and I were best friends, but when the woman most recently proclaimed by *Elle* to be the "It-Girl" says she's only okay, even I have to give in to curiosity.

"You don't sound okay. Is something the matter?"

Juliet sighed loudly.

"You could say that." She paused, and I got the impression that she was wrestling with whether she should say more. "I don't want to talk about it here, but maybe we can talk about it tomorrow, when the event is over."

"Cool," I replied. I'm not pushy…much. "We can go to lunch or something and have a nice long chat."

"Could we do it at your place?"

"Sure," I said while silently brainstorming ways to make a Queens studio apartment not look like a Queens studio apartment. I gave her my address and she typed it into her phone. "I guess we have to let them back in now, huh?"

"Ready when you are," said Juliet, and she was. Our spokesmodel was stunning in red velvet that hugged in all the right places. I made a mental note to go to the gym more, the same mental note I made every day.

I opened the conference room door expecting to find everyone in the lobby sipping sparkling water with lime. Instead, I saw Meredith and Pamela tending to Tanya who was sitting in a chair with her head between her knees, two of her fingers bandaged, while Hoss tried to position the laptop so Dustin could see what was happening and the seamstress looked on disapprovingly. They promptly abandoned the girl, who could have been dying for all I knew, at the sight of Juliet in her finery. The seamstress immediately began pulling and tucking while Meredith and Pamela oohed and aahed and generally sucked up.

"Tanya break a nail?" I managed to ask between exclamations.

"She cut herself trying to twist off the bottle cap," explained

Pamela. "Poor thing. They shouldn't be allowed to put the caps on so tight."

I made another mental note—to hold an office seminar on how to use a bottle opener.

"Well, what do we have here?" A booming voice I recognized all too well snapped me out of my reverie. I turned to greet the big boss, CEO William Waverly of Waverly Communications, but Pamela beat me to it.

"William, you must meet our spokesmodel, Juliet Scott, and our client, Hoss Buckworth," crooned Pamela as she practically knocked me down to get to Mr. Waverly. Our boss, a legend in the beauty PR business and a notorious loud talker, was actually quite a small man. At age eighty, he wasn't as hands-on as he once was, at least not with the business. Whether he was hands-on with VP Pamela Van Princis, well that was the cause of much office speculation.

Taking him familiarly by the arm, Pamela guided him over to Juliet where he took her hand in both of his and peered up into her face because in heels she had a good seven inches on him.

"You look ravishing, my dear. An asset to our team. I can't wait to show you off at tonight's event, which will be one of Waverly Communications' proudest moments, thanks to you and to Pamela's tireless efforts on behalf of Eshellon Cosmetics."

Did you catch that last part?

"I think Jill deserves the lion's share of the credit," ventured Juliet, and my heart leaped at the idea of acknowledgment.

"Jill?" Mr. Waverly looked confused.

Juliet gestured to me, and he turned in my direction but looked at me like I was a stranger. He turned back to Juliet.

"Well, Pamela has always been good at assembling a strong team."

Sigh.

When all the hoopla was over, Juliet, Hoss, and Meredith were dispatched in a limousine, and I retreated to my office for lunch, a little peace and quiet, and a good sulk. My office was small, about six by six, with a window that overlooked the roof of the building next door. I could crawl out the window and onto the roof if I wanted to, and sometimes I did. I shut my door, sat down at my neat-as-a-pin desk, and rummaged through my Behemoth Black Bag for my lunch. That morning I'd had only enough time to grab a yogurt, a granola bar, and a banana, but it was better than nothing.

I started in on the yogurt, and my mind turned to Juliet. She was her usual feisty self that morning, but something was going on in her life. I had no doubt. I wondered what it could be. Bad boyfriend? Substance abuse? (She *was* a movie star.) Illness? Or maybe she just felt unfulfilled by all the money, fame, and adoration. Yeah, right. I let my imagination run wild for a second, as I often do, and then shut it off. I sincerely hoped it was nothing worse than the early signs of crow's feet, but I had a nagging suspicion Juliet had something important to talk about. I mean, she was prepared to schlep out to Queens to talk about it when we could have just ordered room service at the Waldorf Astoria Hotel.

With difficulty, I made myself forget Juliet for the moment and instead thought about all the work that I still had to do before the event that evening: lots of phone calls, then waiting around in Conservatory Garden for all the vendors to show up, then a mad dash home to make myself presentable. (Although after seeing Juliet in that gown, what was the point?) A wave of panic washed over me as I once again pictured the entire event falling apart. I felt overwhelmed. Pamela and Tanya weren't going to help me. The whole thing rested on my shoulders.

Jill Cooksey doesn't fail.

Actually, Jill Cooksey might. After five years in public relations, I'd learned a lot about the business, and I was starting to rethink my career choice. PR was considered glamorous, which meant that you got paid next to nothing to do the job because the job itself was supposed to be the reward. And it was a lot of fun when I got to meet celebrities, go to events, and score goody bags. But the "glamorous" nature of the industry also attracted a few ineffectual do-nothings like Tanya who liked to go to parties but didn't like to do the work involved to make those parties happen. Add a sagging economy that had forced PR firms to operate on skeleton crews and you got my situation—no help from above or below.

As if by magic, my computer started dinging, and an email from my friend Kate popped up on the screen. Kate was my counterpart at another firm, and her situation was nearly identical to mine. We had spotted each other at a cosmetics trade show and struck up a friendship. Kate knew another woman in the same predicament who in turn knew somebody else. We all started hanging out together complaining about our companies, clients, bosses, and underlings, as well as men, fashion, books, and food. In short, we became the best of friends, and in no time we had formed our PR Posse.

The Posse came about because we all found ourselves overworked with our respective PR firms understaffed. We also found that the periods of intense activity at our agencies were sporadic, so we made a little pact. Even though we worked for rival firms with rival clients, we all felt more loyal to our little group and its success than to our companies. So we simply decided to help each other out.

When one of my clients had an event going on and I couldn't handle all the work, I could call on my Posse for help. Whoever had time to help out would, and if more than one of us had a project or crisis going on, we would divide up the group's resources as best we could. It was ingenious. Not only did our secret society ensure its members' survival, it also meant that five women in their mid-twenties controlled a huge amount of the public relations activities in New York, and no one else had a clue. It gave us more than a good chuckle. It filled us with glee.

I quickly emailed my situation to Kate, my feelings of gloom and despair diminishing with every keystroke, and in half an hour I had her working with the theatrical people and musicians, Surya working with the rental company and florist, Liz managing the caterers, and Anupa confirming the car service. I was free to focus on media relations, which is the actual point of my job. I was almost enjoying it.

By 4:00 p.m. all my follow-up calls were made, and my media alerts and social media posts were sent out. Half an hour later, I had boxed up all the press kits and important documents and was ready for one last look at the park before I went home to attempt to make myself glamorous.

I opened my office door to find Tanya fully recovered and doing her nails. Hardly surprising.

"Tell Pamela all is well. Everything is ready," I called out to Tanya with an unaccustomed smile as I sailed to the elevator. "See you there!"

"She's at a mani-pedi," muttered Tanya resentfully without looking up. "But I'll text her." Then she blew on her nails.

CHAPTER 2

J got five text messages from Pamela on my cab ride back to the park. She must have been in the pedicure portion of her mani-pedi. Thanks to my Posse, I was able to answer all her questions reassuringly. That didn't stop her from ending the conversation with "And Jill, don't be late." Ouch. But I had to admit it wasn't quite undeserved. Still, a "Good job!" would have been nice.

The cab arrived at the park. As I entered Conservatory Garden and saw what my Posse had done, I nearly burst into tears. The place looked gorgeous. For the first time that day, I felt hopeful.

Jill Cooksey might not fail.

The subway soon cured me of that. My ride home was a nightmare as always. I was nearly pushed onto the tracks at the 59th Street and Lexington Avenue station, and a wire hanger from someone's dry cleaning tore a hole in the sleeve of my sweater. Still, I comforted myself with the knowledge that an actual automobile would be picking me up to take me to the event. You can't wear an evening gown on the subway. Well, you can, but I don't recommend it.

Much to my horror, my apartment was just as I'd left it that morning. While I kept my office immaculate, my home was a Superfund site. Vowing as usual to clean my apartment the following weekend, I turned my attention to the task at hand, namely to make myself gorgeous or at least presentable. I began the transformation by laying out my gear.

One basic black satin evening gown with spaghetti straps and a slit up the thigh—check!

One black Lycra body shaper to make the aforementioned evening gown possible—check!

One pair of extra-control top, thigh-shaping pantyhose in Barely Black—check!

One extra pair for when the ragged thumbnail that I chewed all day poked through the first pair—check!

One pair of merciless black Italian pumps (nobody does torture like the Italians)—check!

And even though I knew it was useless to think I could shine in the company of celebrities like Juliet, still I'd purchased a beautiful item to spruce up my plain black dress— a gorgeous beaded silk shawl in deep, deep orange. With all my gear laid out on the bed, I ran to the bathroom to plug in the curling iron.

An hour and a half later, I surveyed myself in the mirror and was pleasantly surprised. My blond hair fell in sculpted ringlets to my shoulders and brushed the vibrant orange shawl draped over them. The color made my blue eyes pop. The dress fit like a glove, and all that Lycra paid off in curves that I wasn't ashamed of. My car arrived a few minutes thereafter, a very rude horn snapping me out of my vanity, and I was on my way.

Cruising down Northern Boulevard, I felt like a queen in my shiny black Town Car. Tonight I was escaping my bridge and tunnel existence and hobnobbing with the rich and famous and those who wanted to be. When my car pulled up to the entrance to Conservatory Garden, I was delighted to see three news vans at the curb, including one from the nationally syndicated *Hollywood Report*! The evening was already a success. Just those three hits would score millions of impressions and make my boss and, more importantly, my client very, very happy. Content in the knowledge that I'd done my job and done it well, I was determined to relax and enjoy myself.

I was halfway through my second glass of champagne and my umpteenth canapé when I saw the bush wearing the Nikes. Hallucinating? Drunk? Neither. A second look proved to me that my drink wasn't tainted and that the shoes were attached to legs. Someone was in the boxwood hedge of Conservatory Garden spying on my soiree.

It had to be a paparazzo, one too low to get an invitation. *Gotcha! Magazine* perhaps. That wouldn't do at all!

I made my way over to the hedge and tried to address the mystery paparazzo in a low whisper. While I needed to get rid of the intruder, I didn't want to cause a scene.

"Psst!"

"Psst yourself," came a growly voice from the greenery.

Annoyed, I turned to face the Nike-sporting shrub. "Do you want to tell me what you're doing in that bush, or do I have to call—" My heel caught on an exposed root, and champagne went flying as I lurched forward into the shrubbery. Two strong hands interrupted my fall, and I suddenly found myself in the arms of a stranger—one who smelled like pine trees, campfires, and s'mores all rolled into one. Nevertheless, a nice smelling stranger is still a stranger, so I used my high heel as the torture device it was intended to be. The sound of my wicked Italian heel puncturing a leather sneaker was followed by a strangled scream and a series of very colorful swear words.

"Serves you right!" I was most indignant as I disentangled myself from the hedge and began to pick twigs and leaves off my dress.

A moment later, my assailant came hopping out of the bushes too, making odd strangled noises. People were starting to stare, and I began to panic. Grabbing the pesky paparazzo's arm, I steered him toward a side exit, intent on throwing him out.

"I don't even want to touch you," I spat as I dragged the hopping man along, "but there's no way I'll let a weasel like you ruin this event."

"Now hold on a second!" He jerked out of my grasp, planted himself on a nearby bench, and leaned over his foot, rubbing it and mumbling under his breath, while I stood nearby with folded arms, tapping my toe impatiently. After a moment, he sat up straight, and I got a good look at the jerk.

For a jerk, he was awfully attractive. His hair was a thick, soft brown and stuck out in little spikes, and I could tell that his face would be cute when not twisted with pain. He wore jeans, the now torn sneakers, a rugby shirt, and a drop-dead sexy leather coat. Little bits of boxwood were caught in his hair and clothes.

Like a sap, I softened.

"Is your foot all right?" Was that purring my voice? The voice of a righteously indignant PR professional? Couldn't be.

"If I tell you it is, will you try to maim me again?" I could hear a hint of a smile in his voice. His face relaxed, and I forgot to breathe. He wasn't just cute—he was delicious.

"Mike McCall," he said, offering his hand. I took it, but only because my mother had taught me good manners.

"Jill Cooksey."

"It's a nice party, Jill Cooksey." Now *he* was purring. What the heck was going on here?

"Thanks." I shook my head a little to dispel the fog that encircled my brain. I grabbed a patch of reality and tried to hold on. "But it's by invitation only. I'll have to ask you to leave."

"But I have an invitation," he smirked. I cocked a skeptical eyebrow in return.

"Oh really? What media outfit are you with?" When he said *Gotcha! Magazine*, I was going to throw his cute little butt out on the sidewalk. His smirk deepened, making him even cuter, dang it!

"*New York Gazette*. 'All the news you need to know.'"

Alarm bells went off in my head. Ashton Hillary was the style guru for the *Gazette*, and he had assured me personally that he would be covering the event. He had even promised color photos in the Style section and a skybox on the front page. But Mike McCall looked more like sports than fashion. Had Ashton played a cruel joke?

"So you work with Ash?" I queried tentatively, praying he would turn out to be Ash's photographer.

"No way!" The distaste was evident in his voice and in the way he wrinkled up his adorable (cut that out!) nose. "I'm police beat. Ashton got some bad shrimp salad at some tea party today, and I was the guy unlucky enough to be last to leave the newsroom."

"Was that the launch of the new Adrien Grimaldi salon in SoHo? I so wanted to go, but I had to plan this event." I was eager for news about the competition, but Mike just stared at me like I was on crack.

"How should I know? I didn't go. And you're probably lucky you didn't either because seventeen people who ate shrimp curry are now at St. Luke's puking and eating charcoal, including Ashton whatshisname. Anyway, I was told to come here, but I got almost no briefing, and no one told me it was black tie—"

"Which is why you were hiding in the bushes." My heart had plummeted on hearing that Ash wasn't around, but I needed the *Gazette*, and I vowed to make it happen. "Well, to bring you up to speed, this is Eshellon Cosmetics' launch of their new fragrance Fall Fantasy, the first of four seasonal fragrances. I'll get you a press kit. Is your photographer here?" Fingers crossed.

Mike gestured toward the party.

"Vinnie's somewhere over there. Lucky stiff's wearing a tux."

"Well," I continued in full publicist swing, "as soon as the cocktail hour is up and all the VIPs are here, we'll be sitting down for dinner and the presentation, followed by dessert and dancing."

He grinned. "Sounds like a prom or a wedding."

I struggled to keep my voice level and polite.

"It's a *ball*, and for your information, it's the hottest event in New York tonight."

"A real A-list event, huh? Astors, Rockefellers, McCalls, and…Cooksey was it?" He took my hand and gently raised it to his lips.

"Jill Cooksey," I had to whisper because his twinkling blue eyes had stolen my voice. With all the willpower I possessed, I forced myself to snap out of it. Snatching my hand back, I gathered my wrap around me to hide my consternation, while Mike grinned crookedly at me, cool as a cucumber, as if he kissed ladies' hands every day. The scoundrel.

"Don't worry about your attire." I struggled for a businesslike tone and achieved it, barely. "But if it bothers you, I'd suggest sitting at a table on the perimeter and perhaps not dancing."

"Oh, I won't be dancing. You don't have to worry about that." Adopting an expression of grim determination, he squared his shoulders and marched toward the party like a soldier headed for battle.

I took a moment to compose myself. So far the night was full of surprises. I truly hoped there wouldn't be any more.

The cocktail hour flew by as I greeted and seated the press

and VIPs. Meredith Hopkins arrived on the early side. The client always does. They like to keep tabs and make sure the agency isn't cheating them or doing a slack job. A champagne cocktail and an introduction to the mayor's hot nephew got her off my back. Pamela arrived soon after in a white stretch limo. I looked to see if Meredith had noticed since car services are billed to our clients, but luckily she was too busy flirting.

My boss was stunning in a bronze Prada gown, perfect for fall, as she unfolded herself from the limo and strode down the red carpet. Hard on her heels was Tanya in a very small, very filmy flesh-toned cocktail dress—another avant-garde creation with ragged bits of fabric hanging here and there. She looked like she was molting. The sickly bird was supposed to have arrived when I did to distribute press kits, but she had somehow bummed a limo ride. I hurried over to exact my revenge.

"Pamela, you look terrific!" I cried.

"You're so sweet," she cooed back unenthusiastically. "Now, who's here?"

I quickly filled her in on my media success, and to her credit she did seem impressed. In fact, her brow even wrinkled (must be time for more Botox).

"Well you seem to have it all under control," she said, as close to a compliment as I would get. I grinned pathetically at her. She tried to smile encouragingly, gave up, and went to schmooze the big boss, William Waverly. I had no doubt she would be taking all the credit again. Tanya moved to follow until I firmly hooked my arm through hers.

"Tanya, don't forget to include tonight's hours on your timesheet," I gaily reminded her. She frowned and looked for Pamela's help, but the boss was already seeing and being seen. I steered Tanya to the back of the marquee and ensconced her behind a table piled with press kits.

"Give one to anybody who asks for one."

"But I can't see anything back here, and no one can see me. I'm wearing couture! Will they even bring me dinner out here in the hinterlands?"

"We're here to do a job, Tanya, but I'll make sure they feed you." I wondered if I could arrange a bowl of birdseed to be delivered, but then I told myself to be kind. I left Tanya sulking, but at least I knew she couldn't do any harm back there.

Hoss Buckworth arrived next.

"Mr. Buckworth!" I greeted him cheerfully. I craned my neck to spot Pamela. As Waverly Communications VP, she should have been there to greet the client, but she was off being a socialite. I hoped Hoss wouldn't mind.

"Why, Miss Cooksey! Aren't you a vision tonight?" He was such a flirt. "Looks like you gals have done a great job once again." His bolo tie tipped with turquoise and silver seemed out of place with his black tuxedo, but if there was anyone who didn't care what other people thought, it was Hoss.

"Thank you, Mr. Buckworth," I said and meant it. I was surprised to see him without a date. "So, going stag tonight, are we?"

A pained look briefly touched his face, and I cursed my ineptitude. I'd left a seat open next to him for his date, and if he didn't have one, I was going to have to juggle some place cards pretty quickly. I couldn't have the owner of Eshellon Cosmetics sitting alone at his own event. Still, I could have found out more tactfully. Luckily Hoss recovered quickly.

"So where is that pretty Miss Pamela this evening?" He arched his brows meaningfully, and I flashed back to a dinner in Dallas the year before where, from the look on Pamela's face at the time, I could have sworn that Hoss, who probably interpreted #metoo to mean the more the merrier, had put his hand on her knee under the table. Before I could think of a reply, he leaned in conspiratorially, "She's probably in the little gals' room fixin' her face. I'll just have a look-see around." Now that was the Hoss I remembered. I wouldn't have been at all surprised if he had slapped me on the rump as he strutted off, champagne in hand, to find the stunning Pamela, but mercifully he didn't.

Putting my boss next to Hoss, I finished rearranging the place cards in the nick of time. A moment later, chimes announced seating for dinner. Hoss gallantly held a chair for Pamela, who barely hid her chagrin with the fakest smile I'd ever seen. I sat down next to her, and she whispered angrily in my ear.

"Any idea who's responsible for the seating chart?"

I shrugged my shoulders, tried to look sympathetic, and turned to arrange my shawl over the back of my chair, using it as an excuse to scan the room. Socialites, politicians, entertainers, and journalists were spread out before me, and my chest puffed up a bit at the thought that I, with a little help from my Posse, had pulled it off.

I was busy daydreaming about how I would decorate my corner office after I got headhunted to be VP at a major agency when my reverie was interrupted by a very tall man with a very large camera sitting directly behind me at another table for ten.

"Jill Cooksey? I'm Vinnie from the *Gazette*." I shook his hand and wondered how his enormous paws could hold the camera without crushing it. Vinnie was a big guy. Closer to seven than six feet tall, he was muscular with a thick thatch of black curls crowning a face with a square jaw and a hint of five o'clock shadow. Zeus in a tuxedo. As if on cue, his camera flash went off, and I had to stifle a giggle.

Vinnie quickly reassured me that Ash had briefed him by phone and he knew what was being planned. He then introduced me to his girlfriend, Antoinette (pronounced Antinette), a buxom lass who I knew would also be well over six feet tall when she stood up. Hera, I thought, and for a moment I was aglow with the romantic notion that the universe provides a partner for everyone, regardless of size, until I remembered that I was dateless for the event.

Dinner went off without a hitch: pear and goat cheese salad, roasted red pepper and carrot soup, choice of filet mignon or pine nut stuffed Pocono trout, and wines to accompany each course. When it was time for the presentation, I looked around at the crowd to find them full, content, and not likely to wander off anywhere—exactly what I wanted.

I gave the orchestra leader his cue and sat back to watch the show, fingers crossed. A low roll on tympani was the cue for the lights to dim. Then the orchestra launched into the music that would accompany every Fall Fantasy commercial. It was grand, sweeping, and bittersweet, like the final orchestral surge at the end of a sad romantic movie like *Casablanca* or *Gone with the Wind*. On cue, the shimmery brown, gold, and orange curtains surrounding the stage parted to reveal a forest ablaze with light and fall color, but like no fall color nature ever generated. The leaves, created from fabric, were brilliantly colored, some even metallic. They fluttered in a light breeze.

All of a sudden, angelic female voices rose, blending with the orchestra but singing no words. Pure music. From behind each tree stepped a beautiful singing maiden wrapped in diaphanous brown chiffon, face lightly bronzed and hair streaked with gold. The forest was suddenly alive with wood-nymphs, otherworldly and alluring. I could feel the room hold its breath, wondering what would come next.

Then the stage started to move, and the rows of trees glided around in opposite directions to reveal a much larger tree—an apple tree with leaves of green and gold and branches burgeoning with sparkling crimson fruit. Then the huge tree itself began to rotate slowly revealing the Goddess clad in crimson velvet, perched high in its branches, the train of her dress spilling down the trunk of the tree. The music rose and swelled. The audience burst into spontaneous applause. Cameras flashed like a lightning storm.

Before I even knew she was moving, Juliet had glided down the small steps built into the tree trunk. As she moved forward, away from the tree and the forest, the stage rotated again. The forest came back into view, and with a last surge of the orchestra, the curtains billowed to a close, leaving Juliet standing on the apron of the stage like a queen. The audience was on its feet in a split second, applauding not only her incredible beauty, but also the amazing spectacle they had just witnessed in Central Park.

The music retreated into the background, the standing ovation subsided, and Juliet began her role as spokesmodel for Eshellon's new fragrances. She described the beauty and the special feeling of autumn and the anticipation it carried with it. Then she segued smoothly into a description of the fragrance and the mood and emotion it evoked. The copy I'd written weeks before came alive when Juliet said it to the point that I began to feel like some sort of modern Shakespeare.

I glanced around the table to gauge the client's reaction. Meredith was hanging on Juliet's every word, her brow creased with effort, and I got the impression she was willing Juliet to be perfect, to give the product a flawless introduction. In stark contrast, Hoss Buckworth's face practically glowed as he gazed on the beautiful Ms. Scott. He looked positively smitten.

As Juliet finished her speech, the dryads emerged from the sides of the marquee bearing baskets full of sparkling crimson apples, which on closer inspection were made of glass and contained a cut crystal bottle of Fall Fantasy.

The lights came up as Juliet walked down the stairs from the apron of the stage to be greeted, somewhat awkwardly, by Hoss Buckworth and escorted on his arm to our table where she was seated on his left. The dryads were revealed to be beautiful young women handing out the handsomely packaged fragrance, and we all eased back into reality. I finally exhaled.

The rest of the event was a blur of pastry, music, dancing, flash photography, and champagne—in other words, a smashing success. The party started to thin at eleven, and by midnight the diehards were making plans for an after-party at some hotspot. But there would be no after-party for me. I would remain at the park supervising clean up until the crack of dawn and then go home to bed for a couple of hours of sleep before I had to clean my apartment for my lunch with Juliet. But it was all worth it.

Feeling much like the mother of the bride, I made the rounds to thank and tip the catering crew, the waiters, the orchestra, and the security guards. When I was finished, I looked around the tent to see it empty except for Juliet and the folks from Eshellon who were kicked back at a table finishing off a couple of bottles of bubbly. I made my way to the press kit table at the back of the tent, kneeled down, and reached under the tablecloth for my Behemoth Black Bag and the sneakers I'd stashed therein. When I exchanged my Italian torture devices for sneakers, I heaved a great sigh of relief.

"Caught ya!" I spun around to find Mike McCall in all his rugby-shirted glory grinning at me and my tennis shoes.

"I still have a long night ahead of me," I laughed, pleased that he'd made the effort to talk to me again. He was so cute.

"Just when I'd worked up the courage to dance."

My heart picked up.

"Can I take a rain check?" I pulled a pouty face. "I've been on my feet all night, and they're killing me."

"Sounds like you need to kick back for a bit."

"I have to supervise cleanup."

"You can do that from a chair." He took my hand and led me toward a table that had been bussed. "Those catering professionals know what they're doing. You deserve a nightcap. I stashed a bottle of champagne and two glasses under my coat."

I had a vision of William Holden and Audrey Hepburn.

"You're not going to take no for an answer, are you?" I laughed.

"You already know me too well," he joked.

"Must be the All Blacks jersey." That made him pause.

"You know rugby?" His blue eyes lit up, and I almost tripped over my own feet.

I just smiled mysteriously. The evening had suddenly gone romantic, and I was eating it up. This is your reward for all the work, I told myself and sent a prayer of thanks heavenward.

My reward didn't last. Raised voices from the other side of the marquee interrupted our romantic interlude. I hurried over to the Eshellon folks, Mike hard on my heels, just in time to see a voluptuous girl in a gold minidress and acres of hair that couldn't all be hers toss a glass of champagne at Juliet Scott.

"That's what you deserve, you cow!" the girl screeched. For a moment everyone was too shocked to speak.

"Hey, that's Amber O'Neil," Mike whispered in my ear. Amber O'Neil? She wasn't on the guest list. Amber was Juliet's TV costar. On the small screen they played best friends who shared an apartment in New York. Clearly, they were decent actors.

"Juliet, let me help you clean that up." I rushed to her side.

I could tell that the enraged and vibrating Juliet was trying to decide between a tongue-lashing and physical violence. She didn't get the chance to do either as Amber wasn't finished. She wheeled on Hoss Buckworth.

"And as for you, you ancient, sexually depraved lummox, you wouldn't know true talent and real beauty if it was standing right in front of you!" We all winced as she tried to put her palm in contact with Hoss's face, but luckily she was too drunk, missed, and nearly fell down.

"My mother always said pretty is as pretty does." Was that my voice? "Right now you look like someone's been beating you with an ugly stick!"

It *was* my voice. The righteously indignant, overworked publicist had been loosed.

"Now git! Before I call the police!" Where did that come from? My Virginia roots were showing, and I blamed mental and physical exhaustion, but it was just the thing to scare off angry Amber. Her rage instantly dissolved into deep despair, and she started sniffling and muttering to herself. Without another word to us, she turned and stumbled toward the street.

"I'll put her in a cab," said Mike. I gave him a grateful smile and grabbed a napkin to help mop up Juliet. At that point, everyone recovered from their shock. Hoss Buckworth collapsed in a chair and mopped his brow with his hanky, a turquoise blue bandana. Meredith Hopkins, who hadn't left with the mayor's nephew, surprisingly, helped me mop up our spokesmodel.

"Juliet, let's get you backstage and into some clean clothes," I suggested. Meredith and I moved to help her, but she put up a hand.

"I can handle it. Thanks," was all she said, and, still trembling with rage, she stalked off toward the stage.

When she was gone, I dragged Meredith a few feet away from the others.

"What in heaven's name was that all about?"

"Your guess is as good as mine," she replied. "Looks to me like Amber is a little jealous of Juliet's deal with Eshellon." Meredith's cheeks were flushed, and I could tell she was as stressed out as I was.

"Has Juliet ever mentioned this to you?" I was still trying to make sense of it.

Meredith's gaze narrowed, and she sucked her teeth. "I'm

surprised you're asking me, Jill. You're the one she talks to. I'm just glad this happened after all the reporters left."

Reporters! Mike! Crap!

"Yeah, me too," I mumbled and made a beeline for Mr. McCall.

I found him at the curb on his cell phone, which he pocketed as I approached him.

"Well that's taken care of," I said trying to sound light-hearted.

"Quite a little scene if you ask me," he replied, and my heart sank.

"It was a beautiful event, though, don't you think? I mean, it went off without a hitch." I tried to smile.

Mike smiled back, but his eyes held a mischievous glint.

"Sure, sure. But that was some drama back there, huh? I mean real tabloid stuff. America has no idea those two are such bitter enemies. Quite a scoop."

"For the tabloids, right? I mean, no respectable journalist would report on a little argument like that unless he worked for *Gotcha! Magazine*."

"I guess that would depend on incentive…if he had a reason not to report something like that."

My mind was reeling. What was he saying? All I could manage was a "Pardon?"

"By the way," he continued. "I was hoping I could get your phone number. Maybe we could go out sometime."

It all became clear. Jeez. He was a creep, and he was black-mailing me. A date (to begin with I'm sure) in return for keeping the argument out of the papers.

"Is that the incentive you were talking about?"

He arched an eyebrow. "Something like that."

My mind raced. The story about the event would run the next day—before we could go on a date. What harm would giving him my number really do? By the time he realized I wouldn't date him, the argument would be old news and have no impact. Maybe Mike McCall wasn't as smart as I thought? You have been outwitted, mister hard-boiled reporter!

I flashed him a smile. "Do you have a pen?"

"Better," he said as he pulled out his cell phone. In a minute, my number was stored and he was hailing a cab. Still, I wanted to be on the safe side.

"So you have my number. You're not planning to include the argument in the story, right?"

A cab glided to the curb. Mike opened the door but turned to grin mischievously at me.

"To be honest, I've already submitted my story."

Overcome with rage, I could only manage "You jerk!"

His grin just grew larger.

"Cooksey, I'm hurt. After our moment in the bushes, I thought you knew me better. I don't do tabloid journalism." Then with a wink and a grin and an "I'll call you," he jumped into the cab and sped away leaving me dazed and not a little confused.

The evening had become too crazy. It was time to wrap it up and go home. I hauled myself back to the marquee, but the place was deserted except for Tanya. Oddly enough, I met her coming out of the tent with a tote bag of leftover press kits. Was she actually working?

"Where's Juliet?" I asked.

"In Mr. Buckworth's limo on her way back to the hotel," she mumbled, looking everywhere except at me. "I'm just going to catch a cab home."

"Well, make sure you save your receipt so we can reimburse you. Thanks for your hard work, Tanya." Were those words really coming out of my mouth? "See ya Monday."

"Yeah, see ya," she mumbled and headed for the street.

I was left alone in Conservatory Garden not knowing how to feel. The sweetness of that perfect evening had turned sour.

Had the event been ruined by Amber's appearance? Were my clients still happy with my work? Would we get bad publicity? Was Mike McCall being playful, or was he really just a jerk? I had no answers to these questions, so, on the verge of tears, I made my way to the street to hail a cab.

CHAPTER 3

I awoke to light flickering in through the sheer curtains and the sound of children alternately laughing and screaming. I managed to pry my eyes open and glanced at the clock. 9:00 a.m. I looked around at the landfill I called my apartment—and leaped from my bed. A Hollywood star was coming to my hovel for lunch. Lunch usually happened, oh, around noon. That was only three hours away. Sugar! Honey! Iced tea!

I shut my eyes and tried some yoga breathing while I silently prayed for a miracle. Then I opened my eyes and plunged into a cleaning frenzy.

I stripped the futon, turned it back into a couch, and started a pile of laundry. I threw away the Lucky Charms and Triscuit boxes that were lying under the bed. Then I picked all the papers up off the floor and added them to the junk mail monster on my desk. After I ran the carpet sweeper (a vacuum just seems like overkill in a shoebox studio apartment), I swept and Swiffered the kitchen floor. Then I stuffed the dirty clothes into my laundry bag and crammed it in my closet. By sitting on the floor against the closet door with my legs stretched out, I was just able to push against the opposite wall (yes, my apartment was that small) and shut the closet door. Then I approached my desk. The junk mail monster would take hours to tame, so I just tried to arrange it in stacks. Maybe then I would appear busy and high-powered instead of sloppy and behind on my bills.

With the rest of my apartment approaching order, I turned my attention to the kitchen sink, or rather, the fortnight's dishes in the kitchen sink atop which perched my pet cockroach, Saul. I called Saul my pet because, well, he wasn't going anywhere. His was a master race that defied my best attempts at extermination. Now one might assume that getting rid of the fortnight's dirty dishes might just get rid of Saul, but to get to the dishes I'd have to get past Saul. And as a 5'8", one hundred and (like I'd tell you) pound woman is no match in anyone's books for a four-and-a-half-inch New York City cockroach, I usually adopted the mantra "Discretion is the better part of valor." But today I had no choice. Saul had to go.

I pulled a pair of clunky loafers from under the futon and crept silently toward the sink. There he was, his hard brown back glinting in the morning sun, perched atop a saucepan, surveying his domain.

"Bombs away!" I stage whispered (did I need to? do cockroaches have ears?) as I let one loafer fly. Direct hit! The saucepan and Saul went flying through the air. It only took a split second, I know, but it felt like an eternity as the pot fell to the floor. Saul, an insect Indiana Jones, rode that pan all the way down. Instinctively, I let loose with loafer number two. Saul never saw it coming, and I'll remember the crunch until my dying day. I never expected to actually kill Saul, but I guess something primal took over that Saturday morning.

I decided that the saucepan, like a shipwreck on the bottom of the ocean, was a burial site, and I solemnly carried it with the lid over Saul's not so little yet horribly squished body to the trashcan out front. My landlady, Mrs. Maroulis, was outside sweeping the stoop. A Greek widow about my mother's age, she had swept the stoop every day since I'd moved in, and I'm sure she had swept it for years before then. Clad in a crisp white blouse and black pencil skirt, she spoke with just a hint of an accent.

"Was that noise you?" she asked, not even pausing in mid-sweep.

"Cockroach killing," I replied matter-of-factly.

A grunt and a nod was her only reply, and I could tell she was a fellow veteran in the roach wars. I dumped the pot in the trashcan and resisted the urge to cross myself. (I'm a Baptist, after all.) My solemn mood didn't last, and I caught myself humming a little "Ding dong the witch is dead" on my way up the steps to the front door.

"You know…" began Mrs. Maroulis without looking up from her sweeping. Politely I turned to face her. "If you washed your dishes regularly you might not have such a problem." And then she did look at me from underneath eyebrows like storm clouds, her lips pursing enough to show buckets of disapproval.

"Yes ma'am," I gulped. Was she channeling my mother?

"And you might get a boyfriend. Men don't like messy women." She *was* channeling my mother! Satisfied, she went back to her sweeping.

"Yes ma'am," I muttered as I ran from her disapproval, making a mental note to keep my curtains closed.

Back inside, I attacked the dishes and had the kitchen sparkling in no time. Then I jumped in and out of the shower, blew my hair dry, and pulled on jeans and a sweater. I glanced at the clock. Eleven. I had about an hour to make lunch, or did I? I suddenly realized that I didn't know exactly when Juliet was going to show up. She had left the event pretty quickly after the Amber altercation and before we could settle on a time for lunch. She had been insistent on lunch at my place, but

I hadn't heard from her. I decided to give her a call. It went straight to voice mail, and I left a message. Then I called the Waldorf Astoria Hotel, praying that the desk clerk would be someone I knew who would even admit to me that Juliet was staying there. Ah, the hassle of having famous friends.

I got lucky with the clerk who connected me with her room, but there was no answer. She must be on her way, I thought. Yikes! The panic was back.

What do you serve to a television and movie star when she comes for lunch and you're on a budget? Food Network never covered that scenario. I only had moments to decide, but it came to me in an instant. When you've grown up with the star, you serve her a taste of home. By eleven thirty I had recreated the lunch my mother had always served us when we were kids: pimiento cheese sandwiches, sliced tomatoes and cucumbers, and Fritos. I opted for iced tea in lieu of the Kool-Aid we were addicted to as children. I knew Juliet would appreciate the lunch, and I found myself feeling rather emotional. The tastes of home were comforting and a little depressing.

Truth be told, after six years in New York, I was starting to really miss the outside world. Coming out of college, New York had seemed like the last stop on the road to success, but it wasn't all that it was cracked up to be. Sure NYC is a hot town with lots to do, but you had to have money to do those things, something I was a little short of. And at the ripe old age of twenty-seven, I'd started to realize that, barring any unforeseen circumstances, I might live to be eighty-five or ninety. Six years is a long time to stay in one place and do the same job. Juliet had been a welcome reminder of home as we worked on the Eshellon campaign, and I'd started to wonder if I really had to be in New York to work in PR. Could I go home to Virginia? Was that where I belonged? My Southern had certainly been on display when I confronted Amber. Maybe the South was calling me home.

I pondered my place in New York and the universe for a good half hour, but there was still no sign of Juliet. After trying her cell phone again to no avail, I decided to tackle one of my junk mail piles to pass the time until she showed up or called back. When junk mail pile number one was history, my apartment was still celebrity free, so I moved on to junk mail pile number two. By two o'clock, the junk mail was gone, and I was starving. Reluctantly, I ate a pimiento cheese sandwich. By three o'clock, my apartment was starting to look as if a neat freak inhabited it, but there was still no sign of Juliet.

So she forgot lunch, I thought. Big deal. But I couldn't shrug it off so easily. Juliet had wanted to talk to me about something, and something private at that. Why else would she have proposed schlepping all the way out to my Queens apartment? At the very least, wouldn't she want to vent about Amber's outrageous behavior? Something didn't feel right. I decided to head over to Manhattan. Maybe I'll catch a movie, I thought, and maybe I'll stop off at the Waldorf.

Luck was with me, and the R train pulled into the station as I tripped down the stairs and onto the platform. Ten minutes later I was in Manhattan. I changed trains at Lexington and 59th and headed south toward the Waldorf Astoria Hotel.

CHAPTER 4

*I*n art deco splendor, the Waldorf Astoria Hotel towered above Park Avenue. I'd organized and attended several events here over the years, so I hoped to find a sympathetic staff member to help me track Juliet down. I was in luck. The concierge on duty was my old pal Jean-Paul. As usual he was dressed better than any of the hotel's patrons as he stood behind an exquisite antique rosewood desk and surveyed his domain.

Tall, dark, and ooh-la-la, Jean-Paul was the ultimate metrosexual. He oozed sophisticated charm, and with his Hermès ties, impeccable taste, and sexy French accent, he was the occasional subject of my daydreams. He saw me coming from across the lobby, and his cool gaze never wavered from me. The effect on most people was intimidation, but as I said, I knew Jean-Paul. I'd once seen his custom suit splattered with crème brûlée by a novice waiter at the American Society of Cosmetic Surgeons annual dinner. The sight of custard sliding down his lapel thoroughly humanized Jean-Paul in my eyes. Now that cool gaze, instead of intimidating me, just made me smile. He was so sexy. Consciously, I added a little sway to my walk.

"Bonjour, Jean-Paul," I cooed at him as I sidled up to the desk.

"Bonjour, Mademoiselle Cooksey," he said and smiled the faintest smile while cocking an eyebrow. "How may I be of service?"

"I'm looking for someone, and I'm hoping you can help."

Automatically, his lips pursed a little. While one of the concierge's duties is to be overwhelmingly helpful while remaining chillingly polite, the other is to safeguard the privacy of his guests. This was going to be tougher than I thought.

"Mademoiselle, you of all people should know that I cannot divulge the identities of our guests," he said.

"But it's a matter of life and death!" Was it really? Not so much. But as I hissed the words at Jean-Paul, my imagination kicked in, and I began to imagine all sorts of horrific scenarios that might have prevented Juliet from keeping our date. (I'm not dramatic. Not at all.) I suddenly knew in my gut that it *was* a matter of life and death. To my surprise, Jean-Paul didn't argue with me. He simply cocked another eyebrow and surveyed me calmly before he replied.

"Could it possibly wait for ten minutes? Jean-Pierre will be here then, and I will be at liberty to talk. If indeed someone's life is hanging in the balance as we speak..."

"I can wait ten minutes," I breathed with a sigh of relief.

Jean-Paul directed me to a small cafe around the corner, and I headed there to wait for him.

Cafe Montmartre was full of patrons munching pastry, swilling espresso, and eagerly reading the day's newspapers. I ordered a latte and sat at a table by the front window. As I sipped, I suddenly felt silly for being so dramatic with Jean-Paul. Was it really a matter of life and death? So a friend stood me up for lunch. It happens all the time. What made this situation any different?

Juliet made it different. She had needed to talk to me, and she had suggested lunch at my place out in the hinterlands. It was too odd a suggestion for her just to forget about it. And the scene with Amber the night before had made me realize that even "It Girls" have enemies. Maybe it wasn't life and death, but something was certainly wrong. I needed to help a friend.

As I reached this conclusion, Jean-Paul strode into the cafe. With a slight bow of his head, he sat down, and I swear five seconds later a tall blonde waitress/supermodel (wait, where did she come from? I had to order at the counter) deftly set a double espresso in front of him. He flashed her a smile in thanks, and she smiled back—with her whole body.

"You must be a regular." Now I was cocking an eyebrow. In response, Jean-Paul merely shrugged his shoulders and slightly pursed his lips in that all too French way that neither confirms nor denies.

"Now Mademoiselle, what is this all about?"

I briefly explained my relationship with Juliet and our lunch plans. I could tell by the end of the story that Jean-Paul wasn't buying it.

"So, Mademoiselle, you are telling me that Juliet Scott, star of television and silver screen, decided not to go to Queens, that cultural Mecca, that glittering gem of the five boroughs, to have lunch, and this surprises you?" His smile of contempt was probably the closest Jean-Paul ever came to laughing. My father's animosity toward the French suddenly seemed justified. With reserves of strength I didn't know I had, I suppressed the desire to strangle him with his tie.

"That wouldn't seem so strange if I hadn't witnessed," I leaned in closer, "an altercation, if you will, last night between Juliet and a person who shall remain nameless who most likely wishes her dead."

"Amber O'Neil!" gasped Jean-Paul, suddenly interested. "You mean the story is true?"

My stomach plummeted.

"How do you know about Amber?"

In an instant the look of derision was back on his face. "Mademoiselle," he said with infinite patience, "look around you."

I did, slowly and in extreme shock. Everywhere I looked I saw pictures of Juliet and Amber splashed across cell phones, tablets, and the front page of the *New York Gazette* along with the headline "Starlets struggle in Central Park." The patrons were devouring the story faster than the *pain au chocolat*.

"I'm going to kill that Mike McCall! Jean-Paul, now you must see why I have to find Juliet." He scrutinized me for a moment, his eyes narrowing to slits as he sized up my situation.

"*Alors*," he began finally. "If you accompany me to the hotel and promise to wait in the hallway, I will knock on Ms. Scott's door and see if she is home."

"What if she doesn't answer? What if Amber has murdered her?"

"Murder, Mademoiselle Cooksey? I think not. Not at the Waldorf Astoria Hotel." With that he rose, deposited a few bills on the table, blew a kiss to the waitress (who simpered), and was out the door, all in one fluid motion, leaving me scrambling to catch up.

I tailed him to the hotel and followed him inside, always careful to keep my distance. The hotel could never know that Jean-Paul was helping me stalk a star. I caught up to him at the elevator, and we pretended not to know each other. When we slipped into the car, Jean-Paul pulled out a special card key and inserted it into a slot. Then he hit the button for the twenty-sixth floor. The doors slid shut, and we were alone in the elevator for the ride up.

"Mademoiselle, you are glowing," crooned Jean-Paul. I looked into the mirrored interior of the elevator and was surprised to see he was right. My cheeks were flushed and healthy-looking from running after a concierge who might have been a panther in a past life. My straight blond hair was windblown in an attractive way, and even though my friend might be lying in a pool of her own blood, I was smiling and my blue eyes were shining.

"Perhaps the cloak and dagger stuff appeals to you," purred Jean-Paul as he took a step closer. I just smiled and tried to shrug at him in a French sort of way. I don't know if it worked or if I looked ridiculous, but he did take another step closer.

Ding! The elevator stopped, and the doors slid open at the twenty-sixth floor.

"Now Mademoiselle, stay out of sight while I knock on her door. If she doesn't answer, I will investigate first and call for you when the coast is *clair*, I mean clear."

"Sure thing," I lied, and we headed down the hallway.

At long last, we were at the door where Jean-Paul knocked several times with no answer. He pulled out his master key and was inside Juliet's room in a flash. I counted to around seven before I followed him inside. The look on his face told me he was expecting just such behavior, but it really didn't matter. No body and no blood waited for us. The bed was made. The room was neat. No sign of struggle. The bedspread was a little mussed as if someone had sat on the bed.

Immediately, I went to the closet.

"Mademoiselle!" Jean-Paul was actually a little pale.

"Jean-Paul, we need to establish where Juliet is. Obviously, she didn't sleep here. Did she leave town or did someone take her away?"

"Or is she merely out to lunch?" he parried.

"Jean-Paul, I've tried her cell. I called the hotel this morning.

I grew up with her. She wouldn't have stood me up. Something may have happened to her. We need to know."

I put my hand on the closet doorknob and looked to Jean-Paul. I would have searched the room without his approval, but I'd rather have had it. After a moment, he gave me the nod.

I'd hoped to find everything gone from the closet. That could mean she had left town or changed hotels or something like that. But her big beautiful Louis Vuitton suitcase was there along with a row of gorgeous designer garments that fluttered in the air conditioning like a Seventh Avenue Sherpa's prayer flags. Shoes were lined up on the closet floor with some space between pairs. Might some pairs be missing, or was I just going crazy analyzing the shoes of a woman who could at this moment be waiting outside my apartment in Queens? I slipped my cell phone out of my jeans pocket and dialed her number. It went to voice mail again, and I felt a little better about stalking Juliet and rummaging through her closet. She was still missing.

Next I tackled the gorgeous highboy. Again, there were clothes in the drawers, so I headed for the bathroom. All the hotel-provided toiletry items were there on the vanity along with a few makeup items and a comb. Some personal items might have been missing, but I couldn't be sure. I went back to the bedroom, perched myself on a satin covered Louis XV-style armchair, and pondered.

"Mademoiselle." I turned to find Jean-Paul holding one crimson satin open-toed pump. "I seem to find only one." He cocked another eyebrow. Together we searched high and low, but the shoe's mate was nowhere. And where was the dress? A wild scene of abduction sprang into my mind.

"Okay, Jean-Paul, suppose Juliet arrives home from the event only to find kidnappers in her room. She struggles with them. They overpower her, but not before she loses one shoe. They bundle her up in a laundry sack and take her down the freight elevator, out of the hotel, and into a waiting car that screams off into the night." When I looked to Jean-Paul for affirmation, the skepticism was marching across his face.

"I think perhaps, Mademoiselle, public relations is not creative enough for you. Perhaps you should try your hand at writing science fiction novels."

"Fine. So what's your theory?" My feelings were a little hurt.

"Juliet Scott got up this morning, put on her clothes, picked up her handbag, and went out. Perhaps she went to breakfast. Maybe she went shopping or walking in the park. She is still out, and eventually she will return."

I hadn't thought about the handbag. There wasn't one in the room, and kidnappers don't usually pause while their victim grabs her purse, at least not in all the books I'd read.

"But what about the dress, Jean-Paul? Why isn't the dress in the room, and where is the other shoe?" I had him there. There couldn't be any explanation for the missing dress.

"Perhaps she sent it to our dry cleaner. Didn't Amber toss champagne at her?" *Touché*! Score one for Frenchie, but I wasn't ready to admit defeat.

"Well, I suppose we should check with the dry cleaner, but that still doesn't explain the missing shoe."

Jean-Paul only gave me a pitying smile as he led the way to the hall. Once we were out of the room, he went to the house phone and dialed the operator. In a moment he was connected with the Waldorf's in-house dry cleaner. While I certainly didn't want to look overly dramatic and stupid, I was truly hoping the dress would be there. Then at least I'd have some hope that Juliet was just being a flaky actress, that she hadn't been the victim of a crime. Unfortunately, such reassurance was not to be. The dress was not at the dry cleaners.

My mind was blank. I couldn't think. I don't remember sitting down on a settee near the elevator, but that's where I was when Jean-Paul next spoke.

"Perhaps, Mademoiselle, Miss Scott took the dress herself

to another dry cleaner when she stood you up and went out to explore this fascinating city. At this very moment, she is probably ogling a long-dead pharaoh at the Metropolitan Museum of Art." Jean-Paul was teasing, but his voice was kind. He knew I was worried. I looked up to find him smiling benignly down on me, not a cocked eyebrow in sight. Despite my worries, I found myself smiling back. I suddenly felt a little foolish.

"No doubt you're right, Jean-Paul," I gave in gracefully.

After I said goodbye to Jean-Paul, I headed to the Upper West Side to catch a movie. I figured I'd stay in Manhattan for as long as possible. That way, when Juliet remembered me and finally called, I could run down to the Waldorf. I got a ticket for the six-thirty showing of a romantic comedy that I was pretty sure would be bad. I had an hour to kill before the film, so I went next door to a bookstore to browse.

I was by the magazines pretending to read *The Economist* while actually staring at the fashion magazine covers when I spied the horrible *New York Gazette* headline out of the corner of my eye. Snap! In my concern over Juliet's whereabouts, I'd forgotten Mike McCall's handiwork. I filed *The Economist* on top of *Vogue* and snatched up a *Gazette*. After beating a teenaged girl to the last empty armchair near the periodicals, I finally gave the paper a good look.

"Starlets Struggle in Central Park." The headline was outlandish. It had been a single glass of champagne, not a struggle. Really, the *Gazette*'s standards were in the crapper. The copy on the front page was actually quite short to make room for the stunning photo of Amber's champagne making contact with Juliet's gown. But the story continued on page three, and by the end of it my head was spinning.

The story confirmed a few things I already knew. Both Juliet and Amber had been up for the same movie role, which Juliet had won. Both had been considered for the Eshellon Cosmetics campaign, and Juliet had won that too thanks to my connections and the fact that Juliet exuded much more class than Amber did. The next factoid came as a bit of a shock. Amber had been linked romantically to Hoss Buckworth.

It was hard for me to imagine a hot twenty-something celebrity like Amber with the over sixty-five Hoss. She was making half a million per episode and had been linked with many of the hottest leading men in Hollywood. She had her own money and could date anyone she wanted. Why Hoss? What was in it for her?

More money, of course. I had worked with the super-rich for long enough to know that what seems like a fortune big enough to last a lifetime to the average Joe is never enough for some people. Hoss's cosmetics empire was worth billions. With his fortune, any young woman could ascend to the most luxurious lifestyle imaginable.

Still, she might have loved Hoss, said a little voice inside my head. Perhaps Hoss had filled a void in her life.

Alarm bells started going off in my head. If Amber and Hoss had been an item (and that was supposing the *Gazette* and Mike McCall were telling the truth—fat chance), might Juliet and Hoss have been an item too? And was Amber as angry about losing Hoss to Juliet as she was about the film role and the cosmetics campaign?

I finished the article, and by the end I was not only better informed about the gossip surrounding my missing friend, I was also livid. Mike and his photographer Vinnie had no standards whatsoever beyond selling papers. Ashton Hillary never would have pulled a stunt like that. The entire story was about the fight and contained barely a mention of the Fall Fantasy fragrance.

And how did Vinnie get that picture of Amber throwing champagne at Juliet? He must have been hiding somewhere, but how would he know to hide? He couldn't have known the incident was going to take place. Maybe some passerby saw two famous people and snapped a picture with his cell phone and emailed it to the paper. I looked at the picture again. It was a little grainy, but the framing was good.

At least the TV coverage was going to be good. Or was it? Would the *Hollywood Report* dump the perfume story when they got wind of the scandal as they most certainly already had? Was all my coverage ruined? Maybe not. Certainly all the networks and syndicated shows would want to talk to Juliet about the fight to get her side of the story. Juliet was media trained. If she could slip in enough cosmetics references and maybe turn the interviews toward the perfume…What was I thinking? Juliet couldn't do that because she was missing!

Jill Cooksey does not fail.

My head was starting to spin again, so I headed for the in-store cafe and ordered a calming decaf latte.

"You gonna pay for that paper?" asked the clerk behind the register, a pimply teenager with a red Mohawk and a name tag that read "Alan."

As much as I was loath to purchase that rag, I needed a copy of it. I was sitting down with my latte and the paper when my phone chirped. The number was unfamiliar but had a 212 area code, and I hoped it would be Juliet instead of an irate Meredith Hopkins.

"Hello," I answered eagerly.

"Hello to you too," replied a voice I had no desire to hear.

"It's you, is it? Well, I have a few things to say to you, Mr. McCall, and if you are any kind of man, you'll refrain from hanging up on me and take your medicine!" Vaguely, I noticed the other cafe patrons staring at me. I must have been talking rather loudly, but I didn't care. Mike McCall had it coming.

"Of all the lowdown, dirty tricks to pull! After you claimed to be a respectable journalist. Well, let me tell you, you and that rag you write for aren't worth the two bucks you charge for your garbage. And when I'm finished, every respectable public relations professional in this business will freeze you out. Your name will be mud. No interviews for you. No one will touch you because you, sir, cannot be trusted to do the right thing!"

"I assume you're referring to today's cover story." Mike's voice was strangely calm. I'd expected a fight, but his calm momentarily took the wind out of my sails.

"You know perfectly well what I'm referring to—'Starlets Struggle in Central Park,'" I bit back, my voice dripping with disdain.

"Ms. Cooksey, would you do me the favor of looking at that cover story again, specifically at the byline?"

"What are you getting at, Mr. McCall?" I queried as I reluctantly looked at the paper again. "There is no byline. Evidently, you were too ashamed of your handiwork to let them put your name on it."

Mike was still eerily calm.

"Now Ms. Cooksey, if you would be so good as to look at the tip-top of the front page and tell me what you see."

With an impatient sigh, I scanned the top of the page and was brought up short by a skybox that included a photo of a bottle of Fall Fantasy perfume and the text "Eshellon's Fragrance Fantasia, page D1."

Hastily I turned to D1, the Style section, only to discover the story I'd been promised complete with color photos of my carefully planned spectacular. The text was tight, included great quotes from Juliet, Hoss, and Meredith, and didn't even mention the fight between Juliet and Amber. It was perfect.

Several minutes later I was still engrossed in the story when I heard a voice in my ear.

"I'll take that apology now, Jill."

I'd completely forgotten he was there, so I jumped and knocked over my latte, which spilled across the table, cascaded onto the floor, and splattered the gentleman sitting next to me. Luckily he was wearing dark khakis. I offered to pay for the dry cleaning, but he refused and just moved to a table farther away. I noticed the other patrons were still staring at me and looked thoroughly entertained. New Yorkers are all about cheap entertainment.

"If you won't apologize to me in that charming southern accent, you can at least meet me for a drink." Mike was still there, and he was laughing at me.

"I'm glad the chaos that is my life is so entertaining," I said to him and the other cafe patrons. One smart aleck in the corner actually started slow clapping. "I think I'll be free some-time at the end of the century."

"I was thinking about tonight."

"I'm about to see a movie."

"Alone?"

I hated to admit it, but I did. I've always been too honest for my own good.

"So skip it and meet me."

"Do you know how much a movie ticket costs in New York? A girl on a budget can't afford to waste her hard-earned dollars."

"Fine!" he said to shut me up. "I'll go to the movies too. Where are you and what are you seeing?"

For a moment I considered lying to him, but as I had jumped to conclusions and accused him of yellow journalism, it didn't seem right. Plus, I had an ulterior motive. If he and Vinny weren't responsible for the story in the *Gazette*, I wanted to know who was.

"I'm at 68th and Broadway. But the movie starts in 15 minutes."

"I'll be there in five." Five? He must live close by. Upper West Side address. Nice. "What are we seeing?"

I told him.

"Aw jeez. That piece of girlie crap! I don't deserve this."

I was standing outside the movie theater when he showed up five minutes later. He was in jeans and another rugby shirt, his uniform of choice, and he carried that great leather jacket. I'd taken the five minutes to refresh my lip-gloss and consider what I'd say to him. There was a chance, albeit small, that I did owe him an apology. Maybe he was a standup guy. I settled on buying him a ticket. Shelling out fifteen bucks was easier than saying I'm sorry.

Mike saw me as he walked up and smiled. I started to get some rather pleasant feelings, so I gave myself a mental lecture about how New York men were complete jerks. Mike walked right up and kissed me on the cheek like we were old friends, or something else. I knew I was in trouble.

"I'd better get a ticket before they sell out. Wait, I forgot. It's a crappy chick flick. It won't sell out." He grinned.

"Ha ha. I already bought you a ticket as a peace offering." I gave it to him and we went in. On the way, Mike casually took my hand, and a bolt of electricity went straight up my arm and left me tingling. Was it static electricity or something else?

After a trip to the concession stand for popcorn and a lively debate over Raisinets versus Junior Mints, we headed into the theater. I stopped at the last row.

"Do you mind if we sit back here?" I asked.

"The back row?" Mike looked surprised.

I shrugged. "I always sit in the back row."

"Really?" said Mike softly. His grin was back, and this time it was lecherous.

Gulp.

"We can sit in the front. That's fine too," I mumbled hastily. Why was my face so warm? Was I blushing?

"Oh no, Jill. The back row will do just fine." His lecherous grin grew even wider, and his blue eyes twinkled as he led the way to seats in the middle of the row. Suddenly, I couldn't feel my feet.

Okay, so the movie was pretty bad—a romantic comedy with no surprises. They just don't make them like *When Harry Met Sally* anymore. Mike groaned audibly at every cheesy line until I finally elbowed him in the side. By thirty minutes in, we were stealing each other's candy and fighting over the old maids in the bottom of the popcorn tub. Occasionally, I checked my cell phone, but there was no message from Juliet. After the fourth time, Mike gave me a questioning look, so I stopped after that.

By halfway in, we had settled down, and Mike had his arm around me. Lord, he felt good and warm and smelled like a camping trip. Better yet, I seemed to fit perfectly against his shoulder, and I was contemplating laying my head on it when he reached over with his free hand and began tracing small circles on my wrist with the lightest touch of his finger. My breath quickened, and a wave of delicious sensation flowed from the top of my head to the bottoms of my feet. I turned to find Mike looking down at me. His playful, flirty grin was still there, along with something else. In an instant his arms were around me, and his mouth was on mine. If the man smelled like a camping trip, then his mouth was the campfire and he was melting my marshmallow. Movie? What movie?

Thirty minutes later when the lights came on, the armrest dividing our seats was pushed up. I blinked for a moment as I struggled to remember where I was. Oh yeah, the movies. When my eyes could focus again, they saw Mike, face flushed, hair unrulier than ever, staring back at me with wide eyes.

"Cooksey," was all he said.

Indeed.

After the movie, we decided to go for the aforementioned drink. When we exited the theater, the cool night air helped to dispel the amorous fog that had settled on my brain. It seemed to have the same effect on Mike. I was feeling a bit embarrassed. It was out of character for me to lock lips with a man I'd only known for twenty-four hours. What would my mother say? What would Mrs. Maroulis say? And what if Mike was really the writer of that awful story? Had I been kissing the enemy? My mind was spinning as we silently strolled up Broadway. Mike tried to take my hand, but I pulled away. He gave me a quizzical look, and I tried to smile reassuringly. I'm pretty sure it didn't work. Luckily it was time to turn the corner onto 73rd street, and soon we arrived at a little Irish pub called Meehan's.

The interior was typical of New York City Irish pubs: dark wood paneling, cozy booths, dim lighting, and a long, highly polished bar. It was mostly a local crowd, and some musicians were setting up in one corner. Mike led me to a booth, and we sat down. An attractive older waitress with soft brown hair streaked with gray came to take our order.

"Hey, Mikey. Where ya been keepin' yourself?" Her voice was a bit raspy from smoking and tinged with a trace of an Irish accent.

"I'm a busy man," Mike replied good-naturedly. "Gotta make a living. Mary, this is Jill."

"Don't take any of his sass, Jill, and remember, if his lips are moving, he's lying." She winked at Mike, and he chuckled. "Now what'll it be?"

Mike ordered a beer, and I ordered an Irish coffee light on the Irish. For a minute no one spoke. I was looking everywhere except at Mike when a little voice in the back of my head reminded me that my friend was still unaccounted for and I had some questions unrelated to making out in the back of a movie theater. Finally, I broke the silence.

"It's a nice story. You've got a nice style."

"Wow! Two compliments. That's high praise from you, Jill." He tried to make it a joke, but his eyes gave him away. What I thought seemed to matter to him. Interesting.

"I mean it. The writing was good. I'm no journalism professor, but I practically read newspapers for a living. You can turn a phrase."

His shoulders relaxed.

"Thank you."

"You're welcome. But one piece of advice, you shouldn't write features so well. They might take you off the police beat."

"Not a chance," he said as Mary put our drinks on the table. "I have too many good contacts."

"That's the toughest part of the business, isn't it?" I had several reporter friends who had complained that it took years to make good contacts, to find people they could trust and who would trust them. Reporters who couldn't make good contacts often washed out or ended up with lame beats.

"It was pretty easy for me," Mike said without looking at me. He took a sip of his beer. "I used to be a cop."

Hold on. Time out. Cop turned reporter. Interesting? Yes. Scary? A little.

"Wow," I said lamely. "What was that like?"

"Exciting. Dangerous. Hard work. The stories I could tell."

"So what happened? You suddenly got an itch to write?"

"Not exactly."

The big pause that followed that statement told me something not so great had befallen him.

"Three years ago I got shot on the job. My leg. I don't know if you noticed my limp."

"You have a limp?" It was news to me. Mike chuckled.

"Anyway, they never caught the guy."

He stopped there, and I didn't push him further. We were both silent for a moment. I had so many questions, but it didn't seem right to ask them. Luckily my cell phone broke the silence.

I was expecting it to be Juliet, so I was surprised to see my friend Anupa's name on the screen. I sent the call to voice mail and mentally promised to call her back later. Still, I was spooked. I considered telling Mike about the Juliet situation. Perhaps his law enforcement experience could be of some use. On second thought, nope. He was a reporter. I couldn't trust him just yet even though the fact that he'd been a cop made it less likely in my mind that he'd written the story about the fight. I decided instead to put out a feeler.

"So Mike, here's a police question. Is it true that you have to wait twenty-four hours before you report a missing person?"

"Well, that depends on the situation. The age of the person, the circumstances under which they went missing." His eyes narrowed slightly. "Why?"

"Oh, no reason. It's just one of those things you always hear on TV. I always wondered if it was true." My ability to manufacture cool lies on the spot had me wondering if my profession was getting the better of me. I decided to strike while my powers of deceit were at their peak.

"So if you didn't write the story on page one, where did it come from?" I tried to continue the conversational tone and to sound like I didn't care that much. I thought I succeeded pretty well, but Mike knew a BS artist when he heard one. He threw a sardonic grin my way that made my heart do flip-flops.

"As soon as I saw it, I went straight to my editor and asked. Anonymous tip."

"But where did the picture come from?"

"It's the twenty-first century, Jill. This particular tip took the form of a video message from a cell phone."

So it had been a random person passing by and whipping

out a phone at the first sign of drama. For a moment, neither of us said a word, and I considered the difficulties of controlling publicity in the digital age. Soon conversation resumed, and I felt myself relax as our talk moved away from things journalistic.

We finished our drinks and left the bar. Walking the streets in the evening, I wanted it to feel romantic and date-like again. Reading my mind, Mike took my hand, and the electricity was still there. I was practically humming with tension when we reached the subway, from Mike's touch but also from worry that he would ruin this evening by asking me to his apartment. When I came to New York, I learned pretty quickly that men here have very different standards than they have back home, but Mike surprised me in a very good way. He gave me a smile and kissed me gently on the forehead.

"Good night, Cooksey. I'll call you soon."

And then he was gone. My trembling legs barely carried me down the stairs to the train, but I had something good to think about the whole way home.

That night I had crazy dreams about people wearing only one shoe who wandered around the city spraying people with perfume. Occasionally, one of them would fall through a subway grate and disappear. I didn't find this alarming for some reason, and I awoke around seven o'clock feeling reasonably rested. Lying in bed, I reached over to the bedside table and picked up my cell phone. For a second I hesitated to call Juliet so early, but then I remembered the aggravation of the previous day.

Just like the day before, the call went straight to voice mail, and I hung up without leaving a message. I was filled with contradictory emotions. Part of me was even more worried that I still hadn't heard from Juliet while another part of me, the part that thought she was a big girl who could take care of herself, was annoyed at her for making me worry. I called her again, and this time I left a message.

"Hi, Juliet. It's Jill. I haven't heard from you, and you stood me up for lunch yesterday. I'm getting really worried, and I hope you will call me as soon as you get this message. I saw the papers yesterday, so you may be lying low right now. But in a situation like this, the one person you can talk to is your media relations specialist, especially when she's also your friend. Talk to you soon, I hope." Was that really me laying on the guilt? I didn't care. I was sick of worrying and just wanted to hear from Juliet.

Sunday in New York means one thing, brunch, and I was supposed to meet my PR Posse for brunch at noon. It was only nine o'clock, so I had time to make church beforehand. I quickly showered and dressed in brown corduroy pants, a cream-colored V-neck sweater, and brown leather sneakers. At the last minute, I tied a little brown and blue scarf around my neck. I grabbed my Behemoth Black Bag, and I was ready to go.

One of the beautiful things about New York is that no one really considers church a dress-up affair. At home in Virginia, church meant a dress or skirt, possibly stockings, and certainly heels, but in New York I was free to wear pants—lovely pants— and flats—lovely flats. And my congregation was especially un- picky; the First Mt. Zion Southern Baptist Inner City Ministry, Queens branch, would gladly welcome you in a bikini. First Mt. Zion was a mission of the First Mt. Zion Baptist Church of Charlotte, North Carolina, and it was situated a mere five blocks from my apartment in an old movie theater on Steinway Street. You could have knocked me over with a feather when I passed the church that first Sunday after I'd moved to Astoria. I had just gotten off the phone with my mother who had encour- aged me to find a nice Southern Baptist congregation to attend.

"Mama, I doubt I'm going to find a Southern Baptist church in New York City," I said skeptically.

"Jill, they have everything in New York, from Rosicrucians to Christadelphians. I guarantee you they have Southern Baptists," she replied with certainty.

"Don't hold your breath, Mama."

I did not tell her for several weeks that I started attending First Mt. Zion that very Sunday (oh, that stubborn pride), but I had to. It was like a sign from God. I had attended regularly ever since.

I don't remember much of the sermon, although Reverend Calhoun was in good voice. My mind was too preoccupied with thoughts of Juliet. Eventually, I just gave in and prayed for her, searching for comfort. At the end of the service, as the congregation stood and sang, I slipped out and headed for the subway to Manhattan. The train ride gave me even more time to think about Juliet, and by think I mean worry. As I came up out of the subway station on the East Side, I was on the verge of begging off brunch so I could search for her when Mike called.

"This is a pleasant surprise," I purred into the phone.

"You won't think so in a moment. Amber O'Neil is dead. A maid at the Waldorf Astoria found her this morning with the heel of a crimson satin stiletto embedded in her eye."

CHAPTER 6

On the relatively short walk from the subway station to the Waldorf Astoria, I did some deep breathing exercises and tried to wrap my brain around the situation. Amber O'Neil was dead, killed with what was more than likely Juliet's shoe, and now Juliet was missing. I pushed down the panic that threatened to overwhelm me. The police were going to suspect Juliet. They had to. But I knew her. I knew she couldn't have done it.

Or did I? Juliet and I had been largely out of each other's lives for some years. We had reconnected over the last year, but did that mean I really knew her? She was a huge star now living mostly in Hollywood, and that had never been good for anyone. Had the fame and the money rotted her brain and her soul? I couldn't let myself believe my old friend was a killer, could I?

I entered the Waldorf lobby expecting to find a law enforcement and media circus, but the lobby was its usual sea of calm. I mentally slapped my forehead. If any institution was skilled at guarding and controlling its reputation, it was the Waldorf. All the commotion would be happening via rear entrances and service elevators. I managed only about five steps into the lobby when Jean-Paul appeared at my elbow.

"Mademoiselle, your friends in blue are waiting for you in the basement," said the concierge. He gently took my elbow and steered me toward the elevators. Neither of us spoke on the way down. What was there to say? The friend I was so worried had been kidnapped was now the prime suspect in a murder investigation. Jean-Paul had seen the shoes, most likely both of them. I knew what he was thinking, and part of me was thinking the same thing. I sighed without meaning to, and Jean-Paul gave my arm a gentle, comforting squeeze. The day before, he and I had been in the same elevator headed for Juliet's room. I felt like we were in this together.

The door opened on the basement, and we got off and turned right. This floor was never seen by the guests, and it was a far cry from the luxury of the lobby and rooms. The basement held laundry facilities, kitchens, and all manner of other maintenance departments. Toward the end of a dingy hall, several decorative screens had been set up. Their gilded elegance contrasted sharply with the dim, dirty hallway. I knew that behind those screens lay chaos, and it was there that Jean-Paul handed me off to a uniformed police officer who was standing guard.

The hallway didn't continue far beyond the screens, just one office on the left and one on the right, before it ended at a pair of oversized double doors. One was propped open, and I caught a glimpse of a loading dock outside. A small herd of law enforcement professionals was at work bustling in and out of the offices and the double doors. It looked as though the office on the right had been turned into a makeshift interrogation room for questioning witnesses and whatever else the police did when a murder happened. I watched as a male member of the housekeeping staff was escorted out of the office and toward the loading dock. As he exited, both doors were thrown open, and I caught my first glimpse of the crime scene.

Across the alley, catty-cornered from the loading dock, several uniformed officers were clustered around something on the ground. I saw a photographer moving around the object, focusing her camera, now and then changing its angle. Was the "thing" on the ground Amber with the shoe through her eye? I was starting to feel a little woozy when Mike came out of the office on the left and found me.

"Jeez! You're white as a sheet."

"I don't feel so good." Mike hurried me into the office he had exited and put me in a folding chair. The office was small and contained a battered desk, a couple of folding chairs, a file cabinet, and a telephone. Stacked against the wall were crates of bottled water. Soon he was pressing one of the bottles into my hand.

"Thanks," I managed after a long gulp of the lukewarm water. "I'm fine now. I just started thinking about…"

"The crime scene," he finished. "Try to put it out of your head. There's nothing we can do for Amber right now except help the police find her killer. The detectives just want to ask you a few questions."

And just like that Mike wasn't a reporter anymore. He had morphed back into a cop. With just a few words he managed to put me at ease and direct my attention to the task at hand. It came so easily to him that I wondered just how long it would be before he went back to the force. He was in his usual reporter's uniform of jeans, pullover, and leather jacket, but his manner was one hundred percent policeman.

"They're just finishing up with some of the housekeeping staff." We both looked across the hallway into the "interrogation room" where a young Hispanic woman with red-rimmed eyes was sitting in a chair identical to mine.

"Let me guess," I said. "She found the body."

"This morning. She takes breakfast to her little brother every day. He meets her in the alley. Today she was late, and the little guy started exploring. He found Amber's body behind the dumpster. When she found her brother, he was nearly catatonic. Forensics estimates the body has been there since sometime Saturday morning. Not a pretty sight. She only stopped crying about fifteen minutes ago."

"Poor thing. She looks so young."

He glanced at his notepad.

"Eighteen. Supporting a disabled mother and two younger siblings in Sunnyside." The reporter was back, and I already knew one of the angles he was considering for his story.

"So, any advice before they start grilling me?" I tried to make light but fell flat. There was no getting away from the gravity of the situation. A real life-and-death scenario had intruded on my relatively peaceful and frivolous existence, and I was searching for a way to deal with it.

"Just tell the truth," said Mike sincerely, but a moment later he followed with "You do remember what the truth is, right, even though you're in PR?"

Ha ha. I rolled my eyes at him as a detective motioned from across the hallway for me to join him in the other office. I traded places with the housekeeper who was soon sitting in my vacated chair chatting with Mike. She smiled a little, and I knew that he was comforting her as well as getting his story. It was a fair trade. I turned my attention to the detective.

I estimated his age at about forty. He looked fit, but the lines in his face gave his age away, as did his slightly thinning brown hair speckled with gray. He wore a charcoal suit and yellow tie that only a wife could have picked out for him. On the desk in front of him were a steaming cup of black coffee and a stack of papers. As I sat in the hot seat, so to speak, he filled out some information on a form. It took several minutes, and I started to wonder if he had forgotten me. Then I realized it was part of his procedure.

My father had once shared a business secret with me when I was a teenager. He told me that silence was the best way to get people to spill their guts. He would use it on his employees if he thought someone was up to no good. He'd call them into his office and sit there in silence.

"People hate silence," he told me. "It unnerves them. Make them sit in silence long enough, and they'll be so rattled that they'll tell you what you want to know. Sometimes they'll just blurt it out before you've asked a single question."

Remembering my dad's advice, I smiled just as the detective happened to look up at me. Mistake.

"You think this is funny?" he growled. "A woman is dead."

"I'm sorry. My mind was somewhere else…You remind me of my dad." Well, sort of. Not exactly, but I figured a little charm couldn't hurt at this point.

He grunted at that, but his posture relaxed a little. He went back to filling out papers, pausing only to drain the cup of coffee that was almost instantly refilled for him. Finally, he spoke again. He introduced himself as Detective Donato. He asked me my name, how to spell it, my address, who I worked for, and how long I'd lived in New York. Finally, he got down to business.

"Had you ever met the deceased, Amber O'Neil?"

I told him that I had and described the incident at the launch. He then told me some things I already knew: that Amber had apparently been killed with a shoe; that someone had beat her with it and had managed to puncture her eye with the heel and embed it in her brain; that the shoe was a crimson satin pump.

"Do you know of anyone who owns a pair of shoes like that, Ms. Cooksey?" He already knew the answer to the question. I wanted to shout that thousands of women owned shoes like that, but I only said, "Yes." He waited for me to elaborate, and I told him about the launch, about Juliet's dress and shoes, about her standing me up, my visit to her room with Jean-Paul (he grimaced), and what we found. Then he asked me where Juliet was, but that question I couldn't answer.

A half an hour later, we had gone through it all again, and he was finished with me, sort of. He sent me back to my old chair. The teenaged maid, whose name I learned was Magdalena, was gone, but Mike was still there busily writing in his notebook.

"I'm glad that's over," I breathed as I sat down. I glanced at my watch to find it was only one in the afternoon, but I was exhausted.

"They talked to Jean-Paul earlier. As long as your story matches his, you'll be fine," Mike reassured me. "They were pretty angry when they heard you two had been in Juliet's room."

"We didn't know it was a crime scene, or rather, I thought it had been a crime against Juliet."

"Why didn't you tell me any of this last night?" I could see the bewilderment on Mike's face.

"I wanted to, especially after you told me you'd been a cop…"

"But I'm a reporter now. That's it, right?"

"Mike, my job is to safeguard my client's reputation. That front-page story in *The Gazette* yesterday was bad enough."

"That wasn't my story!"

"I know, but I couldn't risk any other rumors getting out, and that's just what they were—rumors. Honestly, I didn't know if it was just my imagination. I'd have looked like an idiot if I'd shared my worries that Juliet was missing and possibly kidnapped only for her to turn up the next day alive and well."

We both pondered that for a minute. Mike was upset, something I hadn't anticipated, but it wasn't necessarily a bad thing. He was the first to speak again.

"I wouldn't have thought you were an idiot, and I wouldn't have made a story out of it," he said as he touched my hand.

"I know that now." I smiled at him in what I hoped was a disarming manner. "I've only known you for two days."

It worked. He smiled back and took my hand in his.

"What's it going to take for you to trust me, Jill?"

It was a challenge as much as a question, and I had no idea how to answer, no talking points or sound bites that dealt with intimacy, so I just winked at him and asked, "So how come you have a backstage pass for murder? Are you blackmailing Detective Donato?"

Mike snorted. "Not quite. He owes me a favor. I doubt he'll be so obliging next time."

"He seems a bit grumpy."

"Well, he has to deal with murder every day," Mike replied dryly.

Fair enough.

CHAPTER 7

I left the Waldorf at one thirty and headed around the corner to a diner because I'd had to forego brunch with my Posse. My PR campaign was disintegrating around me, and I was stressed out beyond belief. I was planning to eat my feelings and prepare for the round of phone calls I had to make. I ordered chicken and waffles and an iced tea to which I added four sugar packets and stirred as if my life depended on it. Sweet southern nectar! When the chicken and waffles arrived, I doused the whole thing with maple syrup and tucked in. When the plate was clean and my glass was drained except for some sugar sludge in the bottom, I felt a lot better and ready to face the music. I pulled out my cell phone.

The first call was to Pamela, or rather to her voice mail. I was grateful that I didn't reach her in person because I was already a nervous wreck. I didn't need her criticism. What's more, she wasn't going to help me anyway. I left her a message briefly describing the situation and telling her I was bringing Meredith and possibly Hoss in that afternoon for a crisis communications meeting.

Next, I called Jeannie. She made a lot of noise about being

terribly busy, but I distinctly heard her turning the pages of a newspaper and refilling her coffee cup. I shut her down pretty quickly by mentioning the word "overtime" and had her call the never helpful Tanya. If nothing else, she could run out and pick up dinner and some smelling salts.

My next call was to Meredith Hopkins. She and Hoss weren't staying at the Waldorf because she said it cost too much, so we had booked them into the Wellington farther uptown. The phone rang twice before she picked up. I apologized for disturbing her on a Sunday and told her we had a situation.

"You mean that story in *The Gazette* yesterday? I was wondering when you'd get around to calling me about it."

"I'd be happy to talk with you about that story a little later, Meredith." The carbs were making it relatively easy to be polite to her despite her nasty tone. "We have another situation on our hands."

It's rather difficult to gently break it to a client that the spokesperson for her company may have murdered someone. I just put it out there. The announcement was met with stunned silence, which gave me a moment to gird my loins for the onslaught that I knew would shortly follow.

"You brought Juliet Scott to us, Jill Cooksey. She was your idea entirely. I always had reservations about that woman."

Sure you did, Meredith. That's why you ordered champagne and caviar when I announced that Juliet was willing to be the spokesmodel for Eshellon. I held my tongue.

"If this has any impact on Eshellon cosmetics, I will hold you personally responsible. Make no mistake."

I'd expected this reaction, and as in all types of business, the customer was always right unless you were already in court.

"Meredith, let me assure you that I deeply regret the situation, and my team and I will do everything in our power to make sure the impact on Eshellon is negligible." My assurances were met with a grunt of disbelief. I didn't blame her. I wouldn't have believed me either.

Action was required to make everyone feel better and to prevent a rematch of the blame game. I arranged to meet with Meredith, Hoss, and my team (such as it was) at Waverly in an hour to assess the situation and implement the crisis plan.

One problem. My crisis plan didn't cover spokesmodel-as-murder-suspect. In all of our brainstorming sessions, that possibility had never crossed our minds. I had written crisis plans for in case the perfume was tampered with, the ingredients were found to be carcinogenic, or nude photos of Juliet surfaced from somewhere. Murder was a different game altogether. I was going to have to wing it. I left the bar, hailed a cab, threw myself into it, gave directions to the cabbie, and pulled out my cell phone again. I needed a little guidance. Kate, my link to the celebrity world, answered after the first ring.

"Kate, I need some help."

"I know. I've been thinking about it." God bless you, Kate. "Here's what you do. If Scott pleads innocent, you support her. Innocent until proven guilty, right?"

"Well, of course." Please, God, let her be innocent.

"So if they find her guilty," continued Kate, "Eshellon will be saddened and deeply disappointed. Juliet will not only have murdered somebody, but she'll also have let the company down. Eshellon will be a victim, as well."

It sounded so cold and calculating, but that's PR. I had called Kate because I was too close to the situation. Juliet was my friend, so I needed an impartial PR professional to put me on the right path. Cold and calculating it may have been, but necessary nonetheless.

"So what do we do during the trial? How do we keep perfume sales from plummeting?" I needed Kate to keep thinking for me until I could come to terms with the situation.

"That's the best part, honey. You work this right and

perfume sales will soar." Kate was downright cheerful, and part of me was sickened, but the other part of me recognized an impartial professional just doing her job.

She continued, "You tap into Juliet's fan base. If Eshellon openly and vociferously supports Juliet, then Fall Fantasy perfume becomes the next pink ribbon. Women and girls will be wearing it to show they support their favorite girl-next-door. You might even consider some special packaging or including a little apple pin with Juliet's name on it. Something like that."

Somewhere along the line, I started to scribble notes. I thanked Kate for her insight and rang off. She had energized me, and in my head I was already drafting a press release, although the jerking of the cab through traffic made it difficult. Granted, Juliet hadn't even surfaced, and she hadn't been charged with a crime. She might have a terrific alibi and all this could go away in an instant, but PR is about planning for the worst and hoping for the best. Still, a little voice in the back of my head kept calling me a traitor to my friend. I told it to shut up, that I didn't want Juliet to be guilty, that I was just planning for the worst-case scenario. The voice got quieter, but it didn't go away altogether.

Once in my office, I decided to get some answers to some questions. The first was where the heck was Juliet? I flipped through my contacts until I found her agent's home number in Los Angeles.

Sam Herskowitz answered on the first ring. "Hersky here. Talk to me."

"Sam, it's Jill Cooksey." I tried to keep my voice as low key as possible. If he was hiding Juliet, I didn't want him going all evasive on me.

"Jill, baby. I saw my girl getting sloppy with the bubbly, and I don't mean drinking. You plan that?"

"I assure you, Sam, that wasn't my doing. I'm so sor—"

"It's a little lowbrow for my girl's taste, but I've been telling her she needed some grittier exposure."

"Yeah, um, I wanted to talk to her about it, but I haven't been able to get ahold of her today. Have you talked to her?"

"No, baby. I've been holding someone else's hand this weekend." I had to tell him the situation. As Juliet's agent, he would be instrumental in getting her through this. When I finished, he was silent for just a moment.

"Okay baby, it's unexpected, but I've worked with worse. I'll get on the horn with my attorney. You let me know as soon as she surfaces, *capisce?*"

I told him I would, and he hung up. I sat quietly for a moment, wondering at the sangfroid of the people in my industry, including my own.

Juliet's parents in Luthersburg were my next call. When the answering machine picked up, I had no idea what kind of message to leave, so I hung up.

I heard the elevator door slide open down the hall, and in a moment a huffing and puffing Jeannie appeared at my door. Despite her reluctance to come in on a Sunday, she was dressed professionally in one of her work outfits that I felt sure dated from the mid-eighties. A scarf was tied in a huge bow at her throat. Overtime was more of an incentive than I'd thought.

"I couldn't get ahold of Tanya," she said between gasps. "No answer on her phone, and it wouldn't let me leave a message."

"Any sign of Pamela?"

"What do you think?"

Crap! Jeannie and I did not make a full public relations team, and while Tanya and Pamela were hardly assets, my clients needed to see an army on their side.

"That's okay, Jeannie," I lied. "I'm thinking of bringing someone in from the outside to help us in the crisis."

Jeannie, while grumpy, was no idiot.

"Does Pamela know about this?" she asked, her glasses nearly falling off her nose as she peered at me over them.

"Pamela," I replied evenly, "is probably off with Tanya giving their credit cards a good workout." I waited for her reaction. I needed Jeannie on my side, not making things worse.

Jill Cooksey does not fail.

She grunted, nodded her agreement, and headed off down the hall.

"I'll make coffee," she called back to me, and I sighed in relief. Thirty seconds later, I was on the phone with Kate.

By three o'clock Kate, Jeannie, and I were assembled in the conference room. Jeannie had outdone herself on an assortment of sandwiches, cookies, and brownies, along with coffee, tea, sodas, bottled water, and Hoss Buckworth's favorite drink, bourbon, none of which would go on Eshellon's bill. I tried Pamela again with no luck. I wasn't too worried; Kate was a godsend. She and I would both handle media relations, and she'd help me draft all the press materials we would need. Her schedule was clear the next day, so she had called in sick. She owed me a day anyway. I'd recently helped wrangle a dozen stars of a hit Saturday morning show for tweens during their participation in a 5k walkathon in Central Park. Something to do with meningitis awareness. Anyway, the penicillin shot I had to get after a rabid eleven-year-old fan bit me meant Kate owed me big time.

We heard the ding of the elevator, and Jeannie went to greet our disgruntled clients. I wasn't surprised to see Meredith's grim face when they entered the conference room, but Hoss's ashen complexion shocked me. He made a beeline for the bourbon and poured a tall glass, no ice. Then he heaved himself into a chair and stared at the conference table. Meredith took the seat next to him and patted his hand. When he looked up, she gave him an encouraging smile, but he just went back to staring. My speculation over a romantic attachment between Hoss and Juliet suddenly didn't seem so far-fetched.

With my stomach in knots, I started to lead the group through our plan, with strategies and press releases for every eventuality we could come up with: if Juliet were charged, if she denied the charges, if she confessed to the charges. Kate then explained some ways we could spin the situation to Eshellon's advantage if we had to. I asked if Meredith and Hoss could think of any other scenarios we might have missed.

"That's what we pay you for, Jill," said Meredith. Hoss just continued to stare. I replied that we would continue brainstorming and planning to make sure all our bases were covered.

"So until Juliet is charged—" started Meredith.

"If she's charged," put in Kate hopefully. Meredith rolled her eyes.

"Until Juliet is charged," Meredith continued, "what are we telling the press? She has interviews tomorrow about Fall Fantasy and the launch."

"We have to reschedule the interviews," I said.

"What? If she doesn't talk to the press, we'll lose momentum. Fall Fantasy will get lost in the murder coverage." Meredith was frantic.

The time had come to reveal the worst part of all.

"We have to reschedule the interviews," I began, "because we can't find Juliet Scott."

At this, Hoss snapped out of his reverie.

"You don't know where she is?" he gasped.

I explained that she had stood me up for lunch and that I'd been to the hotel and had called her agent, her mother, and her cell phone countless times. Juliet had vanished. Hoss's face turned redder and redder as I explained until he finally pushed away from the conference table, upsetting his chair and his bourbon, and stormed out. I rose to go after him, but Meredith held me back.

"Leave him alone. That man is watching his company, the one he built with his beloved wife, take a beating thanks to your little starlet," Meredith spat. "I expect you to do everything in your power to ameliorate this little PR nightmare, but I'm not getting my hopes up. My assistant, Dustin Buckworth, is flying into town as we speak, and he'll be in this office first thing tomorrow morning to monitor the situation and keep you all on your toes."

Meredith was more worked up than I'd ever seen her.

"Now if you'll excuse me," she said as she snatched up her purse and coat, "I have to see to Mr. Buckworth. I expect reports every hour." She sailed out of the conference room leaving Kate and me gasping for breath.

"Well," said Jeannie as she snatched up a sandwich, "that could have gone worse." I wasn't so sure.

Soon Kate and I were at work rescheduling the interviews. Amber's death had hit the airwaves, luckily without a mention of Juliet—yet. It was easy to tell reporters that she was too shocked and saddened by her costar's death to do interviews the next day. We put them off until Tuesday, hoping against hope that she would turn up.

It was on a trip to the copy machine that I heard the argument. The machine was at the other end of the hall from my office, near a smaller conference room where the employees of Waverly Communications had their yearly performance reviews. Somehow Meredith and Hoss had found their way to it, and although the door was closed, I could easily understand the gist of their exchange.

"You've got to put your personal feelings aside," cried Meredith. "For the good of the company."

"I will not turn my back on Juliet. For heaven's sake, I'm going to marry her!" roared Hoss.

"If she ever says yes!"

I had a hunch that I now knew why Juliet wanted to have lunch with me. That Hoss had proposed to Juliet didn't surprise me one bit. That Juliet would be seriously conflicted about marrying a man her father's age didn't surprise me either.

After a moment, I heard the sounds of soft weeping and of Meredith trying to comfort Hoss. Not wanting to alert them to my presence with copier noise, I crept back to my office without my copies.

I sent Jeannie home at seven, Kate at eight, and I locked up the office at nine and headed for home via car service.

At nine thirty, I opened my apartment door and did a face plant onto the futon. I dreaded the thought that I'd have to be back in the office in less than twelve hours.

My phone chirped, and I snatched it up in a hot second. I knew I'd be doing that until the nightmare was over. Happily, it was Mike.

"How's the world of PR and Eshellon cosmetics?"

"It stinks. Everyone is mad at me, and I didn't even kill anyone."

He chuckled, but I was serious.

"Did you eat dinner?" My mood softened since someone cared enough to ask about the details of my life.

"I had a chicken salad sandwich. I hope it gives me food poisoning so I don't have to go to work tomorrow. How was your day?"

"Busy. Juliet isn't mentioned in my story for tomorrow's paper because she isn't being charged...yet."

"Should I be relieved? Or am I still waiting for the other shoe to drop? No pun intended."

"I think it's going to depend on whose fingerprints show up on that shoe," said Mike. "And Donato told me they'd really like to talk to Juliet. It would be better for her if she would show herself."

"It would be better for everyone. But doesn't Juliet need a motive?"

"Well, the last time anyone saw her, she was being attacked by Amber O'Neil in the park."

"That's a bit thin, isn't it?"

"It's thin, but it's enough to make her interesting to the police."

I had no reply, so we sat on the phone in silence for a while.

"Get some sleep, Jill," said Mike at long last. "Tomorrow could be a rough one."

He was right, so I said good night.

CHAPTER 8

ate and I were the first ones in the office the next day. I had bought her breakfast early that morning so we could plan our strategy. I was going to put her in the empty office two doors down from mine. Both she and I would field calls from the press while we waited to see if Juliet turned up and if she would be charged. We couldn't put any of our crisis strategies into play until we knew what the crisis would be.

We were both installed in our respective offices by eight thirty when Jeannie arrived. I'd left doughnuts on her desk as a thank-you for the day before. Twenty minutes later, she showed up at my door with a half-eaten jelly doughnut in one hand and a cup of coffee for me in the other for which I was very grateful. I thought she would just leave it, but instead she shut my door, helped herself to a seat, and asked the question no one else wanted to.

"So," she began as she peered at me over her reading glasses, "do you think it's possible that Juliet really did kill Amber?"

My temper flashed, I started to say something biting in reply, but I found I couldn't utter the words. Truthfully, anything was possible. I looked Jeannie in the eye and was surprised to find a modicum of sympathy there.

"I don't know, Jeannie. Maybe." For a moment I wanted to cry, but that changed when my office door was yanked open by none other than Juliet Scott.

"Where is everybody? Don't I have interviews in half an hour?"

Jeannie's doughnut landed on the floor with a resounding squish, but we were both frozen in our chairs. Juliet just stared at us like we were crazy.

"Hello? Are y'all okay?"

The next thing I knew I was hugging an utterly confused Juliet.

"Where have you been?" I cried.

"The Hamptons," she replied as if the answer were obvious.

Five minutes later Juliet, Kate, Jeannie, and I were in the conference room with the "Meeting in Progress" sign firmly attached to the door. It was time for answers, which Juliet readily supplied.

After the altercation with Amber, she had gone backstage to change. That's when she decided to get out of the city for the weekend. A friend in LA had loaned her the key to her Hampton's beach house. She took a cab back to the hotel, packed a small bag, grabbed another cab to Grand Central, and made the last train out to Long Island. She needed some time to think.

How logical and yet not.

"Why didn't you let me know?" I asked. "When you didn't show for lunch on Saturday, I got worried."

"I told Tanya to tell you. Let me guess. She didn't give you the message."

"We haven't heard from Tanya since Friday night," said Jeannie.

"When I went back to change out of the dress," Juliet

explained, "Tanya was backstage filling a tote bag with leftover bottles of perfume. I think she was stealing."

"Believe me," I said. "That's the least of our troubles."

She gave me an odd look but went on with her story.

"I handed the dress over to Tanya to take to the dry cleaners on Monday, and I asked her to give you the message that I wouldn't be able to make it for lunch but that I would be back on Monday in time for interviews. I wish she'd given you the message and saved you from worrying."

"Or you could have returned Jill's phone calls," Kate put in quietly.

Sheepishly, Juliet put her hand into her purse and pulled out a cell phone with a shattered screen.

"I sort of took out some frustration on it. I was so pissed off at Amber, among other things. Truly, I'm so sorry that I worried everybody. I promise that I left a message for you with Tanya." The need to please everyone was evident on her face. I was suddenly sad again as I thought about the news I had to share with her because it was obvious she didn't know a thing.

"What were the other things?" asked Jeannie pointedly. "You were mad at the crazy cow, but it seems strange that the fight would send you fleeing the city."

For a moment Juliet was silent. Then with a sag of her shoulders, she coughed up.

"I'm in love with an older man, and I don't know what to do about it."

"Hoss Buckworth," stated Jeannie, whom I was beginning to suspect I'd underestimated. Juliet nodded faintly.

"He wants to marry me, but I'm not sure I should. He was putting the pressure on again Friday night, and I just needed to get away to think. I didn't want to worry anybody."

"Juliet, it's all right," I began. "Now I need to know if you have seen the papers over the last couple of days."

She hadn't, and the cable bill at the beach house hadn't been paid recently, cutting her off from current events. I started catching her up by telling her of the coverage her fight with Amber had received. I told her about my trip to her hotel room and calls to her mom and agent.

Then I broke the bad news about Amber.

All the color drained out of her face, but I kept going, intent on ripping off the band-aid.

"They think I did it," she whispered when I finished.

"Well," added Jeannie unhelpfully, "it was your shoe."

With Jeannie's help, I got Juliet to Pamela's office and onto a small sofa before the breakdown began. I guess I expected her to act the way I would have in her shoes, which would be to yell and scream and get very angry and probably cuss a lot, but all she did was curl up in a ball and cry silently. I raided Pamela's liquor cabinet and made Juliet a vodka and cranberry because I didn't know what else to do. After a few minutes, I left her in Jeannie's care. I had to think.

When I entered my office and shut my door on the craziness outside, I have to admit it felt wonderful. Opening my window and climbing up on the bookcase and out onto the roof, I felt even better. I ducked around a corner to where an old plastic bucket sat overturned—my makeshift stool for sunny days when I wanted to lunch with a little more peace and quiet or when I just needed to get away. I sat and thought.

The first question to hit my brain was whether I believed her, and I was shocked at myself. Everything Juliet had said was plausible and verifiable if ever Tanya decided to show up for work. Moreover, she was an old friend; certainly she deserved the benefit of the doubt. Before any more strange, unfriendly voices could chime in, I settled that question. I was in Juliet's corner for the duration.

The question that naturally followed was what on earth was I going to do?

My phone started to vibrate in my pocket, and I hoped it was the Man Upstairs with the answer to question two.

It wasn't. It was Mike, and instead of letting the call go to voice mail, my hormones made me take it.

"Hey, Mike! What's up?" Could I have sounded any weirder? He was on to me immediately.

"Juliet is with you, isn't she?" he asked sharply.

"I wish," I lied, a little more in control now. "I still haven't heard from her, and I'm worried sick."

He wasn't buying it.

"Look, Jill, if you hide things from the police, it can have serious consequences, not just for Juliet but for you too."

"You're not the police anymore, remember?" Head slap. He got me.

"That's what I thought." I could hear the smile in his voice. "So where does Juliet say she's been?"

"You're joking, right?" Did Mike really think I was the dumbest publicist in the business? "Just because you're attractive doesn't mean I'm going to betray my friend and my client by talking to you."

"So you think I'm attractive." His cockiness knew no bounds. "We can talk all about how attractive I am on our next date, but seriously, have you thought about what you *are* going to do?"

I thought for a moment, and he let me. Juliet would have to make a public statement, and she would have to go to the police. Any other course of action would smack of guilt. Since we had to go to the police, I thought Mike might come in handy. Briefly, without any of the details about Juliet's whereabouts over the weekend, I told Mike my plan.

Two hours later I was back in the conference room with the whole Eshellon team, now including several of their lawyers. Hoss wasn't looking well. I hadn't been privy to his reunion with Juliet, but however it went down, he was not encouraged.

His face was florid and his eyes bleary, a look I'd seen too many times on the subway late at night for me not to recognize a bender. In confirmation, Hoss rose, staggered to the refreshments laid out on the credenza, picked up a glass, and emptied his flask into it. The resulting two fingers of bourbon were unsatisfactory.

"We're going to need some Maker's Mark in here ASAP," he bellowed as he meandered back to his seat between Meredith and Juliet. The Eshellon VP patted his arm encouragingly while Juliet just stared off into space.

She had never really recovered from my earlier revelations. As I watched her, I could almost see the prison scenes floating across her vision. A sob erupted from deep within her, momentarily jogging Hoss out of his drunken stupor, and he took her hand and held it tight. Neither of them said a word or even looked at each other, but that gesture spoke volumes to me. It also seemed to speak volumes to Dustin, Hoss's son, who sat across from him at the conference table.

Short, yet lean and trim, sandy-haired Dustin looked more like a young corporate intern than a PR manager for a large multinational corporation. As if he'd read my thoughts, he donned a pair of light tortoiseshell glasses the exact color of his freckles, and they gave him a bit more authority. His dark blue suit, French blue shirt, and yellow tie gave him a sunny sort of look. A small cloud seemed to pass over that sun as he saw his father take Juliet's hand. He didn't look angry, just resigned.

Pamela still hadn't shown up, and the mood in the room was grim. I was going to have to take charge, not like I hadn't already. With a slight clearing of my throat, I brought the war council to order.

"First, I want to say that we're all so very glad that Juliet has come back to us safe and sound." The lawyers looked a bit startled at this as if they had never been shown the bright side of any situation before. Everyone else just nodded and grunted their agreement.

"Now, it's time for action," I continued. "I have a plan that I think will put Juliet and Eshellon in a favorable light and set Juliet up for the best possible defense."

"But she hasn't done anything!" Hoss interrupted. "This little darlin' is as pure as the driven snow, and I won't have anyone sayin' otherwise!"

"Of course she's innocent," I responded quickly. "That's not what I meant. The police are going to have questions, and they may not believe her the way we all do. The best thing Juliet can do is be as upfront and accommodating as she can…"

Now it was time to drop the bombshell.

"To that end, I have taken the liberty of contacting the police through a journalist frie… associate of mine."

The room went wild. Lawyers were shouting. Hoss was shouting. Pamela and Dustin were shouting. The only person who wasn't shouting was Juliet who just stared at all the shouting people like they were crazy.

I didn't know how I'd get control of the room when Jeannie was suddenly there standing on a chair screaming "Quiet!"

Before shouting could resume, I quickly explained my thinking. Juliet would have to see the police regardless. If they came to the office, she could give her statement with her lawyers present and without being dragged downtown. Then if they decided to arrest her, we could make it as quiet as possible. Moreover, we needed to get her side out to the public as soon as possible. I'd arranged for Mike to be the first journalist to get her statement in return for pulling a few strings with the police. He would run the story in the evening paper before anyone else. Then the firm would release a statement completely in support of Juliet.

The room was quiet as everyone took in the plan. So far, so good. I then called upon Kate to explain phase two should

Juliet be arrested and charged, the "Justice for Juliet" campaign with little apple pins in every package of Fall Fantasy perfume. Provided with another way to support the woman he loved, Hoss seemed to perk up a bit. Dustin frowned, but Meredith seemed impressed. When Kate finished her presentation, Hoss stood up to shake her hand.

"It's a grand plan, little lady," he said as he pumped Kate's arm. He then turned to Juliet and knelt by her chair with only a little wobble. "We're going to get through this. I will not lose you. I want to add one more piece to this little plan. Marry me, and let me show the world how much I believe in you."

The room held its breath. With a sob, Juliet buried her head in Hoss's shoulder and cried uncontrollably. At their end of the table, the lawyers all looked at each other uncomfortably. No one heard the knock on the conference room door, but when it opened to reveal Mike and Detective Donato, I felt a flood of relief mixed with icy fear for my friend.

CHAPTER 9

*D*onato would only let the lawyers accompany Juliet into Pamela's office for questioning. The rest of us were left to sit and wait. Meredith and Dustin both excused themselves to make some calls. Kate went to her makeshift office to research vendors who could design and produce Juliet pins, leaving me with Hoss and Mike who I could see was anxious to get his interviews started. But once everyone else was out of the room, Hoss no longer had to put on a brave face. He sat staring at the table, the occasional tear running down his pink cheeks.

"I can't lose her too," he muttered to no one in particular.

With one hand I squeezed Hoss's arm while with the other I scribbled on a legal pad "Off the record, at least for now" and slid it over to Mike. He gave a little nod, and I turned all my attention to Hoss.

"You're not going to lose her. Juliet didn't kill Amber, so she won't go to jail." Hoss just grunted. I didn't believe me either. Plenty of innocent people went to jail. I certainly didn't believe that the majority of people in jail were falsely convicted, but it did happen.

"I never thought I'd find love again," Hoss reflected. "I never had any trouble finding women, what with my billions, but I never thought I'd find love after Shelley…You know I never thought Shelley would die. She fought the cancer hard, and we thought she'd won. Everyone thought so. The doctors. Everyone. Her hair had even grown back. We were planning a trip to Africa because she always wanted to go there. I couldn't care less about seeing Africa, but it was her dream."

He took another swig of bourbon and belched softly.

"It's so different with Juliet but also the same in a lot of ways. She gets my jokes, just like Shelley did, but she gets me to do different things, stuff I never thought I could do. We went windsurfing once. Can you picture a cowboy like me windsurfing? It was amazing. *She* is amazing."

For the life of me, I couldn't imagine the surfboard that could keep the giant Texan afloat, but I kept that to myself. Before I could ask my next question, Mike asked it for me.

"Hoss, how does Amber fit into all of this?"

"It was just a fling. Nothing serious. I met her at a party in Hollywood. We had chemistry." He blushed. "But that's all we had. Pretty soon I realized she was just looking to be the face of Eshellon Cosmetics. Then you brought Juliet to me, and that was all she wrote. I broke with Amber and a couple of others I was seeing at the time. Juliet's the one."

"Tell me about how you met her, about your courtship," asked Mike. "It would be great for the story, put a real human face on it. It could only help Juliet."

As Hoss told the story, I cast a glance across the room at Dustin and Meredith who had quietly reentered the conference room. He was busy playing with his phone, or so it looked. The expressions that flitted across his face as his father told the tale of his twenty-something girlfriend told me Dustin was listening intently. And Meredith, she was watching Dustin, a look of real concern on her face. Interesting. Meredith and

Dustin? She was certainly older than Dustin, but the age difference was nothing compared to the gap between Hoss and Juliet.

While Mike interviewed Hoss, I half listened in and half pondered a relationship between Meredith and Dustin. When Hoss finished, it was their turn. I hoped their answers to Mike's questions would give something away about their relationship, but they were public relations professionals who knew how to say nothing and make it sound like something. I should have been pleased, but I found myself annoyed instead.

As Mike was finishing with Dustin, one of the lawyers entered the room and signaled to Hoss. The big man was out of his seat in a flash leaving behind a streak of splashed bourbon. I retrieved some napkins from the credenza and started mopping up. Before I could finish, Hoss was back with Juliet in tow. His grip on her was fierce, but she didn't seem to mind. As they entered the room, Mike slipped out, presumably to confer with Detective Donato.

"She's a free woman!" said Hoss enthusiastically. "A free woman!"

"For now," mused Juliet with a weak smile.

"Forever," asserted Hoss. "The police don't know a turkey from a turd."

I had to smile at that, but I noticed that Juliet still looked troubled.

"They still have to check out my story," she cautioned Hoss. "I'm not out of the woods just yet."

"Well, as soon as you are, we're getting the heck outta Dodge. How does St. Bart's sound? Or Fiji?"

"Fiji sounds terrific, Hoss." Juliet stroked his arm lovingly and gazed adoringly into his eyes. The big man melted into a puddle of love.

"I'll just go make some calls. Get the ball rolling." He planted a noisy kiss on her forehead and strode confidently from the room. As soon as he was gone, Juliet dropped the act.

"He doesn't want to believe it, Jill." Juliet's voice, so solid and warm a few seconds before, now held a note of panic. "That's my shoe embedded in Amber's brain. If they can't find a taxi driver or train conductor or anyone who can verify my story, I'm going down for this."

Juliet's hands seemed to be grasping for something to hold onto, so I put mine into hers, hoping my palms weren't sweaty. Hers were soaked, so it wouldn't have mattered anyway.

"Of course they'll find someone," I said in my most soothing voice. Juliet wasn't the only one who could act. "You didn't kill Amber O'Neil."

I turned to Dustin and Meredith for confirmation and support, but Dustin was pale beneath his freckles, and Meredith could only muster a weak smile. Great.

"It's going to be fine," I reasserted as I firmly patted Juliet's hand.

"Help me, Jill," she whispered before succumbing to tears again.

I wanted to pump Mike for info as soon as he got back from talking to Donato, but he came back with a message that the detective wanted to see me. *Gulp.* I searched my brain for anyone who might be able to verify that I went home and straight to bed after the launch. Just Saul the cockroach, and he was dead. But surely Mrs. Maroulis kept tabs on my comings and goings. At least it felt that way.

It turned out that Donato just wanted a copy of the guest list for the Fall Fantasy launch and Tanya's address and phone number. He asked me to call him when she came in to work, and I said I would. I forbore from telling him not to hold his breath.

When I got back to the conference room, Mike was interviewing Juliet. In the wake of her mini-breakdown, she was surprisingly calm, and she answered Mike's questions like a pro. She was deeply distressed and saddened by Amber's death. While they hadn't been close friends, she admired Amber's talent and felt that her death was a great loss. She couldn't imagine *Singletons* without her costar. She deeply regretted that their last conversation together had been argumentative as they had shared some great times over the years. (The cynical part of my brain thought that comment particularly inspired.) She didn't want to comment on Amber's personal life because she wanted to help preserve what privacy she could for Amber.

I thought the interview was going wonderfully well, and I was pondering ways I might thank Mike later until he asked the 64,000-dollar question.

"Juliet, how do you think your shoe ended up being the murder weapon?"

I heard Meredith start to sputter from her corner of the conference room. Juliet opened her mouth to answer, but I managed to get there just in time.

"I think we're done here," I interjected smoothly while shooting dagger eyes at Mike. I rose from the table to signal that it was time for him to leave.

"But that's the question everyone will want to know," he insisted as he jumped to his feet.

"Well, they'll just have to learn to live with unsatisfied curiosity," I rounded on Mike, hands on hips. He had several inches on me, and I had to look up at him—not a hardship as his hair was a glossy brown and his eyes were the color of cornflowers. I struggled to keep my stern expression.

"Like it or not," stated Mike calmly as he turned from me to address the whole room, "Juliet is going to be tried in the court of public opinion as soon as the public finds out that her shoe was used to murder Amber only a few hours after they fought in Central Park. Don't you think Juliet should get a chance to defend herself?"

The fact that Mike was trying to go over my head about this made my blood pressure shoot up about twenty points. What a publicist wants more than anything is control over the information going out, and I was quickly losing it.

"Juliet will only need to defend herself if she gets charged," I pointed out icily. "Until such time, addressing questions like that will only make her look desperate and guilty."

That brought Mike back into the ring with me, which is where I wanted him for multiple reasons.

"Not answering questions will make her look like she has something to hide," he retorted through clenched teeth while shifting a few inches closer. I stood my ground. It wasn't hard to do. His cologne was delicious.

"Juliet is through answering questions, and that is the final word on the subject," I pronounced pompously with a wave of my index finger in the vicinity of his face. I had a quick vision of that finger touching the cleft in his chin and…

"Actually, Jill, I think he has a point," put in Meredith from the corner.

Mike smirked, and I really wanted to kill Meredith. I turned to face her with what I hoped wasn't too hostile an expression on my face.

"Juliet has nothing to hide," explained Eshellon's head of public relations. "Why should she act like she does? Wouldn't an innocent person proclaim her innocence?"

"But she hasn't been accused of anything!" I cried, finally losing my patience. Was I angry because the interview wasn't going my way or because my verbal wrestling match with Mike had been interrupted? Probably both.

"The shoe is out there, Jill," said Meredith. "The shoe alone accuses her." For some reason that statement made me want to giggle, but I stifled the urge.

"You're not considering Juliet's position, Meredith," I argued. "You're just thinking about Eshellon's reputation."

"I'm looking out for Eshellon's reputation because that's what I get paid to do," said Meredith evenly. "And so do you, Jill."

I closed my eyes and took a deep breath. Meredith was right, annoyingly. I was making this personal because Juliet was my friend. But wasn't it Juliet's freedom, if not her life, on the line here? I didn't think it was right for Juliet to do something that might damage her case just because she had a contract with a cosmetics corporation. And I didn't think Hoss would want her to either, even if it cost him millions. He was currently off making plans for Fiji, probably fueling his private jet and stocking it with bourbon, so I couldn't get his opinion. Really though, said the small rational part of my brain, only one person's opinion mattered.

"I think we should leave this up to Juliet," I said.

As it turned out, she was happy to answer Mike's question, but it was a little anticlimactic.

MIKE: "Juliet, how do you think your shoe ended up being the murder weapon?"

JULIET: "I have absolutely no idea."

CHAPTER 10

We did some media training that afternoon to prepare Juliet for the kinds of questions she would have to face from the press at our event the next day, although I think facing Mike McCall of the *New York Gazette* was the best training of all. Hoss returned from making travel arrangements with a calm and cheerful demeanor. I think taking charge of something he could control, like a travel itinerary, had eased his mind. He sat beside Juliet during media training and held her hand. They left around five for the Waldorf where Hoss had now taken a large suite, and Meredith and Dustin soon followed. We were all exhausted, and while I was glad my friend hadn't been arrested, I was still anxious about the future.

Despite our earlier battle, or maybe because of it, I agreed to have a quick dinner with Mike. I was still annoyed with him over the interview, but I wanted to talk over the case. I still didn't know what Donato had told him, but I had a feeling he knew more than would appear in his story the next day. He came back to the office around six to pick me up, and we wandered a couple of blocks over to a gourmet Mexican restaurant. Mike ordered us both margaritas, and the waiter soon returned with our drinks and chips and salsa. Neither of us said much until the basket of chips and our margarita glasses were half empty.

"So who do you think did it?" Mike asked as I was transiting a salsa-laden chip to my mouth. *Plop.* Most of the salsa landed on the menu lying on the table in front of me.

"Someone who hates Juliet, obviously," I replied as I picked up my napkin. "Otherwise why would someone use her shoe?"

"To throw the police off the real killer," Mike said smoothly as he gestured for the waiter. After we ordered, he continued. "This murder could have absolutely nothing to do with Juliet."

I thought about that idea for a moment.

"So how did the murderer get his or her hands on Juliet's shoe? Why not just use a hammer or a baseball bat or a gun if this has nothing to do with Juliet?"

Mike didn't answer the question, and we both pondered it for a while. Eventually, I had to break the silence with the question I was dying to ask.

"So what do the police have?"

"They have a shoe with Juliet's fingerprints on it among others."

"Others? That sounds promising," I said as I reached for my margarita.

"Could be. Depends on how many people handled those shoes."

I choked on the mixture of tequila, Cointreau, and lime juice, and it came just shy of spewing out my nose.

"I touched those shoes! So did the seamstress! Maybe even Jeannie and Tanya!"

"They'll probably be looking for prints that are on the murder weapon that aren't on the mate," said Mike. "Relax."

I took a deep breath.

"So what else have they got?"

What they had so far, said Mike, was a time of death—around 1:30 am. They also had hotel surveillance that showed Juliet arriving at the Waldorf at 12:07 and coming out again at 12:19 with a bag. Cameras on the street showed her getting into a cab. They were still looking for video footage or witnesses to verify her story from that time on. Even though he was checking out her story, Donato wouldn't officially call Juliet a suspect. Without my having to ask, Mike told me he was going to print that Juliet Scott had been questioned by police but she wasn't being called a suspect at this time. I wanted to argue with him about the phrase "at this time," but I knew I'd lose. Then I had a thought.

"Are there any cameras that cover the alley behind the Waldorf and the service entrance?" I asked hopefully.

Mike laughed bitterly.

"Coincidentally, the camera in question was vandalized the day before the murder. Somebody threw a brick at it. If you happen to see Donato again, don't mention it. It's a sore subject. And I probably shouldn't be telling you any of this."

"So the murder was premeditated," I breathed, which had Mike chuckling again.

"Don't go jumping to conclusions, Cooksey. Security cameras get vandalized all the time in New York, sometimes just for kicks."

At that moment our food came, and we were able to put aside murder for the moment. The duck enchiladas were amazing. Instead of a cheese or cream sauce, the chef had used a tangy red sauce to contrast with the rich duck breast.

"Wow! This is so good!" I cried. "You have got to taste this."

Before I knew it, I was feeding Mike a bite off my fork, and it was only as his eyes twinkled at me that I realized what an intimate gesture it was. As he slowly took the bite off the end of my fork, he looked straight into my eyes and, it seemed, into my head where I was suddenly having some very interesting thoughts about him. Trapped by his gaze, I felt my face flush red hot, and it wasn't from the salsa. I finally managed to look away, grabbed my water glass, and took a long swig. When I looked back at Mike, he was busy adding guacamole to his fajita, but he had a big grin on his face. I knew he couldn't have seen the thoughts flitting through my mind, but I also knew that my face gave me away every time. Lucky me.

I went back to my enchiladas until Mike spoke again a moment later.

"You're a lot of fun, Cooksey."

I looked up to find that grin aimed right at me, and despite my blushing, I couldn't help but grin back.

After dinner, we parted outside the restaurant. I was headed uptown, and he was headed across. I started to step off the curb to hail a taxi when Mike grabbed my hand and pulled me to him. His mouth was warm and soft and not too wet. He smelled of leather and camping trips and tasted of chiles and lime. We took our time while around us sirens blared and cars screamed up and down the street. Slowly, Mike's hands ran down my sides to my hips, and he pulled me even closer. I'm pretty sure I whimpered as my arms wound around his neck of their own volition. People walked by without giving us a glance. It was New York. If you didn't kiss goodbye on the sidewalk, you weren't going to kiss goodbye at all. But this kiss didn't feel like "Goodbye." It felt a little more like "Where have you been all my life?" At least, to me. I wondered how it felt to him.

When the kiss ended, I tried to play it cool and sophisticated. I headed for the curb to hail that taxi but instead collided with a fire hydrant. Sophistication went right out the window as I patted my stinging knee and bit my lip.

"Allow me," said Mike with a smirk. Then he walked to the curb and gestured for a cab. He held open the door as I got in, shut it gently, then leaned through the window to plant a kiss on my forehead. With a final smile, he turned and walked away.

The cab headed uptown toward Kate and Surya's apartment where I'd be spending the night so Kate and I could pow-wow before the next day's activities, but while I was physically moving uptown, I was mentally back in midtown with Mike.

When Surya opened the door, I wasn't surprised to see the entire Posse there hungry for information. Kate Vogel and Surya Smythe had grown up together outside Philadelphia. They had been best friends in high school, and they both decided to go into public relations. After college, they teamed up to take on the big city. Surya's specialty was product PR. Her love was art. Long-legged and skinny as a rail, with her pixie cut she reminded me of Audrey Hepburn somewhere between the films *Roman Holiday* and *Funny Face*. When not on the job, she could be found at the Met or the Frick, both within walking distance of the apartment. Kate liked to joke that she had chosen the apartment because of its proximity to legendary French baker Payard, but Surya had actually chosen it because of its proximity to art.

Kate was Surya's opposite in many ways. To look at her, you wouldn't think that she schmoozed the rich and famous every day of her life. Full figured Kate looked more like an elementary school teacher than an entertainment PR specialist. Her clothes were of the highest quality, but she tended to choose styles that were older than her thirty years. I suspected she had a penchant for vintage clothing that she had yet to fully indulge. She worked with film production companies and television networks to promote companies, projects, and sometimes specific people. Kate had met everybody, and while they may not have remembered her, she remembered them.

Their Upper East Side apartment consisted of a living room that also served as a foyer and dining room, a minuscule galley kitchen, two tiny bedrooms, and, oddly enough, a bathroom that was bigger than the kitchen. For four hundred square feet, Kate and Surya paid in rent the equivalent of a house payment on a brick McMansion in the suburbs, but the two women had taken their matchbox and turned it into a jewel box by adding beautiful furnishings. A large white overstuffed sofa took up most of the space on one wall and was the only modern looking piece in the room other than a wall-mounted television. The sofa was draped with silk throws in iridescent blue and pink that complemented the gilt and embroidered Louis XV-style chairs opposite it. In the center of the room was a large, low table painted with pastoral scenes that didn't look like a reproduction to me. Underneath it all on the floor was a worn but beautiful antique carpet. Surya's love of art was evident in the mix of beautifully framed prints from the Met and smaller paintings by up-and-coming artists she had discovered. The effect of it all was sophisticated and utterly feminine.

The Posse was seated around the coffee table on which stood a bottle of red wine, a bottle of champagne, glasses, a teacup and saucer, and the obligatory box of pastry from Payard. The party was in full swing, and as I entered, a cry of welcome went up. I felt like Norm walking into a French provincial version of *Cheers*. Soon I was seated in the place of honor in the middle of the sofa with a glass of champagne in one hand and a cream puff in the other. As heavenly experiences went, it was a close second to kissing Mike on the street corner.

"So Kate has told us all about today," announced Anupa Aranha as she chose another pastry from the box. She didn't have to worry about the calories because she was a party animal who went dancing most nights. Super skinny and able to wear the latest in waif-wear, she had no trouble looking glamorous and getting into the most exclusive clubs in the city. Back in West Windsor, New Jersey, Anupa had been the class valedictorian.

She had double majored in history and chemistry at U Penn. Her parents wanted her to choose between medicine and law, but Anupa had other ideas. Luckily her father understood what she did in financial public relations, and since she dealt with companies that dealt with incredible sums of money, he was willing to overlook her lack of a graduate degree for the time being.

"What I want to know," she said as she extracted a Napoleon, "is did Juliet do it?"

"No, she didn't," I said with cool, calm conviction.

"Is that the company line, or is that how you really feel?" asked Surya. Both she and Kate were eyeing me skeptically.

"I really don't think she did it. I mean, Amber was obnoxious. There was probably a line of people waiting to do her in."

"But did all those people have access to Juliet's red satin stiletto?" asked Liz Gordon mildly before sipping her herbal tea. A healthcare PR specialist, Liz's body was a temple. Tall and toned with perfect ebony skin, she radiated good health and clean living, the result of perpetual training for marathons, triathlons, and other unholy activities. Liz lived in Brooklyn near Prospect Park where she played softball, touch football, soccer, and ice hockey, depending on the season.

I sighed.

"That shoe is the problem. Mike and I were just discussing it at dinner."

Hoots, giggles, and requests for details followed, and murder took a backseat for the moment while I filled them in on our Mexican fiesta. By the time I got to the goodbye kiss, the girls were hanging on my every word. I described our embrace in the best bodice ripper fashion, and at the end of the tale, the entire Posse let out a collective sigh. Then half of the girls reached for more pastry while the other half pushed their pastries away.

"It's such a Romeo and Juliet love story," sighed Surya.

"Neither of them is Italian, and Jill is hardly thirteen," countered Anupa pragmatically.

"But she's in PR, and he's a reporter," said Surya. "It's the Capulets and Montagues all over again."

"The Sharks and the Jets!" cried Liz.

"Which one are we?" asked Anupa. "I'm a Giants fan, so I don't want to be a Jet."

"Promise me you won't rumble with the staff of *The Gazette*," I pleaded with them in a terrible version of a Puerto Rican accent.

"Tanya!" cried Kate.

"No, Maria," I replied. "Her name was Maria. Remember, 'I just met a girl named Maria…'" I sang a couple of bars.

"No, no, no. Tanya!" cried Kate again. "Tanya could have taken Juliet's shoe!"

Thoughts of *West Side Story* took a backseat as I considered Kate's revelation. Juliet had given Tanya the dress. Might she have given Tanya one of the shoes too by accident? What if one of the shoes was tangled up in the dress? Or maybe Tanya took one of them when Juliet wasn't looking?

"But why would Tanya want to kill Amber?" I asked.

"Maybe she has a thing for Branch Matheson?" suggested Kate.

"Who?" Liz, Surya, and I asked in unison.

"Branch Matheson. Amber's ex-boyfriend." When I continued to look at her stupidly, she went on. "He's one of the male leads on their show. Branch and Amber were hot and heavy until she became obsessed with Hoss Buckworth. He's been pining for her for over a year. Don't you guys watch television? It was all over *Hollywood Report*."

"I saw Branch Matheson at Inferno the other night," said Anupa, our resident club kid. "He looks hot on that show but in person not so much. He just sat at a table in the VIP area and polished off a bottle of vodka. Plus, he was wearing jewelry. A lot of jewelry. I hate jewelry on a man."

"Wait a minute," I cried. "Branch Matheson is in New York?"

"He's from here," said Kate as she caught on to the tone in my voice. "He's a suspect, isn't he?"

"He hasn't been, but he should be. Amber threw him over for Hoss Buckworth. She still has a thing…"

"Had," countered Anupa.

"Fine. She obviously still had a thing for Hoss. Why else would she have made a scene in Central Park? She gets murdered while her jealous ex-boyfriend and the guy she left him for both happen to be in town. That makes him a suspect in my book."

"Yes, but how did he get his hands on Juliet's shoe?" asked Liz.

"Maybe Tanya gave it to him. Maybe they met at Inferno. Anupa, did you see Tanya that night?" I asked eagerly. Maybe we were on the verge of cracking the case. My internal monologue was starting to sound like a Nancy Drew novel.

"No. Sorry," said Anupa with a grimace. "I see her out all the time, sometimes with your boss, but not that night."

"Still, she might have met him sometime."

As the night wore on, our theories got wilder and wilder until we were certain that both Amber and Tanya were Russian spies and Hoss Buckworth's cosmetics company was a front for a shadowy syndicate that controlled most of the world's governments, including our own.

The party broke up at about ten thirty, and everyone headed home. Soon I was asleep on the fluffy, white sofa dreaming about Hoss Buckworth, hairless cats, and enchiladas.

CHAPTER 11

The next day found me back at the Waldorf for our postponed press event. We had taken over one of the largest suites in the hotel. The large living room of the suite was turned into a hospitality room where journalists could comfortably wait for their turn to interview Juliet. We had food, drinks, and Wi-Fi at their disposal.

Juliet arrived that morning wearing a cashmere sweater dress in Fall Fantasy signature dark red. Her hair was a beautiful black ribbon down her back, but her face was marred by dark circles. Luckily we had an Eshellon makeup artist on hand who quickly had her looking her best. She was now ensconced in a smaller room off the living area that had been furnished with a comfy sofa for her and a somewhat less comfy chair for the reporters. I was glad that we hadn't done a traditional press conference because I didn't want Juliet overwhelmed with questions about the murder. We had practiced steering the interviews away from murder and onto perfume, but I knew she wouldn't be able to completely avoid questions about Amber.

At nine o'clock, a small group of journalists gathered in the suite. I greeted everyone as they came in and presented them with press materials. Jeannie was in charge of refreshments. Kate had to go in to her own office, but she had promised to take a long lunch and help out. Meredith and Dustin, whom I'd expected to see bright and early, hadn't shown up yet. The day before had been stressful for everyone. Perhaps they were sleeping in. Together? I tried to push the thought out of my mind. Tanya was still AWOL, which made her seem even more like a suspect, and Pamela was probably out shopping, although she had made contact in the form of several irate text messages about the campaign falling apart on my watch. As a result, my breakfast that morning included a large helping of antacids.

I looked at the list of journalists who had RSVP'd. The morning was full of newspaper reporters who were on a deadline, while the afternoon was peopled with magazine writers and television outlets including *The Hollywood Report*. It was going to be a long day, and I knew Juliet would need plenty of breaks and plenty of food to keep her strength and her spirits up.

I was glad to see that Mike was early on the schedule. I wanted to talk to him about Tanya and Branch Matheson to see if Donato was already looking into them.

At 9:20 I made the rounds of the room, passing out bottled water and answering questions. The first interview was to begin at 9:30. Out of the corner of my eye, I saw another reporter enter the suite, and I went to greet her.

Vintage Chanel bouclé suit, helmet hair shellacked into submission, a full face of makeup the likes of which hadn't been seen since the eighties. I scanned my list of scheduled reporters. With that Junior League style, it had to be Hilda Griffith from *The Dallas Sentinel*. I went to greet her and learned I had scored full marks.

"Is Meredith here?" she asked while peering around my shoulder.

"Not yet, but I expect her any minute."

"Oh good. Meredith and I are old friends. We're in the DAR together. I was hoping we could have lunch before I fly back to Dallas. You must love working with Meredith."

"She's very meticulous," I replied diplomatically. I didn't fool Hilda.

"She has high standards. She's very good at her job, and she's helped the Buckworth family so much over the years." Hilda moved over to the buffet, and I followed her.

"Really?"

She picked up a plate and gently set a Danish on it with little silver tongs.

"I guess being a New Yorker you wouldn't know this, but the Buckworths are like royalty in Dallas. They endow everything, send underprivileged kids to college. Dear Hoss even plays Santa every year at Neiman Marcus."

"I had no idea."

"But that family has known so much heartache," she went on. "First Shelley's death just when they thought she had beaten the cancer. Then poor little Dustin's kidnapping…"

"Dustin Buckworth was kidnapped?" I asked incredulously.

"When he was a teenager." Hilda picked up a glass of orange juice and walked over to a small sofa where she sat down. I followed like a puppy.

"Hoss managed to keep it pretty quiet," she continued. "He didn't go to the authorities until after it was all over. He paid the ransom, and the kidnappers let Dustin go, thank the good Lord. Now this murder business."

"And you've covered it all?" I asked.

"Oh yes," she replied proudly. "We take society coverage very seriously in Dallas. Whenever there is a Buckworth story, the editor always sends me."

She leaned in closer and lowered her voice.

"Shelley Buckworth was my roommate at Kilgore College.

She always gave me the inside scoop, and now I get it from Meredith." She winked at me conspiratorially.

"How has Meredith helped them out over the years?" I tried to sound innocent. "Besides helping their image, I mean."

Hilda pulled a small bite off her Danish and popped it into her mouth as she considered the question.

"She practically raised Dustin after his mother died. Hoss was so grief-stricken, you see. She also has a lot of say in the company, you know, new products and things like that."

She went on to explain that Fall Fantasy and the rest of the seasonal fragrance line was Meredith's idea. She had even worked with the chemists on the scent itself. It was her baby. Hilda was a veritable font of information. I decided to try to milk her for everything.

"So did Amber O'Neil ever make it down to Dallas when she was seeing Hoss?"

Hilda made a face and dabbed at the corners of her mouth with her napkin.

"That little baggage was no better than she ought to be. We all knew Hoss was just lonely. It could never be serious, so we just ignored her."

I certainly believed her. A flamboyant actress like Amber O'Neil certainly didn't fit with the picture of devoted husband and philanthropist that the citizens of Dallas knew and loved.

"No coverage, then?" I probed.

"Not a word. They went boating on Lake Lewisville, and Amber took her top off to sunbathe. Can you imagine? Men are frail, as we all know. But we weren't going to give her the satisfaction by noticing her behavior, or his for that matter."

So the citizens of Dallas, including the press, weren't averse to protecting one of their own. I wondered if that extended to murder.

Just then Meredith and Dustin entered the room. Meredith at

once came over to greet her friend, and I discreetly backed away. After waving vaguely at Hilda, Dustin went straight for the buffet. He quickly compiled a plate of muffins and fruit, grabbed a cup of coffee, and went to sit in a chair in the corner. As soon as he sat down, he whipped out his phone and became engrossed.

It felt like a good time to have that conversation with young Mr. Buckworth. I was on my way to his sulky little corner when Mike strolled in. I decided Dustin could wait.

I breezed over to the door, grabbed Mike's arm, and pulled him into the hallway.

"Jeez, don't I get a press kit and a cheese Danish?"

"In a minute. I have to talk to you!" I whispered. Then I noticed what he was wearing. Mike was in a suit—pinstripes, French cuffs, gorgeous paisley tie. He looked delicious, and I must have looked like I was going to devour him because he leered back at me.

"Like what you see?"

"You look fabulous. Not like you, but fabulous."

"I figured it was best to blend in. These feature and magazine writers are a fluffy bunch. Did you see my story this morning?"

"I haven't had a chance. Was there anything in *The Chronicle* about Juliet?"

"Nope," he grinned. "I scooped them!"

I took a moment to ogle him, remembering the way we'd said goodbye the night before. Mike's grin suggested that he could read my mind and was enjoying it, but professional curiosity soon got the better of him.

"You had something to tell me?"

"Cripes! I did! I do!"

I told him about Branch Matheson being in town and about how Tanya might have had access to Juliet's shoe.

"Do you think Donato has already thought of all this?" I

asked. I didn't want to tell Donato how to do his job, but Juliet's innocence was more important than his pride.

"He probably has, but it won't hurt for me to mention it. Let me make a call."

While Mike called Donato, I went back into the suite to glad-hand reporters. It was time for the first interview, and I conducted Hilda Griffith to the interview room and introduced her to Juliet. Her questions seemed innocuous enough, so after a couple of minutes, I left the room. Mike immediately caught my eye, and he gestured me into the hallway.

"Donato knew about Matheson being in town, but he seemed more interested in the Tanya angle. Seems they have tried to talk to Miss Tanya, strictly routine, but no one knows where she is."

"I haven't seen her since the launch," I replied. "Of course, I haven't seen Pamela either. For all I know they're off shopping together."

On cue, my cell phone rang.

"Jill, where is everybody?" asked an annoyed Pamela. "It's Tuesday. We work on Tuesday, but no one is in this office except for me."

I bit back a scathing response about how some people don't work at all. Instead I replied all sweetness and light, "Why, we're at the Waldorf for the Fall Fantasy interviews. Did you forget?"

Awkward silence.

"Not at all…I just didn't expect Jeannie and Tanya to be there too when there is so much to be done here."

"Tanya's not here," I said. "She hasn't been in since the launch. Do you know where she is?"

"Me? It's not my job to know her schedule. Look, I have several important meetings this morning, but I will be over there later today to make sure everything's going smoothly."

She hung up.

"Pamela doesn't know where Tanya is," I told Mike. "That's weird because Tanya is usually Pamela's little shadow."

I glanced at my watch. Time was almost up for *The Dallas Sentinel*. Mike was next on the schedule. Suddenly, something clicked into place in my head.

"Mike," I began. "You aren't doing a story on perfume."

"I'm not?" he replied innocently.

"No, you're not. You cover crime, and you know it."

Mike knew I had spent hours the day before training Juliet to keep the interviews about perfume.

"Mike, you know how much I need this event to be about perfume and not about murder. I have a job to do."

"Well, so do I," he replied evenly. "Part of the story is how Juliet is holding up in the face of suspicion and scrutiny, and that's what I came here to see. I believe it's time for my interview now." He stalked off toward the interview room with me hard on his heels.

"I don't want you to upset her," I said through my clenched teeth. "She has a long day ahead of her, and I need her at her best."

He turned back to me so fast that I ran into him. He smelled great.

"She's a big girl, Jill," he said coolly. "And she's still a murder suspect, albeit unofficial. The fact that she's your friend doesn't change that."

"What about innocent until proven guilty?" I challenged him and tried to get another whiff of his cologne. Was that an Eshellon product?

"I didn't say she's guilty. I said she's a suspect."

On the other side of the suite, Hilda Griffith emerged from the interview room tucking her notebook and pen into her purse. Without another word to me, Mike marched across the suite and into the interview room. I ran after him.

"I will be sitting in on this interview," I announced as I

walked in.

"No way!" barked Mike. "You didn't sit in on *The Dallas Sentinel*!"

"I was there for part of it. It's routine procedure," I sniffed as I sat down next to Juliet. Mike was on the point of replying when we both noticed that she didn't look so good.

Juliet was sobbing quietly into a tissue.

We immediately forgot our quarrel and tried to find out what was wrong. Several minutes later, we finally got it out of her.

"It was that Griffith woman. She was horrible." More sobbing. "She said I was after Hoss for his money, and she asked how I thought Dustin would feel to have a murderer for a stepmother."

So there was more to Hilda Griffith than met the eye. She was a cold, calculating witch, but she was supposed to be Meredith's friend. I'd have to warn her that Hilda was not to be trusted.

I apologized profusely to Juliet for leaving her alone during the interview. Mike brought her a cup of coffee, and after a few minutes she settled down. I was starting to realize just how much of a toll the murder was taking on her, and I wondered if it would be better to cancel the rest of the interviews. Reading my mind, she gave me a wan smile.

"I'm fine, Jill. I can do this. Send in the next reporter." She tried to laugh.

"He's already here," I said and looked meaningfully at Mike.

Juliet leaned over and grasped his hands warmly.

"I'm so glad it's you," she breathed. "After that odious woman, I'm glad to be talking to someone I can trust." A genuine smile lit up her face.

Mike looked sheepish, which pleased me to no end.

"So tell me about Fall Fantasy," he finally managed. I bit my tongue to keep from laughing.

CHAPTER 12

Mike asked a couple more questions, all about Fall Fantasy and Eshellon Cosmetics, and politely took his leave. He didn't look at me, and I resisted the urge to follow him when he left.

After a visit by the makeup artist to freshen her up, Juliet continued with the interviews. Kate arrived half an hour later, and I put her in the interview room with Juliet to keep an eye on the reporters.

With the excuse of checking on our lunch order, I made my way down to the lobby, hoping to see Mike. I saw him all right, with Detective Donato heading for the elevators. Were they going to see Juliet? Something told me they weren't. If Donato was going to arrest Juliet at my press event, I felt sure Mike would give me a heads-up, wounded pride notwithstanding.

Mike and Donato got into the elevator, and the doors closed. I watched the old-fashioned dial over the elevator doors to see where it stopped, just like I'd seen in old movies. The car stopped at the fifteenth floor for a minute. Then the elevator started back down.

I jumped into another car and pressed the button for

fifteen. When the doors opened, I cautiously peered down the hallway. To my right the coast was clear, but to my left a door was open and a uniformed cop was standing guard outside. I casually walked out of the elevator and turned to the right, continuing down the hallway to where it turned a corner and I would be out of sight of the uniform.

Mike and Donato had to be in that room, but why? I was contemplating my next move when I sensed a presence behind me. I whirled around to find Jean-Paul looking at me bemusedly as always.

"Have you lost your way, Mademoiselle?" He arched one perfect eyebrow.

"Not at all, Jean-Paul. Why do you ask?" I glanced around the corner to see if anyone could hear us.

He slid a little closer.

"Because your event is on the tenth floor, and this is the fifteenth. Perhaps Mademoiselle needs contact lenses to read the little numbers on the elevator buttons, or perhaps she is spying on a police investigation."

"All right, all right," I gave in. "Why are the police in that room?"

"Because until recently it was occupied by Amber O'Neil."

"Amber was a guest of the hotel?"

Jean-Paul gave me a critical look.

"She was murdered behind this esteemed hotel. It would seem obvious that she was likely a guest."

"*Pardonnez-moi*, Jean-Paul. It's my first murder. No one mentioned this when I was questioned."

He explained that no one was sure until that morning. Amber O'Neil had registered as one Topaz O'Leary. *Topaz O'Leary?* What's more, she had used a disguise and a fake ID and had paid with a credit card in the name of Topaz O'Leary, as well.

I heard noises from down the hall and peered cautiously

around the corner. Mike and Donato were coming out of the room. Donato shut the door firmly and hung a blue Do Not Disturb sign from the door handle. Followed by the uniform, they made their way to the elevator. When the doors slid shut behind them, I whipped around the corner and down the hall toward Amber's room, Jean-Paul hard on my heels.

I tried the door, but it was, of course, locked.

I turned my best smile on the concierge.

"Jean-Paul, I really need to see inside this room—" He held up a hand to silence me.

"Mademoiselle, I don't know what you think you can find in this room that the trained investigators of the New York City Police Department could not." I started to protest, but a flourish of his hand silenced me again.

"But I do know that you will only pester me until you drive me *complètement fou* unless I let you into this room. So, I will let you in with three conditions. One, you will touch absolutely nothing. Two, you will tell no one you were in this room—"

"But what if I find—"

"You will tell no one. I will not risk my position here to satisfy your curiosity."

Fair enough.

"And the third condition?"

He gave me a long look starting at my feet, ending at my eyes, and lingering at a couple of places in between.

"You will have dinner with me tonight."

My mouth went dry, but I managed to squeak out one word. "Deal." Jean-Paul turned his attention to the door and left me to wonder. What was it with men bargaining with me for dates? Didn't they know they only had to ask? Did I look hard to get?

Guilt stirred in me as I remembered Mike and our amazing kiss the night before. But, I reminded myself, I had only been out with Mike twice. It was hardly a relationship. Moreover, he wasn't really happy with me at the moment.

My reverie was interrupted by a polite cough, and I looked up to find Jean-Paul holding the door open for me. Avoiding his eyes, I walked into the last residence of Amber O'Neil.

I expected the place to be a pit. Sloppy, drunken Amber had struck me as a total slob, but her clothes, while garish and heavily favoring animal prints, were put away neatly. There was no trash on the floor, no drug paraphernalia. I mentally chastised myself for making snap judgments.

The room was not large. It was modest compared to Juliet's with only a queen-sized bed, nightstands, dresser, and two armchairs flanking a tea table. On the table were an unopened bottle of sparkling water, a couple of glasses, and a couple of wadded up tissues. A flash of color caught my eye, and I peered closely at the tissues. Blood. I looked at the metal cap on the bottle and thought I could make out a small brown smear on its sharply scalloped edge. Either Tanya had been in this room or a whole population needed lessons on using a bottle opener.

I knelt down to peer under the bed. Nothing. I felt the hairs on my neck stand up and turned to find Jean-Paul behind me where he had obviously been enjoying the view.

"You have me at a disadvantage, Jean-Paul," I snapped as I climbed to my feet. He held out a hand to help me, which I ignored.

"Don't I always, Mademoiselle?"

I had to brush by him as I walked around to the other side of the bed, and I couldn't deny the frisson of electricity that passed between us. I told myself it was the result of crawling on the carpet in a silk skirt.

Amber slept on the left side of the bed. The covers were pulled back on that side only. A glass on the bedside table held a little water. The phone was on that side too, and next to it was a notepad. Amber, or someone, had written one word on it

—"Topaz"—and had absently doodled two little flowers side by side. The flowers were childlike and consisted of a circular center with circular petals all around. The doodle was rather touching, and I suddenly realized how little I knew about Amber O'Neil.

A sudden cough had both Jean-Paul and me looking at the doorway. Mike.

"You shouldn't be in here, Jill." His look was serious.

"That's exactly what I was telling her," sputtered Jean-Paul. Way to throw me under the bus, Froggy. "I was just about to escort her back down to the tenth floor. Mademoiselle?"

Jean-Paul made a big show of locking the door and securing the Do Not Disturb sign before he led us to the elevators. When the doors opened, I got on, but Mike blocked Jean-Paul.

"I'll see she gets back downstairs. Thanks," said Mike.

"As you wish," replied Jean-Paul, unfazed. He took my hand and raised it to his lips where it lingered long enough for Mike's eyes to narrow slightly. "*L'Étoile*. Eight o'clock," whispered Jean-Paul over my knuckles. Then he was gone and the doors slid shut.

"What's *L'Étoile*?" grumbled Mike.

"I believe it's French for star," I replied primly.

"Yeah, I took French in high school too, Jill," he managed through gritted teeth.

"It's a restaurant, Mike." I was starting to get my back up.

"You're having dinner with that guy?"

"Jean-Paul is an old friend."

"Some friend. He kissed your hand!"

"He's French. I'm just surprised he didn't kiss your hand too."

"So am I," sniped Mike.

It was time to change the subject.

"How did you find me?"

"I went back to the press event, and when you weren't there, I had a hunch you'd found your way to Amber's room."

"I am pretty resourceful."

"That's one word for it."

"So why did you come back to the event?"

"I didn't like the way we left things." He edged a little closer. "And then I find you with the leering Frenchman."

"So?" I challenged.

"Well, I don't like it" was all he would say. I could tell by the look on his face that it sounded just as lame to him. I put on my most detached and diplomatic air.

"Look, Mike, we've been out twice now. It's been great, and I hope we will go out again. But we're hardly at the point of exclusivity, right?"

I saw a flash of panic in his eyes. He unconsciously licked his lips and then managed one word.

"Right."

As I'd expected, the opportunity to define a relationship and commit to a course of action had scared the poo out of him. I wouldn't be hearing any more complaints about dinner with Jean-Paul.

The elevator door opened, and I sailed out.

"Talk to you later, Mike."

I felt triumphant. I'd won a small battle in the war between the sexes. Then that little part of my brain that insists on keeping it real (and which sounds alternately like my mother and Mrs. Maroulis) reminded me that an exclusive relationship with Mike was what I really wanted and that I hadn't truly won a darn thing. I sighed. At least, I countered, I know he'll call again. Even though I knew in my heart I hadn't won anything, to Mike it certainly looked like I had. He would need a rematch.

CHAPTER 13

The rest of the interviews went off without a hitch. After lunch, Kate went back to her real job, and I took over. We had a photo op against a Fall Fantasy backdrop and then more interviews all afternoon. Juliet did a great job deflecting the murder queries without sounding callous, a truly difficult task.

REPORTER: Someone close to you was murdered and you're a suspect.

JULIET: I know a woman is dead, but let's talk about perfume.

Correction—a Herculean task.

During the photo op while all the attention was on Juliet, I took the opportunity to tell Meredith about Hilda Griffith's shenanigans.

"Hilda Griffith is one of Hoss Buckworth's best friends and one of mine. I'm sure you're blowing it out of proportion, Jill," she sighed, but she agreed to call Hilda and exert a little friendly pressure just in case.

I guess I shouldn't have been surprised by Meredith's reaction, but I was. After overhearing her argument with Hoss the day before and learning about her involvement in the development of Fall Fantasy, I felt certain she would be concerned for the company. Maybe she just didn't like me. I wasn't sure how I felt about her.

Dustin Buckworth, who Meredith had told me would be keeping a strict eye on our public relations activities, hadn't said word one all day. The weird little junior executive was glued to his phone and only took breaks from it to eat. I made a mental note to talk to Dustin the next day at Waverly. I had to know if he was a tortured soul with hidden depths or just a spoiled little rich kid with a sinecure who played video games all day.

Pamela swanned in around three o'clock for about five minutes just to make an appearance. Her money radar zeroed in on Dustin immediately, but not even her best efforts to charm the heir to the Eshellon fortune made a dent in his armor. She finally gave up and vented her frustration by grilling me about the press event. It had gone shockingly well considering the spokesmodel was a murder suspect, but, as always, Pamela was able to convey feelings of both skepticism and disappointment that tarnished the day for me. Frustration vented, she hoisted her massive Gucci bag onto her shoulder and was about to venture forth once more into the world of retail when Meredith laid a manicured hand on her arm.

"Pamela, I'm so sorry you couldn't be with us today," said Meredith disapprovingly. I watched their exchange from the table of press materials that I was pretending to organize to hide the fact that I wanted to cry.

I had to give it to Pamela. She could think on her feet.

"But I'm always with you," she countered with a beatific smile. Did she think she was God? "Today I was laying the groundwork for future coverage. I followed up with the editors of some of the biggest fashion magazines and trade publications. (Read: I met some friends for a long, wet lunch, and we hit a sale at Loehmann's.) I think you will be very pleased when the results come in."

I knew Meredith would be pleased because I'd worked with the magazines weeks ago and I knew exactly what kind of coverage we were going to get. Luckily Meredith wasn't a complete fool.

"You will be with us tomorrow at Juliet's appearances at Saks and Macy's, won't you?" The edge to her voice had me warming to her.

"You can count on it," Pamela responded brightly.

I was certain Pamela would be in attendance, and so would her credit cards.

A little after four, a very tired Juliet Scott got on the elevator escorted by Meredith and Dustin and headed up to the penthouse suite that she was now sharing with the Buckworth family. I made her promise me that she would get some rest and call me if she needed anything.

Alone in the suite, I surveyed the damage. The staff of the Waldorf had been very efficient. One table held the remains of the snacks that had been put out around two o'clock, but there wasn't a dirty dish in sight. If only my apartment were in the Waldorf.

I had a few hours to kill until time to leave for *L'Étoile*, but I didn't want to go back to the office. I had my laptop with me, and no one was going to be using the suite until it was cleaned, so I decided to make camp and work right there in the luxury of the Waldorf Astoria Hotel.

I gathered up my things and went into the bedroom that we hadn't used. I deposited my laptop case on the bed, slipped off my heels, and opened the armoire that contained the television. A trip back to the living room procured me a Coke. I plumped the abundant pillows on the bed and settled on it with the TV remote and my laptop.

I powered up the computer and opened a new Word document. I'd decided that the easiest way to pump Dustin Buckworth for information would be to do it legitimately. With the excuse of adding his bio to the press kit, which had to be done anyway now that he was involved with Fall Fantasy, I planned to interview him the next day at Waverly. My fingers flew as I composed a list of interview questions. It didn't take long to come up with the standard questions about education, history at the company, and expertise. The real challenge was inserting questions that would provoke an emotional reaction but that wouldn't seem unprofessional. I couldn't come right out and say "Are you sleeping with Meredith Hopkins, and if so, for the love of Benji, why?"

When I finished my list of questions, it was only a little after five. I popped the top on my Coke and flicked on the tube. Talk shows were on, and I considered the possibility of booking Juliet on a few of them once Amber's actual killer had been brought to justice. I couldn't see how it would help Fall Fantasy, but it might help Juliet recover from the bad publicity. I made a mental note to call Sam Herskowitz about it.

I continued to surf, but I dropped the remote when I hit the cable news channels. There was Branch Matheson crying into a bank of microphones. I recognized him now as the lovable inner-city high school teacher with musical ambitions on the sitcom that he shared with Juliet and Amber. I didn't see any excess jewelry, and he was dressed in a dark suit and tie, the picture of mourning. I had come in at the tail end of the press conference, but thank goodness we have news anchors to sum everything up.

"That was Branch Matheson, star of the hit television comedy *Singletons* and former boyfriend of his costar Amber O'Neil who was found dead outside the Waldorf Astoria Hotel on Sunday morning," intoned a perky redhead in her most grown up voice. "Matheson has organized a memorial service for O'Neil at New York's Cathedral of St. John the Divine that will be held tomorrow at three o'clock in the afternoon. The investigation into her murder is ongoing, but we have learned that O'Neil's costar Juliet Scott is a person of interest in the case."

Groan.

"We obtained this cell phone video from an anonymous source that clearly shows an altercation between O'Neil and Scott that happened in Central Park on Friday night after an event for Eshellon Cosmetics for whom Scott is a model and spokesperson."

Double groan.

In a flash I was on the phone with Meredith Hopkins. Juliet had to attend that memorial service. If she stayed away, she would look even guiltier. As luck would have it, Juliet had seen the report and was already planning to go. Unfortunately, Meredith had also seen the report, and she was so angry she could barely speak. On the bright side, that shortened our conversation significantly.

I rang off and turned my attention back to the news. The focus was still on the Amber O'Neil murder, but now they were talking about its impact on her fans. While a reporter droned on, the B-roll video showed a makeshift shrine that fans had set up somewhere. A life-sized photo of Amber dressed in her signature animal prints and sporting considerable cleavage was the centerpiece of the shrine. Offerings of flowers and stuffed animals, many of them leopards and tigers, were piled up at least five feet high around the photo in front of a building, but I couldn't tell where. Many mourners knelt on the sidewalk holding candles, tears streaming down their faces. In sharp contrast, a dark-haired man in an elegant suit stood off to the side, arms folded, looking at the garish display of grief with evident contempt. Wait a minute. Jean-Paul?

I had to go out a side door and around the corner to get to the front of the Waldorf because the front doors were completely barricaded by the shrine to Amber. I arrived to find Jean-Paul kneeling next to a woman who was trying to embed lighted candles into the mass of flowers, posters, and stuffed animals. He had his hand on her elbow, and he was encouraging her to get up.

"But it would be so pretty," she wailed. "Just like Amber!"

"Madame, it is a fire hazard. *Regardez!*"

Jean-Paul snatched a small stuffed leopard from the spot where the lady was trying to shove the candle. He held its tail to the flame. *Whoosh!* Instant roasted kitty.

With cool grace, he tossed the flaming endangered species a couple of feet away on the sidewalk, picked up a small "We Miss You Amber" poster, and proceeded to beat out the flames. The crowd that had been talking, praying, or singing was silent as everybody stared at the charred and blackened stuffed cat.

"Murderer!" cried a zebra print-clad woman. "That kitty was for Amber!"

More voices joined in. It was starting to get ugly.

Jean-Paul's only response was to straighten his tie and brush some ashes from the sleeves of his jacket. In my head I saw some aristocratic ancestor of his riding along in a tumbrel on his way to the guillotine and refusing to notice the bloodthirsty peasants along the way. His nonchalance had the effect of a candle flame on a pile of stuffed leopards. The crowd went for him.

So he works out, I thought, as Jean-Paul took off down the street and around the corner. He ran with grace and considerable speed, and he reminded me of, well, a panther.

I heard a deep, throaty laugh and turned to find Vinny, the photographer from the *Gazette*, happily snapping away. He saw me, waved, and took off around the corner behind the pack of mourners. Somewhere in the back of my mind, an alarm went off. I'd forgotten something. Something important. I racked my brain to no avail. I'd just have to wait for it to come to me.

No surprise, I didn't see Jean-Paul the rest of the afternoon. I wasn't sure if he would show up for dinner or if he'd gone underground, but I showed up at *L'Étoile* anyway. A deal is a deal. He was there looking fabulous but a little shaken.

He was on the move the rest of the afternoon, he explained when I told him I'd witnessed the conflagration. He had retreated into the hotel, but the mob followed him. Not wanting them to disturb the hotel guests, he had stuck to the service areas. The mob split up into bands, and he spent over an hour dodging them and trying to find a place to hide until they would give up and go back to mourning. No such luck.

"They were out for blood, *Mademoiselle*," he assured me.

"Well, people grieve in different ways."

Finally, the chambermaids smuggled him out of the hotel in a laundry cart.

"It was humiliating, but I live to fight another day, eh? Shall we go in?"

L'Étoile was a restaurant specializing in the cuisine of southern France. I'd never visited Provence, but by the end of that dinner, I felt like I had. Jean-Paul was a gracious host. He wanted me to try everything because everything seemed to be his favorite. He evidently had a relationship with the waiters and the chef because when he wasn't talking to me, he was discussing our dining experience with them. They all spoke the patois of southern France, and the debates about which foods were the freshest, the most in season, and the most delicious seemed to verge on arguments, except that when the conversation was over everybody went away smiling. It was an authentic cultural experience.

I ended up trying more foods than I could keep track of. There was a cold soufflé of eggplant and cheese complemented by an intense tomato sauce, followed by a super spicy squid dish that seemed more Spanish than French, but who was I to argue? Next came grilled lamb redolent of rosemary that I could smell before it came out of the kitchen. I lost track of the dishes six or seven into the meal. I also lost track of the wine. Luckily Jean-Paul noticed my lightweight status after only two glasses of the best dry rosé I ever tasted had me smiling a bit stupidly. After a couple of courses complemented solely by water, I was allowed another glass of wine.

I hadn't known what to expect of dinner with Jean-Paul, but it was completely relaxed and loads of fun. He had stories to tell with every food, stories about France, his hometown, childhood exploits, and his love of the French countryside. I learned a lot about him, and I didn't have to ask a single question. His father had worked in customs in Marseille. His mother had been a homemaker, and the family had lived on the Côte Bleu in a house that overlooked the sea. Jean-Paul was fourth in a line of six children. Two of his siblings had immigrated to the U.S. His brother Claude lived in Napa Valley while his sister Clothilde lived in Washington, D.C. He had innumerable nieces and nephews, and he was very much the doting uncle. I'd suspected all along that underneath his icily efficient exterior Jean-Paul was a bit of a mush. I wasn't disappointed in the least.

Dessert was the best course, as it should be. Jean-Paul ordered *nougat glacé* for both of us. Frozen nougat? I wondered if it would taste like a frozen Milky Way bar, which wouldn't have been bad at all. When the dessert arrived, I discovered a cylinder of what looked like ice cream topped with a golden cloud of spun caramelized sugar.

"You have to get the sugar with the nougat," Jean-Paul directed as he took the spoon out of my hand to construct the perfect bite that he then fed to me. I flashed back to Mexican food with Mike but beat the image away. When the *nougat glacé* hit my tongue, I moaned, and Jean-Paul's face lit up in satisfaction. I had no words to describe or comment on the combination of caramelized sugar, cream, almonds, pistachios, honey, and, oddly enough, citrus. Or was that passion fruit? All I could do was make unintelligible noises, which were enough for Jean-Paul.

After dinner, he took my hand and walked me to the subway where he said goodbye with a peck on the cheek and a flirtatious look. It was the right ending to the evening. I mean, after that dessert, anything would be a letdown. It was only on the subway headed home to Queens that I realized we hadn't talked about murder once.

CHAPTER 14

I woke up on Wednesday to the sound of sanitation trucks picking up the garbage. Crap! I jumped out of bed and ran all of six feet to the kitchen to grab the trash that I'd forgotten to put out the night before, but I was brought up short by a horrible sight.

There on the counter was Saul the demon cockroach.

Dangnabbit! There weren't even any dirty dishes in the sink. The place was immaculate. He was taunting me. He wanted me to know he was still alive and he was back for revenge.

Rational thought kicked in, finally, and I realized this couldn't be the same cockroach. I had personally witnessed Saul's guts smeared all over the bottom of my saucepan (that I needed to replace).

This wasn't Saul.

Saul wasn't alone.

At that cheerful moment, the imaginative part of my brain kicked in again, and I realized that I was most likely embroiled in a blood feud with a cockroach family. I shuddered.

I managed to get to the trash by flattening myself against

the wall opposite the kitchen counter from which Saul's relation was eyeing me ready to pounce. I grabbed the bag from the can, sprinted the ten feet to my apartment door, snatched my keys off the hook, and made it to the trashcans as the sanitation truck was pulling up. Yes! Of course, I was still in my pajamas, pink and lacy this time, which thrilled the garbage men to no end. I beat a hasty retreat to a chorus of whistles and catcalls only to find Mrs. Maroulis glaring at me disapprovingly from the top of the stoop. I knew she had a hotline to my mom. I just knew it.

I had overslept, and my intention of getting to the office early to get ready for the day's events evaporated when I looked at my alarm clock to find it was seven thirty.

Twenty minutes to shower and dress (it was going to be a ponytail day); a five-minute run to the subway to make the shower superfluous; anywhere from zero to fifteen minutes waiting on the train; fifteen to twenty-minute ride to Manhattan (if I was lucky) during which I'd hastily apply makeup; five minute run to the office during which I'd probably sweat off the aforementioned makeup—for a total of about 52 minutes at best, over an hour at worst. No dice. It was time to call Jorge.

Five minutes later, *La Cucaracha* bellowing from a car horn had me leaping from the shower with soapsuds still clinging to my skin. I hastily donned gray flannel trousers, a white blouse, and a fitted navy blue velvet blazer. I stuffed my jewelry, hairbrush, ponytail holder, and hairspray into my Behemoth Black Bag, slipped on a pair of blue pumps without stockings (I'd pay for that later), and bolted from the apartment.

"Good morning, Señora Jill," sang Jorge as I threw myself into the backseat of his Town Car.

"Morning, Jorge," I replied. "And it's *Señorita* Jill." Every. Single. Time.

While Jorge navigated the traffic-choked streets and the

Queensboro Bridge, I brushed my hair, pulled it back into a ponytail, sprayed it into submission, and apologized to Jorge for making him cough. I accessorized my outfit with earrings and a necklace made of chunky clusters of gray, blue, and white pearls (well, pearl beads) and then dug in my bag for my makeup only to find I'd left it behind. It looked like I'd be raiding the Eshellon Cosmetics product closet at work before I headed off to Juliet's appearances.

The Town Car pulled up in front of Waverly at precisely 8:06, only six minutes behind schedule. The Waverly office was quiet, but I didn't spend much time there. Extra samples, brochures, and photographs of Juliet had been sent to Saks and Macy's the day before in preparation for her personal appearances. I wanted to grab some press kits just in case and check my messages. I also grabbed some makeup from the Eshellon closet and hastily enhanced my face. (You can't be PR for a cosmetics company and not wear cosmetics.) Fifteen minutes later I was headed for Saks.

The morning was glorious, one of those crystal clear fall days with a cloudless, deep blue sky. There was a nip in the air that made it seem somehow cleaner and fresher. I'd chosen pumps with a low heel and a rounded toe that morning in anticipation of standing nearly all day, so I decided to walk to Saks. I hoisted the bag of press kits higher on my shoulder and took off. I arrived there ten minutes later feeling very awake and energized.

Saks Fifth Avenue is the jewel in the crown that is Fifth Avenue shopping. The building is like a time traveler from nineteenth-century Paris that just happened to end up in present-day New York. For me it was a tourist destination rather than a place to shop. I couldn't afford to buy anything in the store except for a hot chocolate at the adorable café on the fifth floor. But what a hot chocolate! I did my shopping wherever I could find a deep discount, but I went to Saks for the experience and to view its amazing window displays that were more art than advertisements.

Today the famous windows were ablaze with fall color in honor of the season and Fall Fantasy perfume. I paused for a moment to take them in, and I was struck by the emotion they conveyed. A man and a woman, their clothes made up entirely of crimson-colored leaves, supported each other as they walked toward a fiery sunset. The mannequins' faces were grief-stricken, and I wondered if you could order mannequins with different facial expressions. The leaves that made up their clothes merged with leaves swirling in the air behind them, the trail of airborne leaves leading the eye to a tree ablaze with red and orange leaves. Just like at the launch, apple-shaped bottles of Fall Fantasy were suspended from the branches. And in the center of the tree trunk was a hollow place, lit from below, that contained a single bottle of Fall Fantasy on display. But around the bottle was coiled a bright green snake.

Juliet's appearance at Saks was a big success. The crowd was huge, and she autographed pictures for a good two hours, mostly for suburban housewives and teenaged girls who had come into the city to make a day of it. Still, there were more than a few diehard New Yorkers there. You could spot them easily as they were the people trying hard not to look excited about meeting a celebrity. I also caught a glimpse of Hilda Grif-fith, in a green wool suit that reminded me of a certain serpent, having her makeup done at the Eshellon counter. Funny, I thought. Hadn't she told me she was heading back to Dallas the day before? I made my way past women in black smocks hawking perfume and lipstick to say hello, but Hoss beat me to it.

"Hello, old lady," he grinned at Hilda before he gave her a huge smack on the lips.

"They let a cowboy like you into New York City?"

exclaimed Hilda in mock surprise. "Don't you scare the tourists?"

"They think I'm in the cast of *Oklahoma*," replied Hoss, and they both laughed. Then Hoss spied me watching them.

"Jill Cooksey, get over here and meet my favorite reporter!"

"Hilda and I met yesterday," I replied smoothly. I looked directly at Hilda. "Juliet met her too."

"Charming girl, Hoss," gushed Hilda.

"That's funny," I interrupted. "Juliet said the same thing about you."

"That's sweet," cooed Hilda. "How long will you be in New York, Hoss? I want you at my barbecue next week."

"I don't rightly know," began Hoss. "It all depends on this Amber O'Neil business. Then I'll probably be headed for Fiji."

"Fiji!" exclaimed Hilda. "Whatever for?"

What a liar, I thought as I drifted back to the table where Juliet was signing autographs. I wondered if Hoss had any inkling of how toxic and two-faced Hilda was.

Juliet and Hilda didn't cross paths at Saks, thank goodness, and after a while, when I looked around, Hilda was gone. Juliet seemed in good form; she looked rested and gorgeous in a suit of crimson accessorized with a modest display of diamonds. I hoped the color of her suit wouldn't remind people of a particular shoe and made a mental note to change her wardrobe for all other appearances. As always, Hoss was nearby keeping an eye on her, his love written all over his face. Any tabloid reporter worth his salt would sniff out a story there.

Probably owing to the murder, television coverage of the event was much greater than I anticipated. At around ten that morning, I had peeked out the front door of Saks to find no fewer than five news vans. Reporters and cameramen dotted the sidewalk recording stand-ups that would introduce news packages at five, six, and eleven that night. I only hoped they wouldn't be too harsh.

At eleven, Hoss whisked Juliet past the reporters and back to the Waldorf for a quick lunch before her noon appearance at Macy's. Pamela, who had popped up around ten already sporting a Saks shopping bag, took off upstairs for a little more shopping before the Macy's appearance, and Hilda Griffith reappeared in time to have lunch with Meredith and Dustin. Left alone, thankfully, I grabbed a hotdog from a vendor on the corner, hit an ATM, and hailed a cab. Fifteen minutes later I was at Macy's getting everything ready for round two.

I was putting the finishing touches on the table where Juliet would be signing autographs when I felt a little tug on my sleeve. I looked up and into Mike's face. He had a guarded look as if he wasn't sure of his reception. I couldn't help but smile at him. Ugh! Where was my cool reserve when I needed it the most?

"Hey," was all he said, but I saw his shoulders and face relax in response to my smile.

"What are you doing here?"

"Working. Have you read my latest story on the investigation?"

I pulled a face.

"I haven't had a chance. I've been too busy getting coverage to read any of it." I'd also been too busy dining in culinary ecstasy with a certain Frenchman, but I wasn't going to bring it up. Luckily a news clipping service would be sending me all the stories about Fall Fantasy, Juliet, and, unfortunately, the murder.

"So what's the coverage in *The Chronicle* like?" I asked.

He grimaced. "They used the word 'suspect.' Sorry."

Rats.

"Any news from Donato?" I was almost afraid to ask.

"Prints on the shoe belonged to Juliet, you, and Tanya, who, by the way, has had a little problem with shoplifting in the past."

"Thanks for the tip." I'd have to keep my purse locked in my desk from now on, that is if Tanya ever reappeared. "Have they had any luck locating my erstwhile account assistant?"

"She's vanished. She sublet her apartment and took off, at least that's the theory. They'll keep looking for her," Mike assured me.

"That must make her a prime suspect," I reasoned. "To just take off without a word to anyone right after a murder. It's too much of a coincidence. She must be the killer." And yet Tanya couldn't even wield a bottle opener. Was she truly capable of murder by stiletto heel?

"She might also be afraid," suggested Mike.

"Like maybe she knew the identity of the killer and was afraid he would come for her next?" I gasped.

"That's some imagination, Cooksey."

Mike was right. It was more likely that Tanya had decamped to Delaware for some tax-free shopping. I moved on.

"Well, what about Branch Matheson?"

"Matheson is in the clear. A woman he met at a club swears he was with her all night, if you know what I mean. I'm afraid that isn't good news for Juliet," he said.

"Just because Matheson didn't do it doesn't mean Juliet did," I replied hotly.

Mike sighed.

"They're running out of suspects, Jill. Juliet's prints are on the shoes."

"So are Tanya's and mine!"

"Juliet had a motive," resumed Mike patiently. "So far the police can't find anyone who might have wanted to frame her. She says she took a train to Long Island, but she hasn't shown up on surveillance video. Believe me, Jill, Donato does not want to get the wrong person, and neither does the D.A., but they only have so much to work with here."

"So you agree with them?" I snapped.

"I didn't say that," he sighed.

"Well, what about Hoss or Meredith Hopkins?" I asked. For that matter what about me, Pamela, the mayor, and the guy who'd just sold me a hotdog? I knew I was grasping at straws.

"Donato told me, off the record, that Juliet is their only viable suspect right now," said Mike. "Luckily their case is still too thin to make an arrest, but they'll keep digging."

I heaved a sigh, and all the fight seemed to flow out of me. I felt defeated. Juliet was looking at a murder charge, and the Fall Fantasy campaign was falling apart. *Jill Cooksey was going to fail.* I think Mike could read my mind because he put his arm around me and pulled me close.

"None of this is your fault," he said. "It isn't your responsibility to fix it."

Nice words, but I didn't believe them. I had brought all the players together in this game. I had set this in motion.

"It isn't your responsibility," Mike repeated. "But you are in a better position than the cops to help Juliet, if you want to."

"Of course I want to." I was fighting back tears.

"Then find out if anyone had it in for Juliet."

CHAPTER 15

The Macy's appearance went off without a hitch, no thanks to me because the whole time I was lost in my head pondering Amber's murder. We left the department store at two o'clock to find the cars I'd ordered waiting to take us to the Cathedral of St. John the Divine. Located in Harlem, the cathedral was a haul from 34th Street, and we made it to the service with only five minutes to spare. Juliet had been in contact with Branch Matheson, and our party had seats reserved toward the front of the nave. The cathedral was packed, and as we made our way up the aisle, a low hum of conversation followed us. I glanced at Juliet and was glad we had changed her into a more subdued brown suit before the Macy's appearance. She held her head high as she walked past the crowd of mourners, the stiffness of her posture the only indication that she noticed the buzz she was causing.

Branch met us at the front of the church. I was glad to see him hug Juliet, and I hoped reporters and news crews were watching. I glanced around the church. They were.

Branch also shook hands with Hoss Buckworth, and I saw Hoss say something to him that only they could hear to which

Branch replied with thanks and an even heartier handshake. Probably something to the effect of "Sorry I stole your girl and now she's dead" but not phrased exactly that way.

We took our seats, and Branch made his way to the pulpit to welcome the mourners. Branch might have been called Trunk; he was that tall and muscular. His dark brown hair and tanned face framed brown eyes and shockingly white teeth. I noticed the shimmer of a diamond in one ear, and I wondered if his shirt and tie hid any more jewelry. Just like at the news conference the day before, he wore an exquisitely tailored black suit. The man was hot, I thought, and then felt guilty for thinking it at a funeral. But I couldn't deny that any woman would want someone like that mourning over her coffin.

Of course, there was no coffin in the cathedral. Amber's body had not yet been released for burial because of the investigation. Instead, a series of poster-sized photographs of Amber was set up on easels in front of the altar. Flower arrangements were tastefully arranged around them. The photos ranged from childhood to present day, and they told an interesting story.

The earliest photo was of Amber aged about six or seven in her first communion dress. A white veil framed her golden curls, and a little cross of amber-colored stones hung on a thin gold chain around her neck. For some reason this photo made me look around for her parents. I assumed they would be sitting in the front, but I couldn't find anyone who would be old enough or who looked like Amber.

The next photo was in marked contrast to the first. A preteen Amber was no longer the picture of innocence. Amber aged twelve or thirteen had dyed her hair black, rimmed her eyes with kohl, and painted her nails with black polish. This photo looked like a yearbook picture with its ambiguous background and poor lighting. The girl in the picture looked pained.

In the next photo, blond Amber was back. The blond, however, seemed paler than natural. Amber in her late teens was no longer the shy Goth girl of early adolescence. This Amber was putting herself on display. With smoky eye shadow, glossy pink lips, and an ample display of décolletage, Amber wasn't smiling at the camera so much as challenging it. She was a man-eater.

The rest of the photos were ones I'd seen before: a headshot and a production still from the set of *Singletons*. The first three photos were the interesting ones, and while they told a story, they left out all the juicy details. I wanted to know more.

Unfortunately, the memorial service was just a gloss on the life of Amber O'Neil. Her early life in New York was barely mentioned. Her story, as far as Branch and the other speakers were concerned, began when she went to Hollywood to pursue her dream of becoming a star. Cast members shared stories. Representatives from a couple of charities she had helped sang her praises. A choir sang "Somewhere over the Rainbow."

At the end of the service, the congregants were invited to come forward to pay their respects to Amber. I thought it was a little odd because there was no casket; Amber wasn't there. Instead, people were filing by her photographs, leaving flowers and mementos. A few people knelt to pray, which gave me the weird impression they were praying to Amber.

At first I wasn't going to go forward. I didn't really know her, and I felt a bit out of place. Then I looked at the photos again. The early ones were intriguing, and I decided that I wouldn't mind a closer look.

I had to go to the back of the cathedral to get in line because I'd hesitated, and I could see the rest of the Eshellon party already filing past the altar. As I watched, Hoss pulled out a handkerchief and handed it to Juliet. I thought I could hear her sniffling, but then I realized the sound was coming from the man behind me.

At first glance the man looked very old. At second glance I could see the signs of hard living that had aged him prematurely. He was about my height but emaciated. His eyes were bloodshot, and his face was laced with a web of broken capillaries. The distinctive smell of whiskey that emanated from him when he coughed confirmed my suspicions. His skin was also yellowed and leathered, I suspected from years of smoking. Still, looking carefully I could see the man he once was. His gray hair was once black, and his green eyes once twinkled. Now beaten by life, his shoulders sagged, and he didn't take his eyes off the floor.

I looked at what he was wearing. His gray slacks were worn and too big for him. He paired them with a black dress shirt in a shiny fabric I couldn't identify. He wore no tie, and his collar was unbuttoned revealing the stark outlines of his collarbones and a few wisps of white chest hair. In this nest of bone and hair lay an amber cross on a thin gold chain.

Catching myself staring, I hastily turned around while my mind struggled to formulate a plan. This man had known Amber. I was sure he was wearing her cross, the one from the first communion photo. I needed to talk to him.

Across the sanctuary, the Eshellon party gathered to leave. Meredith gestured impatiently at me and then at her watch. I shook my head at her, and she glared back. I waved at her to go on without me, and with a sigh and an eye roll, she began herding everyone toward the door. I whipped out my phone to send her a text message, ignoring a few coughs of disapproval from people around me.

Don't want to hold you up. Go on without me. Will find my way home. See you tomorrow in the office.

I hit send. A few seconds later I got a reply.

Okay.

Meredith was so eloquent.

Now I had to figure out how to strike up a conversation

with a grief-stricken man who could be Amber's father and pump him for information. I felt like a vulture; nonetheless, I turned to the man and pulled a tissue out of my purse. He took it from me and mumbled a thank you, so I forged ahead.

"Did you know Amber?" I asked softly.

"Oh, yes," he replied quietly, never looking up. I could hear a distinct lilt in his voice. "I knew her better than anyone."

"Are you her father?" I hazarded.

Now he looked at me, and a flash of anger lit his face.

"I am not! Neil will be spinning in his grave to hear that one."

"Was Neil her father?" I tried again, but I got no reply. He shut his mouth and looked back at the floor.

Neil O'Neil? Crazy name, but there were crazier names in this world. Whether Neil was her father, this man clearly wasn't. So how did he come to have her cross?

We were nearing the altar, and I was starting to panic. This man knew something about Amber. I could feel it. Soon we would file past the photos and go our separate ways. I racked my brain for a plan, but I still had nothing as we passed the first of the pictures. I saw the man finger the amber cross as we passed the first communion photo. He moved quickly past the photo of Goth Amber, but he slowed down when we got to Amber the man-eater. His lips moved. He was whispering something. I pretended to stare at Amber's headshot while I strained to hear.

"Oh, Topaz. Topaz, me darlin'. Ye were simply grand," he whispered. Out of the corner of my eye, I could see fresh tears spill down his sunken cheeks. With a shaking hand, he reached into his pocket and drew out a small object. His fingers quaked as he affixed it to the bottom right corner of the photo. When he withdrew his hand, I could see it was a small cluster of rhinestones colored to look like topaz. The circular stones were arranged in the shape of a flower, just like the doodle on Amber's bedside table.

Every molecule in my body wanted to confront this man, but I couldn't make a scene. The memorial service was not the place for this conversation. I was just going to have to follow him.

You're not a detective, I reminded myself. Darby O'Gill, my codename for the mystery Irishman, could be headed for New Jersey, California, or Madagascar when he left the church, and I didn't know thing one about surveillance. But Mike almost certainly did.

Darby was kneeling now to say a prayer. Keeping him in sight at all times, I ducked into a small chapel off to the side of the nave and pulled out my cell phone again. I didn't have time for text messaging, so I dialed Mike.

"Mike," I whispered into the phone. "Are you anywhere near St. John the Divine?"

"I'm nowhere near a saint, Cooksey," he joked lamely. I didn't have time for funny. Darby was hauling himself to his feet with great effort and would be on the move in seconds. I ignored Mike's sad attempt at humor and gave him the bare bones of the situation. Soon he was all reporter. Or was he all cop?

"I'm right out front. Which door is he using?"

Darby had shuffled past all the photos and stopped by a pillar. It looked like he was catching his breath. After a moment he moved again, this time toward me. He made his way to the right aisle of the church and headed for the front doors.

"He's coming out the right-hand door," I whispered into my phone.

"Is that your right or my right?"

Sheesh!

"He's short, skinny, and he looks like he could pass out at any moment. You can't miss him."

I waited several moments after Darby passed me to follow him. As I stepped out into the aisle, I could see him approaching the door. He struggled a bit with the heavy bronze portal, and then he was through.

"I've got him," Mike said in my ear.

I hurried down the aisle and out the door. Mike was on the sidewalk watching Darby make his way slowly up Amsterdam Avenue.

"So who is this guy?" he asked when I caught up with him.

"I think he's Irish. I'm calling him Darby."

Mike rolled his eyes and groaned.

"He knew Amber, but he called her Topaz." That brought him up short.

"You saw the notepad in Amber's room?"

I nodded.

"It's time to move." He looped my arm through his, and we started up the street after the forlorn Irishman, staying about half a block behind him.

The wind had picked up while I was in the cathedral, and it was good to have the warmth of Mike's body pressed against mine as we trudged up the street. I had only my blazer to keep me warm. Mike, who had evidently paid attention to the weather forecast, was snug in his well-lined leather jacket and black scarf looped around his neck.

At 116th Street Darby made a right, and we followed. A few minutes later, he reached the entrance to Morningside Park.

"He's cutting across the park," Mike murmured in my ear. "He's probably heading for the subway to go uptown."

Uptown? We were already uptown as far as I was concerned. We were in Harlem. The only thing farther north was the Bronx.

We followed Darby through a beautiful arboretum. Brown and orange leaves were swirling around us in the cold wind as dark clouds gathered overhead, reminding me of the fabulous launch I'd orchestrated just a few days ago. I'd had no inkling that murder was soon to follow. While Mike led me along the path, my mind wandered through the night of the launch: the dancing, the spectacular show, the mouthwatering dinner, the moonlight, the roses...

Reading my mind, Mike abruptly pulled me into his arms. His mouth pressed firmly against my own, stifling my cry of surprise. In an instant I was responding with equal if not greater fervor. An electric charge coursed through my body leaving every nerve standing at attention. This kiss was going to burn me alive. Mike held me tightly against his chest, but it wasn't enough. Every atom in my body wanted to become one with him. All thoughts of surveillance fled far away.

All too soon I was brought back to reality when Mike suddenly ended the kiss, grabbed my hand, and pulled me down the path. What on earth was going on?

I wrenched my hand from his grasp and refused to go any farther.

"Excuse me," I hissed. "Would you mind explaining what just happened here?'

"Huh?" He looked confused for an instant. "Oh, Darby stopped by the pond, and there was no place for us to duck. I had to improvise."

"That's it?"

He looked confused again.

"Yeeeeeeeah," he replied with not a little trepidation.

"Really?" I was starting to simmer in a completely different way.

"You look upset," he said, eyeing me warily. "Did I do something?"

"Nothing at all," I said icily. "Let's go."

We followed Darby across the park to Morningside Avenue where he took a left. We waited until he was half a block up and then stepped out on the sidewalk after him.

After a few minutes of cold silence, I think Mike was starting to get the picture.

"It was a nice kiss," he tried. I rounded on him.

"It was a bloody marvelous kiss, you ape!"

Men! Why did they have to be so single-minded? Why couldn't they multi-task? Solving crimes and romance didn't have to be mutually exclusive activities. Had we learned nothing from television?

I stalked off down the street without waiting for Mike. When he caught up with me, I could see a smile playing about his lips, which naturally made me angrier.

When Darby ducked into a bodega, Mike pulled me gently into a nearby doorway and enfolded me in his arms.

"It was a great kiss," he whispered into my hair, sending shivers down my spine. I tried to remain aloof, but his cologne was fabulous.

"In fact," he continued, "I look forward to the opportunity to reprise that kiss, this time giving it my full concentration."

I gulped. Full concentration might make me explode.

Mike gently tilted my face up toward his and brushed my lips with his own. Then he was all business again.

"Darby's on the move."

With an eye roll, I followed him out onto the street.

We tailed Darby up to 125th Street and over a couple of blocks to the Metro station. We had to get closer because we could easily lose him when he boarded a train. From 125th Street he could catch the B, C, or D trains. Mike fumbled in his pocket and I in my purse for our MetroCards. With a swipe, we were through the turnstile. Just as Mike predicted, Darby led us to the uptown platform.

Luckily for us, subway platforms are rather long, and we were able to half hide behind one of the I-beams supporting the ceiling. Darby found a bench at the other end of the platform and collapsed on it. He pulled his wallet from his pocket and flipped it open. He spent the next ten minutes looking intently at something in the wallet, and my gut told me it was a picture of Amber. When a D train arrived, he stuffed the wallet back in his pocket, wiped at his eyes with the back of his hand, and climbed aboard. Mike and I boarded two cars down and then moved through the connecting doors into the car next to Darby's. Through the glass doors we could keep an eye on him and see where he got off.

"I'm pretty sure I know where he's going," said Mike. "We're in for a long ride, so get comfortable."

I made myself at home in the crook of Mike's shoulder while he explained his theory to me.

The Bronx was peppered with Irish neighborhoods, he explained. The D train terminated in one particular neighborhood called Norwood that was once a thriving Irish community. In the last twenty years, the character of the neighborhood had changed. With a downturn in the economy, many Irish immigrants had gone back to Ireland or simply moved to other neighborhoods. An influx of immigrants from places other than Ireland had helped to move the exodus along. Now Norwood was changing, and the Irish who were left were hanging on for dear life.

"Darby, your cliché not mine," said Mike, "looks like he's fallen on hard times, just like the neighborhood."

Was Norwood Amber's hometown? I'd never heard of it, but there were a lot of places in New York that I hadn't heard of. And I didn't know much about Amber's early life. Did anyone?

I must have dozed off while thinking about Amber because thirty minutes later I came suddenly awake. The train was slowing, and as it came to a stop, the black and white streaks outside the train windows transformed into individual tiles that spelled out one word—Norwood.

CHAPTER 16

It was dark when we emerged from the subway station. The neighborhood we entered was just as Mike described it. Astoria, where I lived, was not a rich neighborhood by any stretch, but it was bustling and vibrant with families and businesses. Norwood resembled Astoria with its awning-covered shops and brick tenements, but it was more run-down. It possessed less energy and didn't feel like a happy place. As if to confirm my suspicions, the looks we received as we walked down the avenue were less than friendly. Mike took my hand.

We followed Darby for what seemed like a long time. Wherever he was leading us, the neighborhood was getting worse and worse. Despite the darkness, it was still early evening, yet the stores were locked up tight. Every other building was empty and sported a FOR RENT sign. I was starting to wonder if Darby had a destination in mind when he made an abrupt right turn. Mike and I stopped at the corner to see where he was going.

Across the street and several doors down, Darby was unlocking the door to a narrow two-story brick building. The door was a heavy affair and looked like it had been made to resemble the classic pub doors of Ireland; however, all resemblance to a classic Irish pub ended there. Above the door, a faded hand-painted sign read *O'Leary's*. The rest of the first level was brick wall except for a little window way up high covered in bars. I could just make out some old St. Patrick's Day decorations that had been taped to the window and forgotten, green shamrocks now faded to a sad yellow.

The second story wasn't much more inviting. The building was modern, and the two windows at that level were wide expanses of tinted glass covered by vertical blinds shut tight. The overall impression was of a face with empty eye sockets and a crooked mouth and nose. The place was lifeless.

Darby shut the door behind him, and somewhere inside he flipped on a light. Mike and I moved down the street and stood on the sidewalk opposite the bar. The neighborhood was deathly quiet. It occurred to me that I was standing in the seediest and most dangerous place I'd ever been to in my life. Not even when I tried to take a bus to Brooklyn from Queens and ended up in an industrial wasteland in what borough I still don't know did I feel so alarmed. (Note: Only people who know what they're doing should be allowed on buses to Brooklyn.)

"Let me go in first," Mike cautioned.

"Uh, no problem."

We crossed the street, and Mike tried the door. It opened easily, and we stepped through.

When alcoholics went to hell, they went to O'Leary's. The reek of decades of cigarette smoke was the first thing I noticed. The ceiling was streaked with the grime of a million cancer sticks. The walls were paneled halfway up with sheets of dark faux oak. Above the paneling was dingy gray paint that I didn't think had been gray to start with. Posters of scantily clad women dotted the walls: women in cut off shorts and bikini tops, women straddling the hoods of cars, women in little orange shorts and white tank tops, women in cheerleading outfits that were not regulation.

"It's the Hooters from Hell," I whispered. I heard a low chuckle in reply, but I didn't think it was funny. My eyes continued to rove over the joint. It was a train wreck, and I couldn't look away.

Whoever commissioned the "Irish pub" door also had a hand in furnishing the bar. On one wall was a series of booths in dark dull wood that might have looked nice with a lot of Murphy's Oil Soap and elbow grease. The rest of the bar was filled with tables and chairs from Denny's circa 1974—orange vinyl and rusty chrome with a generous patina of smoke, spilled liquor, and plain old dirt.

This wasn't the kind of pub you went to after work for ersatz Irish food and a pint of Guinness. If there was a fryer in the back, I was pretty sure it hadn't been used since the nineties. This was a plain old bar for plain old drinkers. In fact, I had a hard time believing anybody would come here to drink if they had a choice.

Then I saw the stripper pole.

"Now what might ye be wantin'?"

I jumped. I hadn't seen Darby at first. Some of the chairs were stacked on the tables and blocked my view. I shifted over a couple of steps, and there he was behind the bar. His hands rested palms down on its surface, and a little part of me hoped he'd washed it first.

Mike started to lead me over to the bar, but he stopped when he saw the gun resting next to Darby's right hand.

"I think there has been a misunderstanding," started Mike.

"Then why are you following me?" snapped Darby. "You think I can't spot a tail? I've had my head on a swivel for thirty years."

"We're not IRA," said Mike.

IRA? What on earth was going on?

"No kidding," spat Darby. "And you're not FBI, and you're not here for protection money either. So what do you want?"

"I'm a reporter." Mike said it like one would say "I'm a doctor," and I think he expected the same calming results.

"Mary, Michael, and Bride!" cried Darby. "I'd just as soon you were Russian mob. Reporters! Busybodies are what you are!"

"I write for the *Gazette*…"

"I read the *Chronicle*!"

"So do I," stated Mike matter-of-factly, "but they wouldn't give me a job."

Darby eyed Mike shrewdly then picked up a cloth and started wiping down the bar.

"So what have ye come for then?"

I stepped forward.

"We're here about Topaz," I ventured.

"I expect ye are." Darby tossed the rag on the floor and pulled a shot glass and a bottle of whisky from underneath the bar. He filled the glass, threw it back, filled it again, and threw it back. Only then did he look at me.

"Why should I tell you anything about Topaz?"

"Because the story is coming out," I said. "Other people are going to be able to follow this trail too. If we go away, other people will take our place."

"I have enough information to write a story, Mr. O'Leary," offered Mike. "But wouldn't you like the story to be complete, to be *her* story?"

Darby thought about this for a moment and nodded.

"FIRST OF ALL, I'm not O'Leary. I'm O'Neil. Ian O'Neil."

The gun had been put away, and Mike and I were now

seated at the bar. It was only a little sticky.

"Neil O'Leary was my partner. He was also Topaz's father."

"So her name was really Topaz?" I blurted out. Mike gently nudged my foot with his.

"It was," O'Neill challenged me. "Her crazy mother hung around just long enough to name her. Then she was gone."

O'Neil poured himself another drink, but this time he only took a sip.

"Neil O'Leary and I were partners in this dump. He died when Topaz was thirteen."

That explained the Goth Amber in the photo. The little girl in head-to-toe black had been in mourning.

"What happened to him?" Mike asked.

"He was shot, execution-style. The police never found his killer. Could have been a street thug, could have been the mob. I have my suspicions, but that's all I have—my suspicions and this dive."

"When her father died, what happened to Amber, I mean Topaz?" I asked.

"She came to live with me. I was her guardian. Neil left his half of the bar to her, but she was just a kid. I was supposed to manage the bar until she got old enough to take a hand. Then we could run the place together, or I could buy her out if she wanted to do something else."

"Did she want to do something else?" asked Mike.

Not at first, O'Neil explained. In the beginning, Topaz had held on tight to the bar, the only thing she had left of her father. She wanted to be there all the time. She did her homework at the bar every evening, waited tables, and made suggestions for improving the place.

O'Neil walked over to a shelf behind the bar. From under a pile of invoices, he pulled a faded pocket folder, the kind kids took to school to hold assignments. He flipped it open and pulled out a stack of papers.

They were drawings done in colored pencil. Although a bit childish, they conveyed the artist's vision very clearly—a classic Irish pub, O'Leary's as it could have been. In one sketch the façade was completely renovated to look like a pub straight from Dublin's Temple Bar. The green and white painted paneling contrasted tastefully with a bright red door. The only clues in the drawing that this Irish Shangri-La was supposed to be O'Leary's were the two buildings on either side of the pub, resembling the buildings that flanked the pub we were sitting in, and an elaborately painted sign like an illustration from the *Book of Kells*. The sign had been reproduced on the matchbooks that filled a bowl on the bar. I picked one up to examine it. The matchbooks may have been as far as Topaz got with the renovation.

The other drawings were of the interior. Gone were the tacky posters and thrift shop furnishings. In their places were gleaming oak booths and tables and loads of Irish art and knick-knacks. Topaz's vision was exactly the pub you would go to after work or on the weekend with friends and family.

"It's beautiful," I said, and I meant it.

"She had a vision for the place," sighed O'Neil. The look on his face told me he'd soon be pouring another drink.

"So what happened?" asked Mike gently.

Money, of course, or the lack of it. At about the time Topaz was envisioning a great destiny for O'Leary's, the neighborhood started going downhill. The Irish had begun to leave Norwood. Those who were there illegally started moving back to Ireland, and those who had been there for generations went looking for greener pastures in other neighborhoods or the suburbs.

"Topaz thought we could change it. O'Leary's could be the heart of the neighborhood, she used to say. I know now it was a load of rubbish, but back then…she had a way of making me feel twenty feet tall. I thought anything was possible."

She was determined and had come up with all sorts of schemes to draw in customers. When the industry standard food and drink specials and local bands hadn't made a dent in their losses, she got more aggressive.

It was she who had hired the first "exotic dancer" to work at O'Leary's, a former high school classmate. It worked like a charm. O'Leary's was packed every night as long as Colleen was dancing. For the first time in years, they were paying their bills and putting aside some money for the future.

Then one night Colleen didn't show up to work.

"The customers were ugly. They'd come in the door, see there was no Colleen, and walk right back out." As he remembered that night, O'Neil tightened his grip on his glass until I thought it had to shatter.

Colleen called to inform them she had taken an offer from a different bar. Amber panicked.

"She saw her plans, her hard work, falling to pieces. She wouldn't have done it otherwise!" O'Neil's bloodshot eyes began to leak a steady stream of tears.

Topaz had marched over to the sound system and started up Colleen's music. Without a moment's hesitation, she stripped down to her bra and panties and mounted the pole. Customers stopped walking away, and the bar began to fill up again.

"She was glorious," breathed O'Neil. He stared at the vacant pole, and I knew he was seeing Topaz. "She was better than Colleen. The lads adored her."

The lads weren't the only ones, I thought.

"The next night, she showed up with what she called her costume..."

"Pasties," I interrupted. The drawings in her hotel room, the rhinestone flower O'Neil had left at the memorial service—they were pasties.

"Aye. She always wore the topaz pasties. She never took 'em off either. She never went that far."

It probably didn't matter at that point, but I didn't say what I was thinking. The man was tortured enough.

"She told me it was better this way," O'Neil continued. "We wouldn't have to pay a dancer and could keep more money for ourselves. It wasn't forever, she said." O'Neil wrenched his gaze away from the pole and squeezed his eyes shut, but I knew the images he'd been trying to block out for years, images of his best friend's little girl cheapening herself for the sake of a two-bit watering hole, were still there burned on the backs of his eyelids.

"So if you were raking in the dough, what happened to your plans for O'Leary's?" asked Mike.

By the time they'd saved enough money to start making changes, the Irish neighborhood was gone. The clientele spoke more Spanish than English, and they weren't going to be too fond of a new and improved O'Leary's Irish pub sans stripper.

"Then one day Topaz was gone," sighed O'Neil, and all his strength flowed out of him on a puff of air. "She left me a letter on the bar. Said she knew it was hopeless and she just wanted to start over. I couldn't blame her.

"I didn't see her for a couple of years. Then she popped up on telly calling herself Amber O'Neil. The next time she came to New York, she called me and we met secretly. She gave me her half of the bar, you see. Now I own the whole dump," he smiled ruefully. "From then on, every time she came to town she would call me and we would meet somewhere for a coffee or a bite to eat. She told me she always registered at hotels under her real name because it sounded like a fake one. She thought it was funny."

"Where did you meet her this time?" I asked.

"I didn't," O'Neil muttered. "She didn't call me this time."

Mike's eyes met mine. If O'Neil hadn't spoken to Amber,

then someone else knew about her past. And that someone had most likely killed her.

O'Neil was trying to pour himself another drink, but one look told me he'd never get another drink out of that bottle. I gently laid my hand over his and took the bottle out of his grasp.

"The bottle's empty, Mr. O'Neil," I said softly and smiled at him.

"So it is," he breathed. He couldn't quite manage a smile, but one side of his mouth quirked up briefly. I continued to hold his hand. I had to be good cop because I had a feeling Mike's next question would certainly make him the bad one.

"Mr. O'Neil, someone else knew Topaz's story, and that person was most likely her killer. Have you ever told this story to anyone else?"

O'Neil's face crumpled like a piece of paper in the grip of Mike's question. He couldn't speak for a moment, but he managed a nod in the affirmative. We waited patiently while he pulled himself together.

"About a year and a half ago," he resumed, "a gent came in. Bearded fellow with long hair. Tall and dark. Looked like a hippie. The place was empty as usual, but this fellow was friendly. He wanted to talk about the neighborhood, the old days. Soon we were sharing a bottle of twenty-year-old. Oh, he was subtle. We talked for hours before he points to this magazine he brought in with him. Topaz is on the cover.

"That's one beautiful woman, he says oh-so-casual-like. If I hadn't drunk more than my fair share of that bottle, I'd have seen through his blarney, at least I like to think so. But I took his bait hook, line, and sinker. I had to tell him…." A sob caught in his throat.

"What?" I prompted.

He struggled to get out the words.

"Had to tell him…before she was theirs…she was mine."

CHAPTER 17

Mike managed to get O'Neil upstairs to the apartment over the bar. While he was putting the Irishman to bed, I tried to make arrangements for getting home. Neither one of us wanted to brave the streets of Norwood after midnight, so the subway was out. And I certainly wasn't going to spend the night in one of O'Leary's sticky booths surrounded by a panoply of hoochies. That meant a long and very expensive cab ride that luckily Mike could expense to the paper. Unfortunately, as soon as I said Norwood, the dispatchers at three cab companies hung up on me. Waverly's car service politely replied that they were backed up and would be until morning. I was beginning to despair that I'd ever see the delightful streets of Queens again when I remembered Jorge.

I dialed 718-MEXICAR.

"Guadala-Car-a. Where are you?"

"Jorge, it's Jill Cooksey…"

"Ah, Señora Jill. Where are you?"

"I'm at 1835 Conklin Street…"

I said the last part really fast.

"NorwoodtheBronx."

I crossed my fingers and held my breath.

"Fi' minutes."

Shut the front door!

There's no way in heaven, I thought. It would take Jorge at least five minutes to strap on his bandoliers and another hour at the very least to get there.

But five minutes later I heard the distant fanfare of *La Cucaracha*. I ran to the door to see a bright orange Town Car slide to the curve.

"Mike!" I yelled. "Our ride's here!"

Two minutes later we stepped out of the pub. Mike locked the door from the inside and slammed it shut. Then we were sliding across the red velvet back seat of another of Jorge's Queens-mobiles. I saw wonder in Mike's face as he took in the bright red upholstery trimmed with little pompoms, the row of crown-shaped air fresheners in the rear window, and the Chihuahua-dog bobblehead on the dash.

"*Hola, amiga!*" cried Jorge. "*Hola, Señor.*"

"Jorge, how on earth did you get here in five minutes?" It was completely impossible.

Jorge smiled in reply and wiggled his thick black eyebrows at me in the rearview mirror.

"This is my cousin, Juan." Jorge nodded to the man sitting next to him on the front seat. I wouldn't call Jorge short, but he was dwarfed by Juan whose head almost brushed the ceiling of the Town Car.

"He's from Mexico," Jorge continued. "Just got here. We were visiting our *abuela* when you called."

"Would she, by any chance, happen to live in the Bronx?" asked Mike.

Jorge's eyebrows danced again.

I reached over the seat to shake Juan's hand only to find it was busy holding a .357 Magnum. He had the good grace to smile sheepishly at me.

"Did he bring his gun from Mexico, or was that a welcome to America gift?"

"No, no," Jorge reassured me. "That's Guadala-Car-a standard issue. One in every glove compartment. You're lucky we have it. *Ave Maria,* you're lucky we were in the neighborhood."

I introduced Jorge to Mike.

"Any friend of Señora Jill's is a friend of mine," Jorge smiled.

"Jorge, it's *Señorita* Jill," I countered automatically.

There was a burst of rapid-fire Spanish from Jorge that had Juan and Mike (who evidently spoke Spanish) gurgling with laughter.

"What did he say?" I demanded.

Mike wiped his eyes.

"He said you're always so quick to point out you aren't married. You must want him very much." The three men erupted in laughter again. I leaned forward and gently swatted the back of Jorge's head. He ducked.

A burst of music from Jorge's cell phone signaled an incoming call.

"Guadala-Car-a. Where are you?"

As Jorge conducted business from the driver's seat, all the while smoothly and rapidly navigating the streets of multiple boroughs, Mike and I settled down in the back seat and tried to make sense of what we had learned.

O'Neil was technically a suspect, and we would have to tell Donato about him, although neither one of us believed he could have killed Amber. The man was too full of equal parts love and guilt to have harmed a hair on her head.

But someone else knew about Amber's past. O'Neil had never learned the bearded man's name. He had passed out at some point, and when he came to, Grizzly Adams was gone. Mike suggested the mystery man might have been blackmailing Amber about her past. I wasn't so sure. One thing we both agreed on was that whoever had killed Amber had lured her to her death with the knowledge of Topaz the stripper. The doodle on the notepad by the telephone in Amber's room made that clear.

It seemed like hours later when Jorge nosed the Town Car to a stop in front of my building. Instead of dropping Mike off first, he had opted for the longer and more expensive route of Bronx to Queens to Manhattan and back to Queens. I didn't care. While I normally had no scruples about arguing with cab drivers who tried to pad their fares, I was just glad Jorge had been there to save our bacon.

"So this is where you live." Mike put his arm around me and pulled me close. I tried to ignore Jorge leering via the rear-view mirror. Gargantu-Juan was less subtle. He just stared over the back of his seat.

"Maybe I'll get to see inside your place sometime." Mike nuzzled my ear, his warm breath sending shivers of delight in all directions. I tried to say something in reply, but I don't think I managed anything coherent.

Mike kissed me softly, thank goodness. I didn't want to put on a show for Jorge and Juan.

"Goodnight," I finally managed with a smile. Then I was on the sidewalk, up the stoop, and through the front door, which was propped open as usual to make it easy for food deliveries. I waved at Mike, and the cab pulled away.

Luckily my apartment was on the ground floor of the building because, as I fumbled in my purse for my keys, all the strength seemed to go out of me. I was exhausted. What a crazy day!

Maybe it was the fatigue or the countless receipts cluttering up my purse and obscuring my vision, but I was having a hard time finding my keys. I could hear the rattle of my keychain from the depths of my Behemoth Black Bag, but my fingers couldn't make contact. In desperation, I set the bag on the floor and knelt over it, hoping some stability would help. I vaguely heard a thump, and a wave of red light washed over me and then receded, leaving excruciating pain and, finally, darkness.

I AWOKE TO PAIN, blinding light, and a Greek chorus, in that order. Pain emanated from a point behind my right ear, shooting down little highways over the terrain of my skull and down into my neck and shoulder. The intense light piercing my closed eyelids didn't help, and I wouldn't have opened my eyes except that the buzz of Greek voices sounded concerned about something. Then I realized it was me, and my eyes flew open.

Brighter sunshine than the world had ever known was flooding the foyer of my building through the glass and iron front door, at least that's how it felt to me. I was lying on my side, my face against cool and slightly gritty linoleum tile. I hurt.

Mrs. Maroulis's face loomed into view. A smile briefly flitted across her mouth when she saw that my eyes were open. Another stream of Greek filled the air.

I started to raise my head off the floor, and several pairs of hands were there immediately to help me into a seated position. Mrs. Maroulis pressed a cup of water to my lips while an older woman dressed all in black massaged one of my hands and my across-the-hall neighbor, Hector, looked over their shoulders. A hairdresser by trade, Hector was always beautifully bronzed and coiffed, but this morning his face was paler than I'd ever seen it. I must have looked truly awful. I took a sip of the water. Then someone pushed that cup away and pressed another one to my lips. I smelled licorice and took a sip. Fire coursed down my throat and into my stomach. I sputtered.

"Stavros, don't do that!" cried Mrs. Maroulis.

Evidently, Stavros felt that ouzo was good for what ailed you.

The water cup was brought back, and I drank gratefully.

Around me I could make out snatches of English among the Greek.

"It's the Turks. This neighborhood going to Hades!" spat the old lady. Behind her, Hector rolled his eyes.

"Mama, it's not the Turks," countered Mrs. Maroulis. The grim set of her mouth told me she fought this battle regularly.

"It might have been a Turk!" shouted the aforementioned Stavros. He veered into my line of sight, and I recognized the elderly gentleman who lived on the third floor. "This no happen when was good Greek neighborhood!"

The denizens of my building continued to debate the ethnicity of my attacker while I continued to recover. At about the time I was starting to feel better and to protest that I wouldn't need an ambulance, one arrived.

The EMT took one look at me and asked, "What happened to you?"

"It was the Turks!" asserted Mrs. Maroulis's aged mother-in-law while my landlady sighed in exasperation.

"I'm sure it was," the EMT agreed solemnly, and then he winked at me.

With difficulty I managed to convince him that I didn't need to go to the hospital. I had a mild concussion and a lump on my head. While everyone else thought it was the work of a petty thief who had somehow been scared off before he could take anything from my purse, in my gut I felt it had something to do with Amber's murder. I wanted to talk to Mike and Donato.

While I was being examined, Hector held my hand, and Mrs. Maroulis let herself into my apartment with her master key. Through the poking and prodding, I heard doors and drawers opening and closing along with smatterings of Greek.

I turned to Hector to ask him what he thought the Maroulises were up to in my apartment. He was dressed in black slacks and a black t-shirt, the uniform of the high-end salon where he worked in Manhattan. Hector grimaced.

"I have no idea," he replied, "but if there was anything you didn't want them to see, I'd say that ship has sailed."

Shudder.

When the EMT finally left, Hector helped me into my hovel where I discovered that Mrs. Maroulis and her mother-in-law had changed the sheets on my futon, laid out my nightgown, and run a hot bath for me. They reclaimed me from Hector, and he promised to check on me later as he headed off to work. I started to protest that I needed to go to work too, but then I moved too quickly, causing little dots to swim before my eyes. Before I knew it, I was in the tub up to my neck in hot water. It felt like heaven.

Mrs. Maroulis had brought my purse into the bathroom. While I soaked, and while the Greek mother and daughter-in-law were up to heaven only knew what in my kitchen (I heard the occasional *wham* that could only mean a cockroach killing), I dialed Mike.

The first thing out of his mouth when I told him what had happened was a word I don't generally use, but it certainly showed that he cared. He promised that he and Donato would be there shortly.

"See, this is what happens when you don't invite me in," he tried to joke, but I could hear the concern in his voice.

"Ha ha," I replied grimly.

Next, I called Jeannie at the office.

"I need a cigarette" was her reply when I told her about being attacked. I asked about things at work.

"*Everyone* is here: Pamela, Meredith, Juliet, Hoss, Dustin, that reporter from Dallas…"

"Hilda Griffith?"

"That's her. Oh, and Branch Matheson is here too. Every woman in the building has popped by to say hello today."

"What are they all doing?" We had no events planned for that day.

"How should I know!" cried Jeannie. "Pamela's a nervous wreck. Wait until I tell her you're not coming in." She uttered an evil cackle.

"Jeannie, do me a favor, will you?"

I gave Jeannie some specific instructions and rang off. Only then did I start shaking as the magnitude of what had happened began to sink in. Taking a deep breath, I plunged under the bubbly bathwater and wondered if I could stay there forever.

A half-hour later, I was in my nightgown and tucked up in my bed with a tray of delectables straddling my lap. The Maroulis women had given up on my kitchen and resorted to their own. In front of me, I had lovely baked fish, lemon potatoes, hot tea, buttered rolls, and an enormous slice of Baklava swimming in honey. The pain reliever the EMT had given me started to kick in, and as the pain receded, hunger surged to the fore.

The elder Mrs. Maroulis crooked a gnarled finger at me.

"You eat. Eat, eat, eat. No sleep. You concussion. You sleep, you die." Cheerful thought. She stared at me, awaiting some sort of confirmation. I nodded and she nodded back.

The next time I looked up from my plate, the Maroulis women were pulling everything out of my kitchen cabinets and filling a bucket with bleach water.

"Really, you don't have to…" I started, but two sets of resolved and somewhat chilly black eyes stopped me in mid-sentence. I forked up a lemon potato and stuffed it in my mouth. Satisfied, they went back to work.

Fifteen minutes later, Mike and Donato arrived. Luckily Mrs. Maroulis had chosen a very chaste white cotton nightgown with long sleeves, a gift from my mother, but I still felt a little silly sitting in my nightgown with the two men. Thankfully, they had more important things on their minds than my attire. Donato got right down to business and began questioning me, but I wasn't much help. All I remembered was the pain. Pretty soon Donato wandered off to talk to the Maroulises, leaving Mike and me alone, or as alone as you can be in one corner of a ten by twenty-foot apartment with three other people.

"I should have walked you to your door," sighed Mike as he took my hand and held it tight. His expression was positively anguished.

"Then we'd both be sitting here in starched white nightgowns watching Mrs. Maroulis senior clean my oven."

I gestured to the kitchen where the lower half of the elder Mrs. Maroulis protruded from the mouth of the stove—black dress, orthopedic stockings, and black sneakers. That made him smile.

"We're getting close to Amber's killer, aren't we?" I half hoped he would laugh and tell me it was probably just a robber or rapist who had conked me on the head. Unfortunately, he agreed. The killer was spooked and had decided to send a message.

"But why me?"

"Somehow the killer knows we tracked down Topaz. Maybe he saw you talking to Ian O'Neil at the memorial service. However he..."

"Or she."

"Or *she* found out, it's clear we're getting close to finding

Amber's murderer. But attacking you was a panicked move, and it's only going to backfire on the killer."

He was right. Juliet was almost a sure thing for the murder. All the killer had to do was sit back and watch her go down. But since she had no motive for assaulting me, the attack only served to suggest that she was innocent.

So why would any murderer in his right mind show his hand like that? Mike pointed out that the police hadn't arrested Juliet. Perhaps the murderer was afraid I'd find him or her before Juliet could take the rap. But if that was the case, why hadn't the killer taken me out for good? Not that I was complaining about being left alive. A new set of goosebumps popped up on top of the ones that already decorated my arms. I was spooked. I had a feeling that the next time the killer felt threatened, I wouldn't get a warning.

CHAPTER 18

Donato and Mike finally had to leave, the former to question people in the building and the neighborhood and the latter to write a story for the evening edition. Mike made me promise to keep my door locked and chained and not to open it to anyone except close friends. In return, he promised to come back that night to sit with me, so I had something to look forward to.

Ignoring Mama Maroulis's warning about dying in my sleep, I had just dozed off, intent on dreaming about Mike's forthcoming visit, when my cell phone rang. It was Kate.

"I tried to get you at the office, and Jeannie told me you'd been attacked. Are you okay?"

I reassured Kate that I was going to live and filled her in on the activities, violent and otherwise, of the day before.

"I'm schlepping out to Queens to see you later. What can I bring you?" she asked.

I assured her that I was fine and that she didn't have to come. I told her Mike was coming by later to check on me.

"Then I'm definitely coming," she laughed and rang off.

My head was starting to throb again, so I took two more

ibuprofen and settled back on my pillow. Sometime later, my dream about Mike had just gotten good when I was dragged kicking and screaming into wakefulness by a resounding knock on my door.

Muttering oaths, I threw back the covers and stood up only to sit back down again when the room started rotating around me.

"Just a minute!" I called out to the son of a biscuit banging on my door. The room stopped spinning after a few moments, and I slowly stood up and walked four feet to my front door. I peered through my peephole to find Juliet and Hoss in the hallway. At this rate I might as well start wearing my nightgown to work, I mused.

I unchained the door and let them in.

"This is a surprise," I said almost cheerfully.

Juliet threw herself in my arms. Spots again, in a vibrant orange.

"Jill, it's just too awful!" she sobbed. "Why is all of this happening?"

"There, there," soothed Hoss as he gently pried her arms away from my still aching body. I gave him a grateful smile.

"The little lady was so worried about you that I suggested we pay you a visit. I hope that's all right."

"It's fine," I responded brightly. I hadn't had much of a chance to sit and talk to Juliet, what with the hubbub surrounding the launch activities. This looked like a good opportunity to pick her brain and Hoss's.

I gestured to them to sit down, and they took the only seats available, the kitchen chairs that Mike and Donato had pulled into the living room. I crawled back into bed and sat up against my pillows.

Hoss took a good long look at my hovel. I steeled myself for the billionaire's take on a studio apartment in Astoria. I couldn't decide if I wanted a relative of Saul's to pop up or not.

"Jill, you don't get paid enough," he finally said.

"I agree. You won't mind if I add a little something to your next bill to take care of that problem?" I joked. We all chuckled, even Juliet, though weakly.

Without the benefit of a professional makeup artist, she looked terrible. Dark blue shadows pooled under her eyes, and worry lines I hadn't noticed before creased her brow.

"So how are you holding up?" I asked her as if I couldn't tell.

"Well, no one has tried to kill me," she said wryly. "So I guess I'm just fine."

"The killer has shown himself!" exclaimed Hoss. "I hate to see you in pain, Miss Jill, but at least this dark cloud has a silver lining."

The lining was more like bright red and throbbing to me, but I understood what he meant. The attack on me had to throw suspicion off Juliet.

"I know you've been asked this before," I asked her, "but can you think of anyone who has it in for you? Anyone at all who would like to see you suffer?"

Hoss answered before she could.

"Juliet's a movie star. She's rich, and she's going to get a lot richer if she'll ever name the date…"

"Oh, Hoss…" she tried.

"Who wouldn't be jealous of this little lady? I'm surprised someone didn't try to kill her instead of Amber."

Something occurred to me.

"What about you, Hoss?"

He looked appalled, and I realized he had misunderstood. I hurried to explain.

"What I mean is do you think someone has it in for you? Think about it. An old girlfriend killed, a fiancée under suspicion for murder, horrible publicity for the company just when you're launching a costly new line, not to mention your private life of the last several years paraded in front of the public. This has not been good for you, Hoss."

With this fresh perspective, Juliet looked more miserable than ever. Hoss, on the other hand, concentrated on the question, eyes narrowed.

"Nope," he said finally. "I can't think of anyone. I have business rivals, sure, but the rivalries aren't acrimonious. Heck, I go huntin' with most of 'em."

"What about Dustin?" I asked tentatively. I hated to suggest that his son might be involved, but it had to be done.

Hoss was adamant that Dustin was innocent, but Juliet seemed a bit more skeptical.

"Dustin doesn't like me," she said. "He won't talk to me."

"Just give him time," pleaded Hoss. "Dustin has never said anything negative about you. In fact, before we started dating, he used to watch your show religiously. Even if he has taken against you, it takes a lot more than dislike to make someone commit murder."

"What about millions of dollars?" I asked.

"Dustin doesn't have to worry on that score. There's plenty of moolah to go around, even if I remarry and have more children." He looked significantly at Juliet who blushed prettily.

"Plenty means different things to different people," I put in.

Hoss just laughed.

"I'm a billionaire, Jill," he said. "I think that's plenty in any language." I could see his point.

"Besides," he continued. "Dustin and I are okay. It was hard after his mother's death, hard on both of us. I'll admit I got lost in my own pain for a while, but when Dustin was kidnapped, it all changed. I vowed that nothing would come between us again, and I meant it. If I thought marrying Juliet would come between us, I wouldn't do it."

I liked Hoss Buckworth, I decided. He seemed open and

genuine and felt things deeply. It was plain to see that he cared about both Juliet and Dustin. He was all right in my book.

"So how surprised were you to find out that Amber had been a stripper?" I asked absently as I rearranged my pillows to better support my aching neck.

"Come again?"

I looked up to find Hoss and Juliet's jaws on the floor and gave myself a mental slap. Of course they didn't know. I had just found out myself. Without going into too much detail, I briefed them on my trip to the Bronx the night before.

"I never had any idea," said Juliet.

"She always was quick to take her top off," mused Hoss.

So I'd heard.

"You told the police all this, right?" asked Hoss anxiously.

I assured him I had, and a big grin broke out on his face. He grabbed Juliet for a big hug, but she still seemed to be processing the revelations about Topaz the stripper. Hoss's excitement seemed to confuse her even more.

"Don't you see, darlin'? You're in the clear. Amber, Topaz, whatever her name was, her killer had to be someone who knew about her past. That combined with the fact that you have no motive to attack Jill and an alibi for last night means you can't be a suspect anymore. It's over, darlin'!"

I watched Juliet's face relax as she slowly took this in.

"It's over," she repeated. Then she launched herself out of her chair and grabbed me in another painful hug.

"Thank you, Jill!" she cried into my shoulder. "Thank you for not giving up."

"You're welcome," I replied with more enthusiasm than I actually felt. It didn't feel over to me.

Hoss and Juliet left a few minutes later intent on talking to the police and the pilot of the Eshellon private jet, hopefully in that order. Before they left, I reminded Juliet that we still had a late-night television taping the next day and a morning show appearance on Saturday. They couldn't jet off to Fiji just yet.

Now wide awake, I lay in bed with my mind racing. It did seem like Juliet was in the clear, but there were still too many suspects.

Or were there?

Dustin had never seemed very likely, especially as he had been in Dallas at the time of Amber's murder. Moreover, he had plenty of money and a father who loved him. Branch Matheson had an alibi. Meredith Hopkins had a lot to lose if Eshellon went belly up, and Hoss Buckworth had even more to lose than Meredith. Plus, he was happily in love with Juliet. Still, I made a mental note to check on their movements after the launch. Ian O'Neil was a wreck, and I couldn't see how he could have orchestrated a killing using Juliet's shoe. It was too far-fetched. Hilda Griffith as hitman for the outraged citizens of Dallas was even more far-fetched. Besides, what was their motive? Hatred of bad taste?

"Well, at least I know I didn't do it," I said to myself as I finally drifted off to sleep.

CHAPTER 19

"Jean-Paul, I think this is the beginning of a beautiful friendship," said Mike as the two of them walked off into the sunset and someone gently knocked on my door.

I woke up feeling confused. Not only had my dream ended with Mike and Jean-Paul the best of friends, but I had flown away in an airplane with Branch Matheson. Bizarre.

Throwing back the covers, I stood up slowly, and the room stayed put. My head wasn't hurting anymore either. Excellent. A glance out the window told me it was dark out, and my alarm clock confirmed that it was after six.

At my door, I peered through the peephole to find my entire Posse waving back. A few minutes later, we were all piled on my futon/bed. While Liz examined the bump on my head, Anupa pulled a manicure kit out of her bag and started in on my nails. Kate, ever the PR professional, grabbed the remote, flipped on the TV, and settled on a cable news channel. Then she and Surya sashayed into the kitchen with an enormous paper sack. The scents wafting from it led me to believe it was Afghan food from my favorite place on Ninth Avenue.

The two women opened cupboards, correction—cupboard, to pull out plates and glasses.

"Holy Moses!" cried Surya. "How did this place get so clean?"

"I didn't know your countertop was green," added Kate.

I told them about the amazing Maroulises while they dished up plates of spicy lamb and aromatic rice with almonds and raisins. As if we'd rung a dinner bell, there was a knock on the door. It had to be Mike. Anupa jumped up to get it, and all the Posse girls smiled at each other with excitement. Oh boy. I hoped it wouldn't be too painful.

Mike seemed a bit startled to find a gaggle of women, but he covered up his chagrin and was soon charm itself. While we ate, he submitted to interrogation, and he seemed to pass inspection. Never married. No kids. Educated. No inappropriate tattoos or creepy piercings. When the Posse had extracted all the information they needed to pass judgment, the conversation turned to Amber's murder.

For those who hadn't heard, Mike and I told the story of Topaz O'Leary. Then I explained the problem that had been bothering me earlier.

"No one feels right for it," I finished. Mike agreed.

"I have to admit, I'm pretty stumped too."

For a moment we were all quiet, chewing on the bits and pieces we had learned that didn't seem to add up to much.

"Well, there's always Tanya," offered Surya. "The person who runs away is usually the guilty party."

"She couldn't make the copier collate much less plan and execute a murder," I observed to nods and grunts of agreement all around.

"Maybe someone was hired to kill Amber," ventured Anupa.

"Quite likely," said Mike. "But who did the hiring?"

"Well," began Liz. "Maybe you just haven't done enough research."

"Exactly," agreed Kate. "There's got to be more to the story."

I suddenly felt tired. I was a PR professional with a full-time job and not enough staff to help me. How was I supposed to do my job and research all the suspects?

"Aren't the police supposed to do background checks?" I asked Mike.

"Yes, but they're understaffed and overwhelmed with cases. They may find the information we're looking for, but it'll take time. And when they find it, don't assume they're going to share any of it with us."

And all the while a killer would be out there. Wait a minute! Not out there. I'd learned the hard and painful way that the killer wasn't wandering around somewhere far away. The killer was among us. Goosebumps resurfaced on my arms.

"I guess we'll just have to keep looking," I said to Mike.

"Yes, we will," piped up Surya. "Let's face it. You need some help here."

"Yeah, and I think it would be cool to catch a killer," said Anupa with a diabolical gleam in her eye.

Yes! The PR Posse rides again, I thought, but I didn't say it because it was far too corny.

Pretty soon we had a plan. Kate, with her access to celebrities, was going to research the history of the Amber O'Neil-Branch Matheson love affair. Surya, whose clients included a Dallas-based snack foods company, was going to check with her media contacts about Hilda Griffith. Anupa offered to look into the financial health of the key players: Hoss, Dustin, Meredith, Amber, Tanya, and Juliet. I started to protest Juliet's inclusion, but Mike said it couldn't hurt. He was headed back to the Bronx to delve further into the early life of Topaz O'Leary and to see if he could pin down the mystery man who had learned her story. Liz, whose schedule was tight due to an expected FDA ruling on one of her pharmaceutical clients, would remain in reserve. And myself, I was going to spend some time with Dustin Buckworth.

In the midst of our discussion, my cell phone chirped. A glance told me it was an unknown number. I decided to let it go to voice mail. Mike, the Posse, and I finished our scheming and polished off the last of the Afghan food. Then with hugs from the girls and a sweet kiss from Mike that had the Posse pantomiming swoons behind his back, they all took their leave.

As I was drifting off to sleep, I remembered the mystery phone call. Groggily, I groped for the phone and played the voice mail. My grogginess disintegrated as soon as I heard the recorded voice.

"Jilly Elizabeth Cooksey, this is your mother."

Swing low sweet chariot!

"Why didn't you call to tell me you'd been attacked? And why didn't you call to tell me Juliet Scott was a murder suspect? I had my doubts about you moving to New York City, and this has done nothing to alleviate them. Mr. and Mrs. Scott and I are on Amtrak right now. A nice young man has loaned me his cellular phone so I could call you. We will be staying at the Waldorf-Astoria Hotel. Juliet has been kind enough to put us up. She called *her* mother. We will be getting in very late, but I will call you first thing in the morning. I love you. Bye, bye."

Hell's bells.

CHAPTER 20

I opened the curtains before dawn the next morning to find the wind raging and rain pelting down from swirling gray clouds. A low rumble of thunder convinced me it wasn't going to clear up any time soon, and I flipped on the television to check on the forecast. A nor'easter was raging up the coast. Why was this the first I had heard about it? Probably because New Yorkers were the most weather oblivious people on the planet. I'd once seen a funnel cloud race by over midtown Manhattan during a summer thunderstorm, and no one had batted an eye.

As it was not a day for skirts and heels, I opted for plum-colored pants, a soft brown belted cardigan, and boots with a chunky sole and heel that would keep my pants legs out of puddles. I topped my outfit off with a trench coat and umbrella, grabbed my Behemoth Black Bag, and headed out the door. I nearly collided with a gift basket filled with shampoo, conditioner, sugar scrub, hair gel, mascara, eye shadow—it had to be from Hector. I hauled the surprisingly heavy basket back into my apartment and pulled the attached card from its envelope.

Dear Jill,

You looked a fright yesterday, so I thought some product might help put you to rights. Just kidding! You deserve some pampering after what you've been through. I hope you're feeling better. Let me know if you need ANYTHING, even a foot rub.

XO Hector

XO Hector? Foot rub? He was my neighbor, but we weren't close. This note felt more than neighborly, or was I reading too much into it? And why were all these men showing me attention all at once? It would have been nice if they could have spaced themselves out over the last five years.

With a shrug and a sigh, I headed out the door again and soon found myself enjoying my walk to the subway. Despite the lingering bump on my head, I felt refreshed from all the rest and good food. Having spent so much time in bed the day before, I was up earlier than usual, which was fortunate because I had a lot of work to catch up on. Also, I had plenty of time to stop for doughnuts and coffee at the little shop on the corner near the subway station. I leisurely ate a cruller on the ride into work, saving a powdered sugar doughnut for once I was in the office.

The only person at Waverly when I got there was Walt the mailroom guy. A sweetheart of a man in his mid-fifties, he always came in first, unlocked the office, turned the lights on, and started the coffee. I topped off my cup with his blessed brew and headed toward my office.

I sat at my desk, fired up my laptop, and logged on to the web site for the clipping service that monitored the media and collected any coverage of Eshellon cosmetics for us, be it print, web, or TV. I could download all the coverage into a clippings report, write my analysis, send it electronically to my client, or print it off and hand it over to Tanya to photocopy and bind. Unless she miraculously reappeared, it looked like I'd be taking care of that step myself.

While I was waiting for some stories to download, Walt strolled by and asked how I was. With a smile, I assured him that I was fine. No big deal. Usually Walt was too busy being the nerve center of Waverly Communications to stop and chat, but he lingered by my desk.

"Boy, Jill, it was weird around here yesterday."

"What do you mean?"

"Those Eshellon people were here all day. I mean *all day*."

"That's not so strange. Clients from out of town usually work from our offices when they're in New York."

"That's just it," said Walt as he absently smoothed down the few gray hairs combed over his glossy, balding head. "They weren't working. They were just sitting around. And that TV guy..."

"Branch Matheson?"

"Yeah, him. He was with them all day. They finally went to lunch around one, all of them. Then they were back, all except Mr. Buckworth and Ms. Scott."

"Branch Matheson came back too?"

"Yep. And then they just sat there again. It was weird. I mean, if it were me and if I were in New York and didn't have any work to do, I'd take in a show or something."

"That *is* weird," I agreed. Walt raised his eyebrows significantly in reply and wandered off again. I guessed it was inevitable, what with Amber's murder, that the rest of the Waverly staff would start talking and trying to solve the case. But Walt had reinforced what Jeannie had told me the day before—my clients were acting squirrelly. I looked forward to witnessing their strange behavior with my own eyes, but at that moment I needed to look at the clippings.

The clippings started at the beginning of the month, and I'd made it through the first week when my mother called. I still couldn't believe she was in New York. In the five years I'd lived there, my mother had only come to New York once, and that was to move me into my first apartment. Actually, it was just a room that I rented in someone else's apartment. Funny, I thought, five years later I was still living in one room.

Not funny. Sad.

Anyway, since then Mama had avoided New York, but then I made it easy for her by coming home for every holiday and during vacations, especially after Dad died two years before.

Loretta Cooksey née Carter was a petite woman, about three inches shorter than I. Beyond the height and the obvious age difference, my mother and I were practically twins. I had a few more freckles than she, mostly because I was not as fastidious about applying sunscreen and using the freckle fading remedy Carter women had sworn by for generations. Her blond hair was streaked with white, but instead of aging her, it just looked frosted.

Where my mother and I differed, however, was in personality. While I tended to second-guess myself, Mama was a self-assured rock who always knew her own mind. She was also certain that she knew everyone else's. With a tendency to take charge, she liked to "fix" things, especially for the people she loved. There was a reason I hadn't called to tell her I'd been attacked.

After two rings, I picked up the phone,

"Hi, Mama."

"Well, you're still with us, thank the Lord," breathed my mother. "You know people do die in their sleep after a concussion."

"I'm one hundred percent fine," I laughed, remembering the elder Mrs. Maroulis's warning.

"It's no laughing matter, Jilly," lectured Mama. "What's that sound? Are you at work?"

I'd been trying to type quietly, but my mother, who still had twenty-twenty vision at age sixty, could also hear like a bat.

"I was home all day yesterday, Mama. This afternoon Juliet has to tape a late-night show—"

"*Nighttime with Jackie Jordan*! Juliet said we could come for the taping."

I suddenly had difficulty breathing. While I was glad Jackie Jordan had momentarily distracted my mother from worrying about my health, I wasn't so sure it was a good idea that she and Mr. and Mrs. Scott tag along. Late-night hosts were notoriously temperamental. Unless there happened to be empty seats in the audience (fat chance), the three Virginians would have to spend the afternoon in the greenroom, if we were lucky enough to get them in. The image of my mother in the greenroom chatting up celebrities and offering them tips on tomato cultivation and flaky biscuit baking, not to mention their love lives if they happened to come up, had me giggling and worrying at the same time.

I didn't mention my concerns to my mother because she was enjoying herself too much while reminiscing about the time she had seen Elvis on the *Jackie Jordan Variety Hour* many years before I was born. I'd be calling the Jackie Jordan people later just to check in before the taping, and I vowed to do my best to get Mama in. Then something she was saying brought me back to Earth.

"And he says Juliet isn't a suspect at all anymore."

"Who says, Mama?"

"Hoss Buckworth. Jilly, have you been spacing out again?"

Before I could answer the accusation, she rolled right over it.

"Hoss says the person who attacked you is the killer, and of course Juliet would never attack you. You're practically family. So the police have got to look elsewhere. We were worried for nothing."

I felt Hoss was overselling it a bit, but again I held my tongue. They were in New York, and I wasn't going to rain on their parade. A glance out my window told me Mother Nature would do that all by herself.

"Not that I wasn't concerned about you, baby," she quickly added after misinterpreting my silence for hurt feelings.

I laughed.

"I'm fine, Mama. And I can't wait to see you."

That was good, she said, because they were coming in to Waverly with Juliet and Hoss after breakfast. Just then a knock at her door signaled that room service had arrived, and she hung up.

I WAS HALFWAY through the second week of September in the clippings when Jeannie arrived. She was wearing an enormous cowl-neck sweater that appeared to be made of yak hair over black slacks, and her reading glasses hung around her neck on a necklace of chunky beads and Buddha heads. This was Jeannie at her most exotic, which I knew from experience meant Jeannie at her most agitated. Without even a "hello" she marched into my office, shut the door, and flopped into a chair.

"Thank heaven you're back. I couldn't take another day like yesterday." She saw the white paper sack on my desk.

"Doughnuts?" she asked.

"Help yourself."

While she munched my powdered sugar doughnut, Jeannie confirmed what Walt had told me about my clients. They'd been underfoot all day and for no good reason.

"I told them you weren't coming in. There was nothing for them to do. But they sat here all darn day. And Branch Matheson's not even a client, not that I'm complaining. The man is hot. But that Hilda woman is a pain in the butt. She kept asking for things like I didn't have work to do. I tell you, it was strange. Something is going on."

"Did Branch say why he was hanging out here?"

"Nope," she said and paused to lick her fingers. "He just acted like he owned the joint."

"How did he and Hoss get along?"

"You mean in light of the fact that Amber gave Branch the old heave-ho in favor of Hoss?" Jeannie, a born gossip, quickly got to the crux of the matter.

"Right."

"Well, they weren't exactly slapping each other on the back, but they did seem to get along fine."

"Am I wrong to find that a little weird?" I asked.

Jeannie thought about it for a moment.

"Death can have a strange effect sometimes," she pronounced.

Then I asked her about the special instructions I'd given her the day before. I had asked her to watch people very closely when she told them I'd been attacked to see if anybody gave anything away. I suppose I'd read too many Agatha Christie novels, but it couldn't hurt.

"I got zilch," stated Jeannie flatly as she tried unsuccessfully to dust powdered sugar off her black pants.

According to Jeannie, Hoss was outraged and had a lot to say on the matter. Juliet was upset too and echoed his feelings. Meredith, Dustin, Hilda, and Branch Matheson had seemed completely surprised, even shocked, by the revelation.

"They might have been faking," said Jeannie. "But it was a perfect performance. Meredith turned pale, and Dustin dropped his phone. And you know he loves that phone."

She had noticed too.

"And Branch Matheson's an actor. Who can tell if he's faking?"

Jeannie was just saying how much she hoped they wouldn't

be hanging around all day again when there was a knock on my door. It was Meredith. To her credit, she asked how I was feeling before she launched into her request. There was a meeting going on in the conference room, and was there somewhere else she could set up for the day? She sounded a bit miffed, and if she hadn't had the grace to ask how I was, I would have reminded her that she wasn't the company's only client. (Actually, I wouldn't have, but it sounded great in my head.) I told her she could use the office I'd put Kate in earlier in the week. Before Jeannie could show her to it, she spied the stories that had appeared on my computer screen.

"Are those the clippings?" she asked excitedly. Before I could reply in the affirmative, she asked when she would be getting the clippings report and if I had any idea yet about the total number of impressions the campaign had generated so far.

"It will be ready in a couple of days," I replied calmly as I led her into the hallway. "As you know, our assistant seems to have gone missing, so I'm on my own."

"I noticed," said Meredith as she started toward her temporary office. "You should talk to Pamela about hiring more staff. I'm not sure you have enough manpower to handle our account properly."

"I'll be certain to do that the next time I see her." And Pamela would most certainly turn that question back on me to imply that I wasn't working hard enough.

In mid eye roll, I caught sight of Dustin Buckworth hovering near Jeannie's desk. I quickly left Jeannie to show Meredith to her new digs and hastened to Dustin's side.

"There's a meeting in the conference room," he said by way of explanation.

"You can use Pamela's office today," I said with sudden inspiration. There was only a fifty-fifty chance my boss would show up today, and if she found the handsome heir to a billion-dollar fortune ensconced in her office, I doubted she would mind.

"Actually Dustin," I began as I showed him into Pamela's inner sanctum, "I need to interview you today if you have time. I need to write a bio for the Eshellon press kit."

"Sure," he said pleasantly as he settled into the leather executive chair and pulled his phone out of his pocket. "Just give me an hour to return some emails."

I told him that would be perfect and headed back to my office. I'd just stepped through the door when my cell phone rang. It was Mike.

"So you made it to the office safe and sound?" He sounded worried.

I assured him that I'd made it just fine. Then I told him about how squirrelly everyone had been acting the day before.

"Are they back again today?"

"Only Dustin and Meredith so far."

He seemed okay with that.

"Just remember, Jill, any one of them could be the person who knocked you over the head and murdered Amber O'Neil."

Gulp.

"I don't think anyone would try anything at your office, but keep your eyes open. I want you safe."

I felt a flush of warmth, well, everywhere.

"You do?" I whispered, barely able to breathe.

His low chuckle had me blushing.

"I still owe you a kiss, remember? The one with my full concentration."

I couldn't speak.

"I think I like you speechless, Cooksey," he purred, reading my mind. Then he laughed, and the spell was broken.

"Don't get your hopes up, McCall."

He was about to board the subway, he told me, for another visit to Norwood, and he promised to call me in a few hours.

As I rang off, I wondered what, if anything, Mike and the rest of the Posse would find.

I turned back to my computer. With the issue of murder once again foremost in my brain, I scrolled down the list of clips until I found the one I was looking for. I hit download just as a looming figure appeared in the doorway. I jumped.

"Did I scare you?" asked Branch Matheson with a smile. He was dressed down today, but the effect he achieved with artfully disheveled hair, strategically ripped jeans, and unnaturally layered shirts screamed one word—stylist. He was certainly good looking, but I found all that artifice to be something of a turnoff.

"I'm fine." I managed to smile at him as my heart rate returned to normal.

"We didn't get a chance to meet properly the other day," he smiled back. "It's Jill, right?"

I replied that it was and offered him the chair next to my desk. As he insinuated himself into it, I was glad that the door to my office was open because I was pretty sure Branch would have no trouble getting most women to provide him an alibi.

"I really admire the work you do," he said.

"Uh, thanks." Where was this praise was coming from?

"Most of us, you know, actors, wouldn't have much of a career without public relations."

While we were both chuckling lamely, I noticed Jeannie lingering at the credenza in the hallway across from my door.

"Well, we PR professionals couldn't do it without our administrative assistants," I said a little louder than was natural. In response, Jeannie scurried in the direction of her desk, but I also saw Branch wince.

"You don't by any chance keep something in the office for headaches?" he asked as he began to massage his temples.

Only the fact that the man had a headache kept me from laughing loud and long. I kept a veritable pharmacy on hand,

and because I was still recovering from a concussion, that pharmacy had doubled in size.

I dug into my Behemoth Black Bag for the bottles that I took with me everywhere.

"Aspirin, acetaminophen, naproxen, or ibuprofen?" I asked as I rummaged. Branch requested aspirin, but, as usual, I was having trouble locating what I wanted in my purse. I started pulling items out and plunking them on my desk: wallet, keys, hand sanitizer, earbuds, matchbooks, pocket calendar, metro cards, makeup bag, paperback, e-reader, etc.

"Found it." I pulled my bottle of aspirin from my purse with a triumphant flourish and looked up to find a suddenly pale Branch staring at my desk.

"Are you okay?" It took a moment for my question to register with him.

"I'm fine," he replied finally. "I was just surprised by *that.*"

He pointed to my computer screen where the clipping I'd started downloading had popped up while we were talking. It was Amber's obituary from the *L.A. Examiner* complete with a color headshot.

"I'm so sorry for your loss," I said and reached over to pat his hand gently. His grief seemed genuine, but I wanted to be sure.

"You loved her very much, didn't you?" I asked softly. In response, he pulled his hand away and ran it roughly over his face.

I didn't know what else to say, so I opened the bottle and poured out two aspirin. I set them on the edge of the desk and went to get a bottle of water from the kitchenette. Outside my door, I nearly smacked into Hilda Griffith who was hovering nearby. Had she been eavesdropping? She was a reporter, after all.

"I was just coming to see you," she smiled. "Have you seen Meredith? I popped into the conference room, and I must say a whole lot of people stared at me quite rudely, but Meredith wasn't among them."

I directed Hilda to the office where I'd put Meredith and continued toward the kitchenette for water. On my way back, bottle in hand, I ran into Jeannie. She was worried about Branch.

"Do you think Branch needs anything?" she asked in a huskier-than-normal tone. Jeannie's face was flushed, probably from carrying around all that yak hair, and I had a pretty good idea where her mind had been all morning. It hadn't been on her job.

"There is something Branch Matheson needs that only an experienced woman could give him," I replied gravely. "Are you prepared to give it to him?"

Jeannie stared at me. Her face flushed even more deeply, and a thin line of perspiration sprang up on her upper lip as she considered my words. She nodded almost imperceptibly.

"All right then," I said and thrust the water bottle into her hand.

She pressed her lips tightly together in anger, but I grinned nonetheless.

"Drop dead, Jill," she said and turned on her heel. I noticed, however, that she took the water bottle with her and headed for my office, so I took my time getting back, stopping at the little girl's room and saying hello to a few colleagues. When I returned, both Branch and Jeannie were gone.

My tête-à-tête with Branch reminded me that I still needed to call the Jackie Jordan people. Juliet had been pre-interviewed by Jordan's talent booker the week before, and I knew she was scheduled to arrive at one o'clock to get ready for the two o'clock taping. Still, it was good form to check in, or so I'd been told by Kate, who routinely booked celebs on Jackie Jordan's show. In beauty PR, I didn't work with celebrities all that often, and I was excited about my first late-night booking. I dialed the number for the show, and the intern manning the phones answered. I identified myself, and before I could ask for anyone in particular, the line was ringing again and someone was answering.

"This is Simone Resnick, Jill. How are you today?"

My heart skipped a beat. Simone Resnick was Jackie Jordan's head talent coordinator and a legend in the business. Whether you were bona fide royalty, rock-n-roll royalty, or just a child star with a bad attitude, you did not cross Simone. Maybe it was the gray hair that enveloped her head in a barbed wire cloud or the piercing black eyes that never seemed to blink, but she had an effect on everyone she met—fear. Word on the street was that if Simone had worked for Ed Sullivan back in the Sixties, that whole kerfuffle with The Doors never would have happened.

"I…I'm well, thank you," I stammered.

"Good," she said in a voice that made it clear that she couldn't care less. "This business with Amber O'Neil, it's tricky. Jackie thinks it would be better to reschedule for sometime in the future, once things have calmed down. I just got off the phone with Sam Herskowitz, and he agreed."

Of course he did, I thought. Simone was a gatekeeper to the hottest late-night show, and Sam was a talent agent. He had to agree with Simone Resnick. I, however, with the most important campaign in my whole career going down the toilet and a killer on the loose who might want me dead, had nothing to lose. *Jill Cooksey does not fail.*

"Simone," I began, "now is the perfect time to have Juliet on the show."

"For Juliet, maybe," she replied. Simone was no fool. An appearance on *Nighttime* would do wonders for Juliet's image during a time like this. "But Jackie usually avoids interviewing murder suspects, at least until after they're cleared of all charges."

"But Juliet hasn't been charged with anything!" I pleaded.

"But she's the prime suspect in the case, according to *The New York Chronicle*," she snapped.

"Not according to *The Gazette!*"

Silence followed, but I thought I could hear Simone grinding her teeth.

"Look Jill," she said at last. "Juliet's shoe ended up embedded in Amber's brain. How are we going to get around that? What's Jackie supposed to say? How do you feel about the death of your costar who, strangely enough, was murdered with your shoe? It just won't fly."

I didn't have a good answer. Simone had a point.

Just then there was some clicking on the line.

"Hold on," she said. Then her voice was replaced by an annoying commercial for *Nighttime with Jackie Jordan*. A moment later she was back.

"Today's your lucky day, Jill. The Biebs just canceled. New York Highway Patrol clocked him going 120 on the Gowanus. We'll keep Juliet."

"Oh, thank you!" I breathed as the adrenaline flooding my bloodstream began to ebb. Then I heard some mumbling in the background. A moment later Simone was back.

"Jackie wants Juliet to wear flats," she said.

I chuckled.

"I'm not kidding."

CHAPTER 22

I was a bit shaken after my conversation with Simone Resnick. After a few deep breaths and a bite of dark chocolate from the stash in my desk, I sat down and turned my attention back to the clippings, specifically Amber's obituary.

I read Amber's obit slowly and carefully looking for any new morsels of information, but after my trip to the Bronx, I knew more about Amber than the obituary writer did. I closed the document and went back to the list of clips. I started to scroll up to where I'd left off in the second week of September when a clip caught my eye. The clippings service listed the headlines or the titles of the articles, and I had to click on them to download the whole piece as I'd done with Amber's obit. The headline that caught my eye was bizarre: "Two Bucks with One Shot." Had a story on hunting been included in our report accidentally? I clicked on the headline and waited for it to load.

It turned out to be a photo from last Friday's style section of *The Gazette*, and it was no mistake. The photo had been taken the night before at Rasta, a reggae club in the East Village. One of the "Bucks," according to the caption under the photo, was a twenty-something man sporting a shaggy beard and dreadlocks. He was identified as Daniel Winston, the owner of Buck-boards, the popular surf and snowboard company. The other "Buck" was none other than the heir to Eshellon Cosmetics, Dustin Buckworth.

Daniel was all smiles for the camera, happy for the publicity I was sure, but Dustin didn't look too happy to be having his picture taken. Small wonder, I thought. He wasn't supposed to be in New York on Thursday.

My mind whirled as it processed this new information and attempted to come up with all its implications. According to Meredith, Dustin was holding down the fort in Dallas until he joined us on Monday. Had he been playing hooky from work, and did Meredith and Hoss know? If he was in town on Friday, why hadn't he come to the launch? Several disturbing possibilities presented themselves. It was time to talk to the heir apparent.

I unplugged my laptop and headed for Pamela's office.

"Knock, knock," I said with a smile as I poked my head through the door. "Ready?"

Dustin was, so I sat down in a chair in front of Pamela's desk. While I opened my laptop, I took a good look at the Eshellon heir. In a tweed jacket, Oxford cloth shirt, navy tie, and tortoiseshell glasses, he looked more like an English country vet than a public relations professional. A closer look, however, revealed a diamond-encrusted Breitling Chrono-graph watch on his wrist and a shimmer in his hair that indicated the use of ample pomade to achieve that tousled, bedhead look. His appearance was as contrived as Branch Matheson's. But was it intended to conceal?

The interview was pretty straightforward to begin with. I covered all the basics like where he went to school, what he'd studied, and how long he'd been working for Eshellon. As expected, Dustin had attended a prestigious prep school in Dallas. He stayed close to home for college, attending Rice

University where he majored in graphic design and minored in business. After graduation, he bummed around the Caribbean for a couple of months as a graduation present from his father. After that, he went straight to work in Eshellon's in-house PR department.

"Why PR?" I asked.

"Why not?" he replied cryptically. "I'm very savvy with social media, and I like working with Meredith."

"You've known her for a long time, haven't you?"

"I've always known Meredith. She worked closely with my mother."

"So the two of you are close?" I probed.

"I guess you could say that. Is that going in the press kit?" He eyed me doubtfully.

"Probably not. I just like to get to know my clients," I added, realizing I'd have to tread a bit more carefully.

"So do you come to New York very often?" I asked in the manner of small talk.

"Not really. I'm more of a West Coast person."

"What do you like to do in your spare time? Do you work with any charities? Are you an athlete?"

"I like to surf and ski." He didn't elaborate, and I remained quiet for several seconds, hoping my silence would make him talk. No dice. The stillness was eventually broken when the sound of steel drums playing "No Woman, No Cry" filled the room.

"Sorry about that," murmured Dustin as he silenced the phone.

"No problem," I replied politely. "That's quite a phone. I need a new phone myself. Would you recommend that one?"

He certainly would, and he spent the next ten minutes telling me all about its features. It had more gigabytes of memory than my laptop and could hold more music than I could listen to in a lifetime. The phone doubled as a satellite phone, in case the user was ever too far from a cell tower, was waterproof, and possessed three different cameras. For the first time, I saw Dustin come out of his shell and communicate all because he was passionate about his phone. I couldn't imagine him ever getting so excited about cosmetics. I decided to try to capitalize on his newfound gregariousness.

"So your father was telling me how close you are."

He snorted, and I sensed that I was touching a nerve.

"Do you hang out much?"

"We used to," he replied, eyes downcast. So he *was* jealous of Juliet.

"When was the last time?" I asked, hoping he would answer before he realized just how intrusive the question was.

"We went windsurfing on Lewisville Lake, outside of Dallas."

That must have been the windsurfing trip Hoss had spoken of, except he hadn't mentioned Dustin. Maybe the kid had a right to be jealous.

"Was your Dad any good at it?"

"No, he was awful." There was definitely a note of resentment in his voice, so I took a chance with my next question.

"What about Juliet? Is she any good?"

"She's very good," he replied, the note of resentment in his voice taking on a bitter flavor.

"Are we done here?" he asked suddenly. I cursed myself for pushing too far too fast. Dustin's wall was back up, and I'd barely scratched the surface. I scrambled for a new strategy.

"I just want to ask you a couple of questions about...the kidnapping," I replied almost smoothly.

He sat up straighter in his chair.

"The kidnapping? What does that have to do with Eshellon?"

"I'm not sure the kidnapping will go into the bio, but I want to cover all my bases." It was lame, but I needed an excuse.

Dustin sighed and pulled at his spiky hair.

"The kidnappers grabbed me, pulled me into a van, and put a bag over my head," he recited while looking at anything but me. "I never saw them. After a couple of days, they dropped me in the middle of nowhere and took off. A few hours later, my dad showed up to get me. That's it." He recited the story as if he'd told it a million times, yet the memory of it seemed to cause him a lot of anxiety. Was it post-traumatic stress?

"Do you remember any sounds or voices? Could you tell how many kidnappers there were?" I pressed him.

"There were a bunch of voices, men and women. It was a whole gang, I think, but I told you I was blindfolded." The color was rising in Dustin's face, and he was squirming more than a teenaged boy on prom night. I felt a pang of guilt for asking him to relive the nightmare until I remembered that he had lied about when he arrived in New York and that he could be a murderer. What else might he have lied about?

"What was the hardest part of your ordeal?" I continued to pry. "Being tied up? Fearing for your life? Being blindfolded for…how many days did you say the kidnappers had you?" As expected, this sent Dustin over the edge.

"I already told you everything I remember!" he cried as he jumped up from the chair and started pacing the office. "It's a very painful memory, and I just want to put it behind me. Can you understand that?"

"I just thought it might be good PR to show the world your strength and resilience." I was shoveling BS as fast as I could make it. "It might be good for Eshellon if you shared your inspiring story with others, maybe counseled victims of kidnapping and their parents…"

"Holy crap!" he moaned as he stumbled around the office like a caged animal searching for an escape. "I need some air!"

He couldn't get out of the room fast enough. I made it to the doorway in time to see him heading through reception on the way to the elevators.

In the last few minutes, I'd learned a couple of important things about Dustin Buckworth. He certainly harbored some resentment about his dad's relationship with Juliet, and he was still stressed out about the kidnapping. Did it help me? I wasn't sure, but I felt like I was on to something.

His phone started buzzing, reminding me of the whole point of this "interview." In his haste, Dustin had left it behind on the desk. I had a feeling Dustin Buckworth's whole life was on that phone. I picked it up and was relieved to see it wasn't passcode protected. That didn't surprise me. People who use their phones a lot often forego passcodes because they get tired of typing them every time they use the phone. I myself was guilty of this security lapse. The first thing I saw upon opening Dustin's phone was that he had a new picture message. I didn't even give my conscience a chance to weigh in. I hit open.

I had to scroll down to see the whole image, but it was clearly of a young man. Sporting long dreadlocks and a shaggy beard, he was shirtless and wearing board shorts.

Daniel Winston, the CEO of Buckboards, and he wasn't in New York anymore.

Flanking him on either side were two elaborately painted surfboards. The deep red board on the left was crisscrossed with black and silver streaks while the board on the right was a robin's egg blue with a band of brown flowers down the middle. At the top of each board where it came to a point was an elaborate B in a gothic style font. I wondered if Dustin was having a surfboard custom made. The one on the right seemed a little feminine to me, but I didn't know his taste. I scrolled down past the photo to the message and got a confirmation: "Which one do u like?"

I quickly scrolled through the rest of Dustin's text messages because I didn't know how much time I'd have with the phone.

Dustin might have headed to the newsstand in the building lobby to get a Coke, or he might have gone for a walk. I was pretty sure that as soon as he realized he'd left his phone behind, he'd be back.

As I scrolled, I noticed several text messages from "Single-fans," the *Singletons* TV show fan club. Either Dustin was still a fan of the show, or he was just too lazy to cancel his membership. There were also countless messages from Daniel Winston.

"How hard is it to order a surfboard?" I wondered. I closed the text-messaging window and opened Dustin's pix folder. I chose the slideshow view to save time and began flipping through them. Almost immediately, I hit pay dirt.

The first few pictures were of more surfboards, but the next few were of workers building the surfboards. The picture after that wasn't a picture at all. It was a graph. I zoomed in to get a better look and found that it was a chart depicting surfboard sales over the past year. Last piece of the puzzle. Dustin wasn't having a surfboard made; he was making surfboards, and I was pretty sure no one else knew it. But why would Dustin need to keep his business a secret? And why was he working in Eshellon PR when he had his own company?

"Stay focused, Jill," I told myself, and I continued to flip through the pictures. Two photos later I was staring at a scene I knew all too well. On the edge of Central Park, a livid Amber O'Neil was slopping champagne on an outraged Juliet Scott. I recognized the photo as the same one that had graced the front page of the *New York Gazette*. Mystery solved. I was certain that if I looked at the video files on the phone, I'd see the whole thing in action as well. Without pausing to think too much about it, I kept going past the shots of Central Park. The next two images put things in greater perspective. The first was of Dustin, Juliet, and Hoss with blue sky and blue water behind them, probably taken during the infamous windsurfing trip. In the next picture, however, Hoss was gone, cropped out.

From far off I heard the faintest ding from the elevators and jumped out of my chair. I quickly closed the pix file, replaced the phone on the desk, grabbed my laptop, and left the office. I scurried over to a credenza, yanked open a file drawer, and dumped my computer into it. When Dustin passed by, I was busily searching through files.

"Oh, Dustin," I called to him. "I accidentally knocked your phone on the floor." I did my best to sound sheepish. "Sorry. It landed on the carpet, so I think it's okay."

He grimaced and hurried toward Pamela's office.

CHAPTER 23

When I got to my own office, I shut the door, let out a huge sigh, and collapsed in my chair. From the looks of his phone, Dustin was in love with Juliet Scott. So why would he expose her to bad publicity if he loved her? Maybe he saw it as bad publicity for Amber, you dumb-dumb, I chastised myself. After all, Amber was the one starting fights and tossing drinks. And maybe Dustin was angry enough with Amber to kill her for insulting the woman he loved. Crazy people had killed for less. Or maybe, a different voice broke in, Dustin's unrequited love had turned to hate, leading him to frame Juliet for Amber's murder and to try to bring down his father's company with bad publicity. Dustin potentially had two motives for Amber's murder, which was more than anyone else had.

Eager to share my news, I tried Mike's phone. It went straight to voice mail, which meant he was probably on the subway. I left a detailed message and hung up. A few minutes later, I was lost in thought when my door burst open. Jeannie.

"They're doing it again!" she sputtered.

"Who's doing what?"

"The Eshellon people, plus Branch, plus Hilda. They're sitting in the conference room again acting weird."

"I'm on it," I replied. I gathered up my laptop and my phone for the millionth time that day and headed to the conference room. Before I could check it out, however, my mother came bursting into the lobby followed by Mr. and Mrs. Scott, Hoss, and Juliet.

"Jilly!" she cried as she enfolded me in a big hug. Then she made a big show of looking at me as if I were a six-year-old who had just grown three inches. Then there were hugs from Mr. and Mrs. Scott, better known as Dud and Shirley.

"Dud" was David Scott, a tall, thin country lawyer who during the Vietnam War had the misfortune to catch a live grenade that had been thrown at him. (David had been a baseball star in high school, and everyone in town reckoned the instinct to catch couldn't be drummed out of him.) Amazingly, the grenade had been a dud, and a nickname was born. The people of Luthersburg thought he was the luckiest person in town, and it was not unusual to see people touch him when he walked by.

Shirley Scott née Zaricor had been my mother's roommate at Sweet Briar College and was now her best friend. She was descended from some of the original settlers of Luthersburg who were, not surprisingly, Lutherans from Switzerland. At some point during the last two hundred years, her family had turned Baptist. Now Shirley was the organist and choir director at Mount Pleasant Baptist Church. She was also my mother's partner-in-crime for everything from canning peaches to directing the Christmas pageant.

Mama was looking terrific. She was clad in cruise wear, as always, and today she looked youthful in a long-sleeved, blue-and-white-striped boatneck shirt and navy blue pants with little white anchors embroidered on them. After Dad's death, Mama, never one to give in to grief, had taken up cruising as a hobby—it was now a lifestyle. I was sure she gave the cruise directors a run for their money.

A tour was demanded, and I spent about fifteen minutes showing everyone around Waverly. The highlight was certainly the Eshellon product closet. I hooked everyone up, including Dud, with skincare products and let the ladies choose an assortment of lipsticks, eye shadows, blushes, and mascaras. They were having a blast, and I noticed how easily Dud Scott was taking skincare advice from Hoss Buckworth.

"At first he was rattled to find out his daughter was dating someone his own age," confided Mama. "But Hoss speaks hunting, and that'll go a long way with Dud. I'll swan, Jilly, I always thought Juliet had a good relationship with her daddy, but he did spend a lot of time hunting with her brother. That could explain it."

I did *not* want to discuss the psychology behind Juliet's relationship with an older man. What I needed was to get to the conference room, so I decided to end my tour there.

Jeannie hadn't lied. It was pure *Murder on the Orient Express* in that room. I could feel the tension envelop me like a cloud of bus exhaust as I walked through the door. The suspects had arranged themselves around the conference table, and they all looked up when I led my tour into the room.

"Mind if we join you all?" I asked the group.

"The more the merrier," crooned Branch. It looked like he had recovered from his earlier discomfort.

"We're not interrupting anything?" I asked innocently.

"Not at all!" drawled Hilda. I was descended from a long line of Southern women. I knew fake friendly when I heard it. Hilda bolstered her performance by getting up to greet Hoss and plant a kiss on his cheek. He seemed genuinely glad to see her, but I noticed that Juliet kept her distance. Then Hoss was introducing Hilda to my mother and the Scotts. Soon Branch, Meredith, and, reluctantly, Dustin were shaking hands with them too. It was all a bit surreal. My worlds were colliding.

Since it was about ten thirty and Juliet and her entourage needed to be at Jackie Jordan's midtown theater by one o'clock, I suggested that everyone camp out in the conference room and have a bite of lunch. Safety in numbers.

Everyone arranged themselves around the conference table. I chose a seat near the door with Juliet and Hoss on my right and Hilda Griffith on my left. From there I had an excellent view of Meredith and Dustin inhabiting opposite corners of the room. My mother and the Scotts went to sit across from Hoss, Juliet, and me, and my jaw dropped as Branch Matheson gallantly held a chair for my mother all the while asking for her impression of New York. On the other side of Branch, Shirley Scott looked expectantly at Dud, but he was too busy discussing the finer points of pheasant hunting with Hoss to pull out her chair.

With the door at my back, I could make a quick escape should anyone morph into a homicidal maniac, but that was only if I wanted to leave my mother behind, which I wouldn't. I was pretty sure that if anyone morphed it would be Dustin, and I was a little alarmed that he was sitting only a couple of feet from Mama.

Since Branch was busy charming my mother, who was enjoying every minute of it—the little cougar—and Hoss and Juliet were entertaining the Scotts, I opened my laptop and logged on to my email. Sooner than expected, there was a message from Anupa. Eshellon's financials seemed to be solid, and Hoss, Juliet, Meredith, and Dustin seemed clean, although her access to their private finances was certainly limited. Tanya, on the other hand, had a rock-bottom credit score, most likely due to excessive credit card debt. No surprise there. I emailed Anupa back asking for everything she could find on Buckboards as soon as possible.

I minimized my email window and went back to the clippings report, all the while keeping an eye on the group assembled before me. To my left, Hilda was on her laptop, and it looked like she was editing a document, maybe her latest society piece. To my right, Hoss and Juliet were chatting away with her parents, and it was nice to see Juliet so relaxed. To the right of the Scotts, Meredith was on her laptop too. Dustin, at the other end of the table, near my mother and across from Hilda, was working the wonder phone as always.

Only none of these people were actually doing what they pretended to do.

Although he was conversing with my mother, Branch kept darting glances at Meredith who kept looking over at Hilda who had her eye on Dustin who was intermittently staring at Hoss and Juliet. It was fascinating! What on earth was going on?

I had half a mind to flat-out ask them, but I doubted I'd get an honest answer. Were they all suspicious of each other, and were they waiting for the murderer to make his next move? Like that was going to happen in a room full of people! (At least I hoped not since four of those people were dear to me.) Or were they in it together? For the first time, I wondered if it was a conspiracy. Perhaps they had all worked together to kill Amber O'Neil simply because she had been such a pain in the butt. I quickly threw that idea out as too absurd and mentally scolded myself for letting my imagination run away with me. The only way I'd figure out what was going on would be to observe them until someone gave something away or until my Posse came up with the missing piece of evidence.

Just then Jeannie poked her head in to tell me that Pamela was in her office and wanted to see me.

My boss was gorgeous as usual in a deep green sweater dress that clung to all her curves. Her desk was uncluttered as always, and her computer screen displayed a high-end shopping web site. She had eleven items in her cart. Pamela was not a dumb woman. How could she have risen to her position and managed to maintain it without doing a lick of work if she wasn't smart? A couple of images did come to mind. Even so, Pamela was no fool.

"Who are all those people in the conference room?" she asked loudly before I could sit down. I tactfully closed her office door and explained about the visit from the Scotts and my mother. She frowned a little and looked confused by the idea of parents visiting their children who were injured or in trouble. I wondered not for the first time about Pamela's upbringing. I then explained who everyone else was. Pamela confirmed my suspicion that she was smarter than she looked with her next question.

"Why are Hilda Griffith and Branch Matheson here?" I could only shrug in response. "Well, just make sure all these people don't get in the way. This campaign, such as it is, isn't over yet."

Boy did I know it. At this point, I was torn between wanting to use every opportunity to turn the campaign around and wanting the crash and burn to be over with so I could slink back to Virginia with my mother and lick my wounds.

When I went back into the conference room, I was determined to find out why Hilda and Branch were still hanging around. Hilda was an old friend of the Buckworths and Meredith Hopkins, and she was a society reporter to boot. That might have explained her hanging-on, but didn't she have a job to do back in Dallas? Branch was tougher to explain. He was Juliet's friend and coworker, but he had been much closer to Amber. Why would he be hanging out with the prime suspect in her murder? He must have thought Juliet was innocent, or did he? Was he waiting for her to slip and do something incriminating?

While I was talking to Pamela, lunch had arrived, and all my suspects and loved ones were tucking into pasta, salad, and rolls from the Italian place around the corner. I helped myself to some penne with vodka sauce and went back to my laptop.

Just then the lights in the room flickered and went out for a second before coming back on.

"That's a doozy of a storm out there," said Jeannie as she came into the room carrying a large cheesecake covered in strawberries and whipped cream. My mother and Shirley's faces lit up at the sight of dessert, and I marveled at the compulsion tourists felt to eat cheesecake while in the Big Apple.

"You know tomorrow is Shirley's birthday," said Mama as she reached for the purse she had stowed at her feet under the table. She rummaged in the bag and came up with two candles in the shape of a six and a one.

Shirley Scott's face pinked up with delight.

"Loretta, you are such a card," she cackled. Mama was already leaning across the table to insert the candles in the cake.

"Now we just need some matches," said my mother.

"I've got some," I said and ran back to my office. I'd picked up a matchbook from O'Leary's pub, and I dug into my purse for it. Before I could find it, movement in the doorway made me jump. It was my mother.

"We've just got a moment, Jilly," she said slightly out of breath. "Am I correct in assuming Amber O'Neil's murderer may be in that conference room right now?"

Flabbergasted, I could only manage "Uh-huh."

"That's what I thought," crowed my mother. "I just want you and Juliet to know that Dud and Shirley and I are on the case."

On the case? I shook my head a little, unwilling to believe what I'd heard.

"Mama..." I started but didn't get to finish.

"Dud Scott is a lawyer, and Shirley and I took a criminal

justice class at the community college last semester. We're not going home until the murderer has been brought to justice. Only then will Juliet's name be cleared and will you be safe."

"Mama, I don't want you getting involved. It could be dangerous."

"Oh, piffle. Do you think we'd come unprepared? Dud's got a Beretta under his sport coat, Shirley has a Glock in her purse, and I've got The Queen of Sheba." Mama lifted her pants leg to reveal a shiny purple .380 in a little elastic holster. "What are you carrying these days?"

"Fingernail clippers," I croaked.

"Then we got here just in time," said my mother as she rearranged her pants leg and smoothed a crease.

"Lord in heaven," I whispered. My mother was going to get arrested, of that I was certain. Didn't she know that the only people in New York who carried guns were criminals?

"Don't blaspheme, dear. We have permits to carry concealed."

"In Virginia!"

I decided to try reasoning with her.

"Mama, the police are investigating…"

"Investigating the wrong person."

"Which is why I'm doing some digging on my own."

"Have you taken a criminal justice class, young lady?"

Thanks for the reality check, Mama. I gave up.

"Fine, Mama, but whatever you do, don't let people know you're 'investigating.'" I made quotation marks with my fingers. Mama looked insulted.

"You were always reluctant to ask for help," she observed dryly.

"Okay, okay," I sighed. "You win."

"Of course I do," she said, her good nature restored. "I'm going to focus on Branch Matheson because I think he's taken a fancy."

I couldn't go there if I tried, so I stuck with practicalities.

"You might want to find out why he's hanging around," I suggested. "It's a little weird." Surely that little bit of snooping couldn't hurt, and I couldn't think of a reason why she would have to draw her weapon while following that line of inquiry.

"I'm on it, baby." And she was gone.

Unable to come to terms with what I'd just witnessed, I turned to the simpler task of finding the matchbook. After a couple of minutes, I realized it wasn't there. But hadn't I seen it just a couple of hours ago when I was rummaging for pain reliever?

I went back to the conference room to find Hilda Griffith lighting the birthday candles. A familiar green matchbook was lying on the table next to the cake.

"Where did you get those matches?" I asked Hilda who seemed a little taken aback at my forceful tone.

"Why, I found them in the hallway," she answered mildly. "Are they yours?"

I didn't want to make a scene, but there was no way I had dropped those matches. I didn't smoke. Had Hilda been snooping around my office? I decided to let it go because there was no way to confront her in front of everyone without sounding childish.

"I must have dropped them," I replied and attempted a smile. I glanced over at my mother to find her eyeing me narrowly.

After the impromptu birthday party, I went back to my computer, but the brief power outage had messed with either our server or our wireless Internet access, and I couldn't receive email. I paid a visit to our two IT guys who looked as hassled and harried as always.

"We're working on it," they growled in unison before I could even open my mouth. I slowly backed away before I got bit.

My next stop was the product closet. I put together a deluxe gift bag for Simone Resnick full of every product Eshellon offered and said a silent prayer that today's booking on Jackie Jordan wouldn't be my last. I also put together a gift bag with two of the special cut crystal bottles of Fall Fantasy. Juliet was supposed to present it to Jackie Jordan on the show, ostensibly for his wife, and he was scripted to try it out and make some funny but flattering comments about the scent. Then he was supposed to send his interns out on the street to spray random people with the perfume as a gag.

At twelve thirty we were assembled in the lobby waiting for Hoss Buckworth's limousine to take us to the historic

Tennessee Williams Theater in Times Square where Jackie Jordan had taped his show since time immemorial. By "we" I mean Juliet, Hoss, Meredith, Dustin, me, my mother, the Scotts, Hilda Griffith, and Branch Matheson. Simone was going to freak.

Outside the building, the rain pelted down from a leaden sky, and the street was a river in full flood. The long black Buckworth stretch limo cruised to a halt at the curb like a small steamship arriving at a dock, and the driver got out and scampered toward the door with a golf umbrella. Five trips from the lobby to the limo and we were all in the car and not too wet. Even though the limo was large, we filled it. I was just glad the ride to the theater wouldn't be too long as I was squished between my mother and Dud Scott and I was afraid of getting shot. (By accident, of course.)

On the ride over to the theater, my mother managed to whisper in my ear, "Branch says he's here to support Juliet. He also said no one but people who knew Amber could understand the depth of his pain."

"Do you buy it?" I whispered back. I thought about his anguished expression in my office that morning.

"Not for a minute."

Just then my phone rang, but we had piled our bags and coats all together, so I couldn't reach it. I hoped it wasn't Simone calling to cancel again or Mike with some key piece of information.

Ten minutes later we came to a halt in front of the stage door to the Tennessee Williams Theater. This time it took only a couple of trips to get us inside as several interns with umbrellas came to our rescue. The intern in charge of welcoming talent and escorting them to the greenroom was certainly surprised by our number, but she was too polite to say anything. Her facial expression said quite enough, and I hoped Simone would be too busy to visit the greenroom that day.

A few minutes later, we were sitting on sofas with soft drinks in our hands. Juliet had been whisked off for hair and makeup, and Hoss had dutifully followed. Branch was regaling my mother and the Scotts with stories about his own appearances on talk shows, and Meredith, Dustin, and Hilda had resumed their prior activity—pretending to work while watching everyone around them. It was getting old. I just wanted them to go away while I finished the Fall Fantasy campaign activities with Juliet. The Texans were starting to unnerve me.

An aging rocker burst through the door, pushing a baby stroller containing two-year-old twins. A sling across his chest sported a newborn with soft blond hair, an odd accessory for a man clad in multicolored spandex with feathers in his hair and glitter around his eyes. Hard on his heels was a lovely young woman who looked like she'd stepped out of a Talbots catalog. At second glance, she had. I recognized her as the prominent model that had married the rocker who was more than twice her age. I was starting to sense a trend.

Branch knew him—correction—knew her, and introduced himself, my mother, the Scotts, and me. The world was getting more and more surreal. While my mother was hobnobbing with rock-n-roll royalty, I took the opportunity to look for Simone. I wanted to give her the deluxe gift bag and thank her personally, and I hoped to forestall a trip to the greenroom.

My appearance in the hallway was met with astonishment by the interns who didn't quite know what to do with me. There was a lot of shoulder shrugging and muttering. I found it a little odd but sallied forth. I asked one intern named Stephanie to direct me to Simone's office.

"Now might not be a good time," she said as she tried to push me back into the greenroom.

"I just want to thank her personally and give her this little gift," I insisted. "It will only take a second."

Stephanie looked intently at her watch.

"Okay," she said finally. "But we're going to have to move fast."

Before I could reply, she was off like a shot, and I was racing to catch up. We sprinted down the corridor to a stairwell, raced up two flights of stairs, and emerged into another corridor. We passed a huge oak double door decorated with gold stars and continued past several other plain doors that I thought must lead to offices. Halfway down the corridor, one of these doors opened, and an intern emerged carrying a highly polished silver serving tray covered in a lace doily and supporting four Twinkies arranged with military precision.

"Coming through!" shouted the intern. "Make way!"

"Are those the…" I started to ask Stephanie.

"Yes, they are," she snapped and quickened her pace.

I'd heard about the legendary Jackie Jordan Twinkies from Kate. According to entertainment industry lore, Jackie Jordan had once suffered from a bout of laryngitis that had been inexplicably cured minutes before showtime when he ate a Twinkie. Since then, Jackie had eaten a Twinkie before every show. Over the years, the Twinkie ritual had grown and evolved. Now Jackie required four Twinkies without blemish before every show. The color of the Twinkies could be no darker than a golden brown French fry and no lighter than unsalted Irish butter. The cream filling had to be at least two centimeters from the outside of the Twinkie on all sides and surfaces, and this last stipulation required a dedicated intern to use a magnifying glass and a surgical probe no thicker than a human hair to examine the Twinkie without causing damage. I hadn't quite believed Kate, but now I'd seen the evidence with my own eyes.

I was still pondering the curative powers of Twinkies when we suddenly stopped and Stephanie rapped on a door.

"Enter!"

Stephanie opened the door and led me into Simone Resnick's inner sanctum.

I was a little disappointed.

The inner sanctum of the most powerful talent booker in the world was a rather dreary office. Sure the walls were covered in celebrity photos, but the piles of papers on every surface spoke volumes about how hard Simone Resnick worked. My respect for her, already immense, was now boundless.

"Jeez, Stephanie! Do you want to keep your job?" barked Simone as she jumped up from her desk to intercept us. Her wiry hair quivered with anger and frustration. I wondered what the problem was.

"We have just enough time, Ms. Resnick…" Stephanie tried to explain, but Simone cut her off with a wave of her hand.

"Simone, I'm Jill Cooksey," I smiled at her. "I just wanted to thank you for working with me during this delicate time.…" I didn't get a chance to finish my carefully rehearsed speech.

"You're welcome. Now get out," said Simone. When I just stood there with my mouth gaping open, she took the gift bag from my grasp, pushed the intern toward me, and used the door to shove us both back into the hallway. Stephanie grabbed my hand and started pulling me back the way we came. What on earth was going on?

We hadn't traveled ten feet before the oak double doors we had passed at the other end of the hallway opened.

Stephanie froze, and all the color drained from her face.

She muttered what sounded like a prayer under her breath. Then she flattened her body against the wall and looked at her shoes. When I just stood there looking at her like she was a nut, she briefly looked up at me. Fear filled her imploring eyes.

"For heaven's sake, do what I do!" The terror in her voice was unmistakable and prompted me to flatten my body against the wall next to her.

"Avert your gaze," she whispered, this time without looking up.

I looked at my shoes, still wondering what was up. Avert my gaze? Was this Saudi Arabia? No, it was New York City.

A moment later, heavy footsteps resounded through the corridor. They grew louder as the mystery walker approached us. Only after he had passed did I look up to see the back of late-night legend Jackie Jordan. As soon as I looked up, however, Jordan paused as if he could feel my gaze on his back. I averted my eyes, and he continued to the stairwell at the end of the hall. When he was gone, I let out the breath I'd been holding. Stephanie, however, practically fainted.

We made it back to the greenroom with me supporting the failing intern with an arm around her waist. On the way back she explained that no one was allowed to see Mr. Jordan before a show. He considered it the ultimate in bad luck. The last person who had made eye contact with Mr. Jordan before a show, she told me, had been whisked from the theater to a waiting car and hadn't been heard from since. It sounded like a rumor to me, but then I thought about the Twinkies.

CHAPTER 25

At showtime, Juliet, Meredith, Dustin, and I left our parents, Hoss, and Branch having a merry old time swapping diaper rash tips and cookie recipes with the aging rocker and his trophy wife who had shown themselves to be warm and wonderful people. At last sighting, Branch, Hoss, and Dud all had children under three bouncing on their knees. I took a moment to consider Branch who was turning out to be quite a mensch: friendly, outgoing, polite, and charming. I couldn't help but like the guy, and I had the urge to take him off my list of suspects. He did, after all, have an alibi. I wondered what her name was.

We followed another intern through a maze of stairs and corridors until we were backstage. Juliet was to be the first guest on the Jackie Jordan show that day, and he was just starting his monologue.

Jackie Jordan was a throwback to a time when cool meant a tailored suit, a skinny tie, and a glass of single malt. He had started as a comedian until Hollywood drafted him for a few lackluster pictures. He hit real stardom with a variety show that had everyone in America tuning in. When variety shows started to lose their popularity, Jordan stayed ahead of the power curve by transforming his show into a late-night talk show. His ingenuity and willingness to change with the times had led to career longevity, but it was still a wonder that his show could pull down such fabulous ratings in an age of three hundred channels by cable or satellite, not to mention streaming services. Jackie had only himself to thank for his success.

His monologues weren't stellar. His jokes were sometimes political but mostly harmless. The audience laughed anyway because they adored him. What they loved about Jackie was his rapport with his guests. He flattered them, insulted them, and flattered them again, and in the process, he managed to make himself laughable.

Backstage we watched a large monitor as Jackie capped off his monologue with a joke about the latest celebrity to go to rehab, this one for hoarding. He was in good form for a man of his indeterminate but undoubtedly considerable years. His snow-white hair was thick and lustrous, and it capped a face full of good humor, at least when he was performing. His navy blue suit was crisp and clean and contrasted attractively with the muted golds and browns of his set. The suit rested on a tall, broad frame without an inch of fat, except in his cheeks, which dimpled when he smiled.

At the commercial break, Jackie went to his desk, took a sip from his mug, and settled into his chair. Juliet was up next. We had dressed her in a sleek but safe black dress with a plunging neckline. All her goodies were properly covered, but the neckline was certainly suggestive.

All part of the show.

When Jackie introduced her and she walked out on the set, he got to make a big show of reacting to her sex appeal. His fascination with her décolletage continued through the first minute of the interview and had the audience rolling in the aisles. Juliet took it in stride and laughed along. Eventually, Jackie got down to brass tacks.

JACKIE: *You've had a rough week.*

JULIET: *Tell me about it.*

JACKIE: *I'm sure I speak for everyone when I tell you that I'm sorry for your loss.*

JULIET: *Thank you so much. That means a lot.*

(And we were over the hump.)

JACKIE: *So what brings you to New York in the middle of a nor'easter?*

AUDIENCE LAUGHS. JULIET CHUCKLES.

JULIET: *I'm here to launch a new fragrance for Eshellon Cosmetics called Fall Fantasy.*

JULIET PULLS OUT THE GIFT BAG THAT HAD BEEN STRATEGICALLY PLACED NEXT TO HER CHAIR DURING THE COMMERCIAL BREAK.

JULIET: *I have some here for your wife.*

JACKIE: *Do I have to give it to my wife?*

EVERYBODY LAUGHS

JULIET: *You can give it to whomever you want.*

JACKIE LEERS AT HER CLEAVAGE. JULIET LAUGHS SOME MORE. JACKIE GETS SERIOUS AGAIN.

JACKIE: *How it smells will determine whom I give it to.*

JACKIE FUMBLES WITH THE BOTTLE.

JACKIE: *Jeez, it's worse than a brassiere!*

MORE LAUGHTER.

JULIET HELPS HIM UNCAP THE BOTTLE.

JACKIE: *You're very good with your hands.*

MORE LAUGHTER.

SHE SPRAYS SOME FRAGRANCE ON HIS WRIST.

JULIET: *You want to apply it to pressure points.*

JACKIE: *I bet you've got terrific pressure points.*

MORE LAUGHTER.

JACKIE SNIFFS HIS WRIST.

JACKIE: Oh that's very nice. That's so lovely we need to share it. Where are my interns?

And with that, the band let loose on the intern song, the jingle they played every time Jackie Jordan decided to send his interns out into the world to do crazy things. It was all scripted of course. Jackie himself didn't come up with any of this stuff.

"They're young and they're clever, or maybe they're just crazy," chanted the band while several of the interns danced about the stage in t-shirts with the word "INTERN" printed across the chest. "We beat them, but we feed them. We never call them lazy. They're working here for peanuts, and some of them might be nuts. They're interns!"

When the chaos was over, two interns were left on the stage, my good friend Stephanie and a petite African American woman who Jackie identified as Charniece. He handed them the unopened bottle of perfume from the gift bag and instructed them to head out into Times Square to share Fall Fantasy with the masses. The two interns took off followed by a cameraman. Backstage we watched on the monitor as they raced through the halls of the Tennessee Williams Theater and out the stage door where another intern had already wrangled a victim, I mean participant.

I wasn't sure if he had followed directions because the unlikely participant he'd snagged was a mime. The intern and the mime were huddled under a huge umbrella, but the rain had eased considerably since our journey from Madison Avenue. I wondered for a moment why a mime would be working in any kind of rain, but then I remembered what New York City rents were like.

While Charniece held another umbrella, Stephanie worked the microphone and explained to the mime that they wanted him to try the perfume and let them know his opinion. The mime made a big show of smelling a silk flower to demonstrate his love of fragrance, and he pantomimed opening a perfume bottle and dabbing some on his wrists and behind his ears. He was quite funny, but he was taking his time. Someone must have chirped a warning into Stephanie's earpiece because she suddenly pulled the top off the bottle and sprayed some Fall Fantasy in the vicinity of his neck and face, the rest of his body being covered by a long-sleeved black leotard and white gloves.

The mime made a hilarious face intimating that the fragrance wasn't to his taste. I looked at Meredith and Dustin to see how they were taking it, and they seemed to be fine. As long as other people later in the show said something nice about Fall Fantasy, we would be okay. Besides, no one took these late show gags seriously. Just being on the show would garner sales.

I looked back at the monitor to find that the mime had dropped to the wet sidewalk and was writhing around, his face contorted.

He's going a little too far, I thought. It's not funny anymore.

The audience, however, found it hilarious, at least until the mime started vomiting and the interns started screaming.

CHAPTER 26

*T*eaching. That was a safe profession. Kids were cute, weren't they? Of course, the last time I'd hung out with kids, one of them had bitten me. Or cooking. I could go to cooking school. But head chefs were known for throwing pans and knives at their underlings. I needed a safe career, and it looked like I'd need it soon.

I'd just taken a tongue-lashing of the first magnitude from Eshellon VP Meredith Hopkins. Several hours had passed since the *Nighttime with Jackie Jordan* debacle, and we were now in the Buckworths' suite at the Waldorf. Meredith, trying to pour a drink with unsteady hands, was still shaking with fury but had taken a moment to regroup. I wanted to protest that it hadn't been me who'd put cyanide in the bottle of Fall Fantasy that almost killed the mime, but I didn't think it would help. Meredith was watching her pet project go up in smoke, Waverly Communications was looking at a billings loss of at least two million dollars a year, and Hoss, who had collapsed in an armchair after several tall neat bourbons, was anticipating the arrest of his almost fiancée. I was contemplating the events of the day and the effect they would assuredly have on my life.

When the mime started seizing and vomiting, the technical director cut the feed to the monitors in the studio and backstage, leaving the audience abuzz over the incident. With a quick word to Meredith instructing her to keep an eye on the situation on set, I took off for the stairs. Whatever was going on at street level, it involved my client, and I needed to help.

I emerged on the sidewalk sixty seconds later to find a policeman rendering first aid to the unfortunate mime and the two shocked interns holding each other and crying. I felt bad for them, especially Stephanie whose day I'd managed to ruin twice. I tried to comfort them, but a moment later I was distracted when Hoss, Juliet, our parents, Hilda, and Branch came trooping out the side door. One look at the convulsing street performer had Juliet near hysterics. Luckily the Buckworth limo was parked nearby, and Hoss and the Scotts managed to get Juliet inside just in time because a crowd was starting to gather.

Soon an ambulance appeared, and the EMTs took over. A few minutes later, Meredith and Dustin appeared at the stage door. Meredith reported that Jackie had announced that the young mime had suffered an allergic reaction to the perfume but was headed to the hospital. That seemed to calm the audience down, but taping resumed without Juliet Scott and Fall Fantasy. Meredith and Dustin were noticeably grim. We all were.

Amid the chaos of EMTs, police, hysterical clients, and perplexed parents, I caught sight of Simone Resnick who had come to take charge of the interns and assess the damage. I started to approach her to ask if any of Juliet's interview could be salvaged. After all, I was still a public relations professional, and I had to at least try to rescue the situation. Before I had taken two steps toward Simone, she spotted me. Her fierce expression stopped me in my tracks, and I watched in horror as she slowly drew her index finger across her throat. It was at that moment that I realized my career in public relations might be coming to an end.

Jill Cooksey has failed.

I felt a pat on the back and turned to find my mother.

"I think my career's over, Mama," I managed despite the lump that was rapidly forming in my throat. "Maybe I should move back to Luthersburg. You haven't turned my bedroom into a craft room, have you?"

"Nonsense, Jilly," my mother sniffed. "After what I've seen today, life in Luthersburg would have you in the booby hatch inside six months. You'd be bored to death."

That's my mom. A kick in the butt (she would say "bottom") just when you needed it most.

"Of course," she continued, "a person can have a bit too much drama in her life. There is a line."

"Yeah," I agreed as we climbed into the limo. "And we crossed it a week ago."

With a tender kiss for Juliet and instructions to his driver, Hoss sent us back to the Waldorf and went straight to the hospital to watch over the mime who had come very close to death. His name was Frank Ferguson, and he had come to New York from Michigan to be a Broadway star. When that didn't pan out, he had taken to street performing to make the rent. But I had a feeling Mr. Ferguson's days as a busker were over. Most likely he would never have to work another day in his life, at least as soon as his lawyers were done with Eshellon. Probably sooner, I thought, as Hoss Buckworth had taken the man's attempted murder hard. Racked with guilt, he waved off every attempt I made to assure him that he wasn't to blame. These scenes only served to infuriate Meredith even more.

The cops arrived at the Waldorf right after the lawyers. Perfect timing, I thought.

Detective Donato was looking haggard like he hadn't slept in days, and I thought I knew why. One woman dead, one attacked, and the attempted murder of a mime made for three crimes, most likely by the same perp, and no arrests. When Donato commandeered one of the suite's several bedrooms for use as an interrogation room, no one put up a fuss. No one wanted to go to the police station. We were all wrecked.

Juliet was the first in for questioning, then Meredith, Dustin, me, Branch, my mother, Dud, and finally Shirley. The three Virginians emerged from questioning looking energized and animated.

"Well, that was exciting," chirped my mother.

"You know, I've always regretted not going into criminal law," mused Dud. "That's where the action is."

"That police detective looks terrible. What do you think he takes in his coffee?" asked Shirley.

The rest of us just stared. Personally, I felt like I'd had a close encounter with a semi.

During my oh-so-exciting session with the police, I had taken Donato through my day, including making up the gift bag of perfume, the ride to the theater, and everything that happened once I got there. Then I took him through it again. By the sixth time, a vein on the left side of my head was starting to throb and my left eye was twitching.

As he had at the end of each recitation, Donato finished up with the same question: "And Ms. Cooksey, was there any time throughout the day during which you were separated from the gift bag of perfume?"

A tiny muscle above my right eye began to beat. I think it was doing the samba. Although Donato sounded like he was wrapping up the questioning, I knew he wasn't. He had asked me the same question five times before, and each time he had followed it with "Now if you will just take me through your day one more time." I'd had enough.

"In the limo, it got covered with coats and purses," I enunciated fiercely. "I left it in the greenroom when I went to see

Simone Resnick." My consonants were so crisp that little bits of spittle were flying from my mouth like sparks. "Then an intern took it from me. The next time I saw it, it was sitting on the set. You can ask me a hundred more times, but the answer is going to be the same!"

He let me go after that.

After his second session with Juliet (I was not envying her at all), Donato took his leave. With a last tired look at the assemblage of suspects and hangers-on, he muttered, "Don't anybody leave town. I'll be in touch." Then he was gone.

Hoss arrived from the hospital a few minutes after Donato left. It was around seven o'clock, but it felt much later. Hoss said he'd given a statement to a detective at the hospital, but I had a feeling Donato would be back to put him through the wringer. Then Hoss threw back several bourbons and collapsed in a chair. I tried to comfort him to no avail. It was then I'd received a thorough dressing-down from Meredith about my ineptitude as a PR professional. When she was finished, there didn't seem to be anything I could say or do to make things right for her or Hoss, so I decided to go where I thought I could do the most good.

I went to check on Juliet and found her in the bedroom/interrogation room asleep with her head in her mother's lap. My mother and Dud were also seated on the bed. It was a touching scene, these loving parents clustered protectively around one of their children. Part of me wanted to crawl into my own mother's lap and drift off to sleep. I settled for giving her a warm smile that she returned with a knowing look. Satisfied that Juliet was in good hands, I returned to the living room to find Hoss alone. The doors to Meredith and Dustin's rooms were closed, and I wondered where Branch had got to.

I tiptoed over to Hoss. His eyes were closed. I didn't think he was sleeping, but I decided to leave him alone for a bit.

Not really knowing what to do, I opened my Behemoth

Black Bag and took out my cell phone. I had silenced it at the theater, and what with talk show hosts, interns, poison, and mimes, this was my first opportunity to check it. I'd missed nineteen calls and my voice mail was full. Ye gods and little fishes!

The call from the car turned out to be Mike. He had left a message saying that the trail in the Bronx was cold. He had also suggested a dinner date for that night. Fat chance! How I would have loved to be curled up next to Mike in that cozy little pub in the Upper West Side instead of caught up in a murder investigation. The second call was from Mike again, but he hadn't left a message. The rest of the calls were from reporters who wanted a statement from Juliet or Eshellon and to schedule interviews. Well, no one would be talking to reporters anytime soon.

As much as I wanted to talk to Mike, I didn't call him back. The idea of rehashing the nightmare that had been my day provoked a visceral response in my gut. Instead, I opened up my laptop. The Waldorf Wi-Fi worked well, and I was pleased to see that my email was up and running again.

The first email I saw was from a producer at *Wake the Nation*, the morning show Juliet was supposed to appear on the next day. Crud! I'd all but forgotten the final piece of our strategic communications plan for the launch of Fall Fantasy perfume. I supposed I would have to email the producer back to cancel. I started to type the message of regret and apology but paused. Maybe there was some way to save the campaign that I just hadn't thought of. I decided to put off responding to the producer for another hour or two.

The next email was from Surya. The subject line read "RE: Hilda Griffith."

Holy moly! Where was Hilda?

I distinctly remembered her coming out of the theater to stand with us on the sidewalk, but somewhere in all the chaos, she must have slipped away. With all the tragedy swirling about us, no one had noticed her absence, not even Meredith and Dustin. Weird. Anxious, I opened the email.

"Society reporter, my foot!" Surya had written. "Take a look at these clips and call me." Attached to the email was a zipped folder. Inside the folder were several PDF files. I opened the first one to find a news story from the *Dallas Sentinel,* including photos. The headline read "Transit worker says drivers pimped from city buses." The byline belonged to Hilda Griffith. Not exactly the debutante ball.

The story was an exposé of bus drivers who used their buses as hubs for prostitution during their late-night shifts. Hilda had managed to get someone inside the Dallas transit authority to talk and had set up a sting operation. The story was gritty and well-written and most definitely not about polite society. I eagerly opened the next file.

"Doctor's Flu Vaccines Fake" was another exposé, this time of a doctor who had sold flu vaccines to his impoverished, immigrant clientele that turned out to be merely saline solution. Another story was about animal cruelty in a slaughterhouse, while another was about a man convicted of murder who was vindicated by DNA evidence after twenty years in prison. Hilda Griffith was a hard-hitting reporter with a nose like a bloodhound. What was she doing following a perfume launch?

Surya had saved the best story for last. "Dallas Mourns an American Original" was a profile of Shelley Buckworth. While Hilda had remained emotionless in the writing of every other story in the file, her love for her friend was unmistakable in this piece. From a simple statement that Shelley Buckworth had passed away peacefully in her sleep at home following a struggle with cancer, Hilda flashed back to Shelley's childhood. She then took the reader on a journey through Shelley's impoverished early life, to her academic successes in high school and college, to her early years in business, and finally to her aha moment and the birth of Eshellon Cosmetics. Along the way, Hilda shared humorous anecdotes that only a real friend could have known. She talked about Shelley's marriage to Hoss as if it were a love story for the ages. Then came tremendous joy at the birth of Dustin followed by tremendous anxiety at the diagnosis of cancer. Years of fighting the disease with an indomitable spirit made Shelley Buckworth my new hero, but just as she received a clean bill of health from her doctors, Shelley's body had given out. The years of chemo and radiation had taken their toll.

I was still recovering from both the revelations about Hilda Griffith and the intensely moving story of Shelley Buckworth when Hoss shifted in his chair. I looked over to find him hunched over, his head in his hands. Slowly he looked up at me.

"Jill, I did it. It was me."

CHAPTER 27

"Come again?" I stammered. Had Hoss just confessed to killing Amber O'Neil?

"I did it," he repeated. "I had you attacked. I'm so sorry."

It took a moment for me to comprehend what he was telling me, but when it finally sank in, I jumped to my feet.

Rage. That's the only word to describe what I was feeling, what was coursing through my veins and making me clench and unclench my fists. Trembling with fury, I wanted to scream obscenities at Hoss Buckworth. No, I wanted to punch him in the face. No, I wanted to scream obscenities while punching him in the face. Unfortunately, I was so upset I could barely speak much less move. I finally got one word out.

"Why?"

"I was afraid for Juliet. I didn't want to lose her. I couldn't go through that again!" Then the giant Texan dissolved into tears that washed away a little bit of my rage. As his tears turned to sobs, more of my anger melted away until I would have been happy just giving him a scolding and a good spanking.

"You did it to help Juliet." I was calmer now and trying to

reason it out since Hoss was incapable of speech. "If the killer struck again but Juliet had an alibi, she would be in the clear."

Hoss managed to nod.

I remembered how excited he had been after my attack, how optimistic that the worst was over. In hindsight, it seemed perfectly clear. Why hadn't I suspected it?

"Because you're too trusting, Jilly-Bean," I heard my father say.

I couldn't quite bring myself to comfort Hoss, but I did sit down again to wait until he cried it out. A few minutes later, he was over the worst and able to speak.

"If you hadn't been attacked," he began, "if Juliet were still the prime suspect, then the killer wouldn't have tried to kill Jackie Jordan."

Slow. You're really slow, Jill.

The poison in the bottle was intended for Jackie Jordan. It had been a game of Russian Roulette. Jackie sampled the first bottle and gave the second to the interns, but what if he had chosen the poisoned bottle first?

Visions of Jackie Jordan convulsing on the set of *Nighttime* in front of a studio audience made me shudder. I reached over and picked up Hoss's latest glass of bourbon. There was still about a finger left. I threw it back and then coughed until my eyes watered.

Hoss had forced the killer's hand by having me attacked. Because Juliet had an alibi for that night, the police had probably been forced to look more carefully at other suspects like Ian O'Neil, Branch Matheson, Meredith Hopkins, and Dustin Buckworth. The killer had to throw suspicion back onto Juliet, and what better way than to have her kill someone with poisoned perfume in front of an audience of hundreds while being recorded?

Forgetting all about Hoss Buckworth for the moment, I grabbed my laptop and opened up a blank document. I needed to organize my thoughts.

I began by going through the list of suspects.

Ian O'Neil. While the man was tormented and knew all about Amber's past, how could he have put poison in a bottle of Fall Fantasy perfume? I had taken the bottles from the product closet. Only someone with access to Waverly Communications could have tampered with one of them. But how could anyone know which bottles I would take off the shelf to put into Jackie Jordan's gift bag? No one could. My feet turned to ice as I realized that somewhere between my office and the theater the killer had made a switch. Was it in the lobby, in the limo, at the theater? There was no way to know. Fending off feelings of panic, I moved on from Ian O'Neil.

Branch Matheson. Hoss had stolen his girl. How better to get revenge than to frame Hoss's new girl for murder? He had an alibi for the night of Amber's death, but it was thin. Moreover, he had been hanging around Waverly for the last couple of days—plenty of time to take a bottle of perfume and doctor it. He had also been uber-charming to my mother and the Scotts to the point that I was really starting to like the guy. If I were a killer, that's exactly how I'd act. Branch was a prime suspect.

Meredith Hopkins. Complete harpy, I typed as I remembered the dressing down she'd given me earlier. She irked me something fierce, but that didn't make her a murderer. Fall Fantasy was her creation more than anyone else's. She had no reason to sabotage it. Still, there were so many secrets swirling about this group of people—perhaps she had one of her own. More to the point, did she have an alibi for Amber's murder? Meredith had never been discussed seriously as a suspect, and I hadn't heard of any alibi. For that matter, I hadn't heard about Hoss's alibi either. Curious, I turned to him and found him looking much better. Evidently, confession and a good cry had eased his soul.

"Hoss, the police never considered you a suspect for

Amber's murder. You must have had an alibi. Just out of curiosity, what was it?"

Hoss's newfound serenity vanished in an instant. I watched his brow wrinkle and his chin quiver. Big fat tears began to roll down his cheeks.

Oh, for Pete's sake! Gargantuan Texans in boots and Stetsons were not supposed to cry at the drop of a hat. Hadn't Hoss seen any John Wayne movies? This crying cowboy routine was getting on my nerves. I stifled the urge to tell my client to get a grip.

"Meredith is my alibi," he said softly.

That answered my question. He had been with Meredith after the launch.

I looked again at his tear-streaked face. My breath caught in my throat.

He had *been with* Meredith after the launch.

The shock must have shown in my face because Hoss hastened to explain.

"Juliet and I had been fighting, and I'd been drinking heavily the night of the launch."

When didn't he drink heavily?

"I barely remember getting back to the Wellington. Meredith had to help me upstairs. She helped me undress." His voice was quivering in time with his chin. "One thing led to another." Hoss buried his face in his hands and hiccuped one big sob.

I looked over at the door to Meredith's bedroom. The last thing I wanted was to involve her in this conversation. It was awkward enough. The door was shut. I did a double-take. No, it wasn't. Instead, it was barely cracked like someone hadn't shut it firmly. Had it been shut all the way when I first noticed she'd gone to bed? I looked over at Dustin's door to find it slightly cracked as well. Were they both standing on the other side of those doors listening to Hoss spill his guts? None of it would be news to Meredith, except for the part about Hoss hiring a thug to bash me over the head. But all of it would be news to Dustin. I wondered how he would take all these revelations. He was, after all, carrying a torch for Juliet.

Well, the genie's out of the bottle, I thought and turned my attention to Juliet's door. Shut firmly, thank goodness. I could only imagine the ruckus that would ensue should Juliet or her father hear us. I wanted no shots fired in the Waldorf Astoria Hotel.

After a few more sobs, Hoss was able to continue.

"The next morning was awkward." Good, I thought. "But Meredith was a lady. We agreed never to speak of it again, and we wouldn't have except the police needed to know where we were."

"When are you going to tell Juliet?" I asked in a surprisingly firm voice.

Hoss looked at me with pleading eyes. I looked back with as much steel as I could muster. *Either you tell her, or I will.* The message passed silently between us. Hoss let out a huge sigh.

"I'll tell her soon. I promise. I don't want to start a life together based on lies." He squared his shoulders and wiped away the remaining tears.

Just then I heard a knock at the door.

"What now?" I wondered as I hauled myself to my feet.

I opened the door partway. It was Mike.

"I got here as soon as I could," he said. "How are you?"

"I'm fine." When I didn't open the door further, Mike cocked an eyebrow.

"Can I come in?"

"Now isn't a good time," I replied. "It's been a hard day, and Mr. Buckworth doesn't want to see any reporters."

Plus, he'd just admitted to having me beaten up and cheating on Juliet. A headline of "Buckworth indicted for attempted murder" would be the rotten cherry on top of the ecoli laced sundae that was the Fall Fantasy campaign at this point. From behind me, I could hear that Hoss had resumed sobbing and sniffling. It was not the time to meet the press.

"What are you hiding, Jill?" asked Mike. His eyes were narrowed in scrutiny. Had he learned to read my face in exactly one week?

"I'm not hiding anything," I lied. "Can you not hear someone crying? This is not a good time."

"Is it ever going to be a good time for you to trust me, Jill?" Mike turned on his heel and headed for the elevator.

I barely restrained myself from slamming the door. When I turned back to Hoss, he was shambling toward his bedroom. He closed the door quietly behind him, but it wasn't thick enough to muffle his sobs and sniffles. For pity's sake! I wondered if everyone else could hear it and looked at the other doors only to find them now firmly shut. Good grief.

This was turning out to be the longest day of my life, and my patience, fortitude, and love for my fellow man were quickly running out. I looked longingly at Hoss's empty glass and then at the bar on the other side of the room. Tempting, but it wasn't my style. My style, I thought as I went back to my computer, was a gallon of sweet tea, a big think, and lots of lists. Lists were comforting, and sometimes they worked.

I went back to my inventory. After making a few notes next to Meredith and Hoss's names, I called room service and ordered the aforementioned tea. Then I moved on to Hilda. She wasn't a suspect in my book. Hilda was after a story, but what was it? There seemed to be no end to the Buckworth family secrets. Her story could be about any of them or all of them. My mind returned to the loving tribute to Shelley Buckworth that Hilda had written. I had a hard time imagining Hilda out to get the family of her beloved friend. Maybe she was here to protect Hoss from gold diggers like Amber. If that was the case, maybe she had stabbed Amber and tried to frame Juliet, killing two birds with one shoe. It was quite a stretch, and I didn't buy it. I didn't know what Hilda's game was, but I had a hard time believing it involved murder.

The last person on my list was Dustin.

Dustin!

I did a mental head slap as I realized I hadn't shared what I knew about young Mr. Buckworth with the police. Nobody else knew that he'd been in town on Friday and had tipped off the media about the Amber/Juliet fight. Maybe the police were looking at Dustin, and maybe they weren't.

Just then a ding signaled an incoming email. It was from Kate.

"Hey girl," Kate began. "I heard about the Jackie Jordan mess. What is going on? More importantly, how are you holding up? Call me when you can. I've attached a collection of clips about the Amber-Branch love affair. Hope it helps. Kate."

Somehow just reading an email from a dear friend gave me renewed energy, that and the sweet Southern elixir delivered by room service. Fortified by friends, sugar, and caffeine, I opened the clips. They were mostly from magazines, the kind that line the checkouts at the supermarket, and they were in chronological order. The first, dated two years before, was about a rumor that Branch and Amber were secretly dating. The second had the headline "Yes, we're a couple, confess Amber and Branch." That story included photos of a private vacation in the Caribbean. Most likely when presented with the photos, the couple had no choice but to take their relationship public. In the photos, they looked gorgeous and very much in love. The third story had the novel idea to call the couple "Bramber," but thankfully it didn't stick. The fourth story hinted at wedding bells for the A-list couple after Amber was spotted coming out of a bridal boutique in Hollywood, and I was struck with an overwhelming sense of déjà vu. Hadn't I followed the same relationship countless times in the tabloids?

As a result, it was far too easy to predict the subject of the next story.

"Amber cheating?" was about the inevitable rumors of trouble in paradise. The cover art was just as predictable. A photo of Branch and Amber at a premier had been "torn" in two, the two halves set at odds. In the pictures, Branch and Amber were smiling and had been holding hands before being separated by Photoshop, and it just made the headline more shocking. I looked at the date on the magazine—a little over a year ago. Sadly, the tabloids had it right.

I looked at the two people in the picture and searched for a sign of impending doom, but there wasn't one. Amber was all smiles, dressed in a zebra print sequined evening gown with impossibly large earrings, and while her clothes were over-the-top, she still looked amazing. She had been a beautiful woman in need of a good stylist. And Branch was looking devilishly handsome as always in a drop-dead sexy tuxedo. His hair was longer, down to his shoulders, and he sported about a week's worth of beard, but he looked fine just the same, like an Armani-clad pirate.

I hesitated to open the next clip because I knew what was coming. I don't like sad endings, but it was the climax of a real tearjerker. I double-clicked the file.

"Amber to Branch: I don't love you anymore," claimed to be about their last fight on the night they broke up. Supposedly this fight had happened at a club in Hollywood in front of many witnesses, but none of the sources were identified by name. I was more interested in the photos than the poorly written story. One photographer had managed to get a shot of Amber dressed down for the weekend, coming out of a coffee shop in Beverly Hills. The hunted expression on her face spoke volumes. Her hands were shoved into her pockets, the collar of her jacket was turned up, and if she could have shrunk down to subatomic size rather than face the paparazzi, I'm sure she would have.

The subject of the other photo was, of course, Branch. On location in Montana where he was starring in the story of a famous mountain man, he was covered in furs from his head to his foot. Mountain man chic. But I was more interested in the fur on his face. Branch the sexy pirate had morphed into Branch the wild man of the wilderness with long shaggy hair and an even longer beard. The photo had me transfixed. It almost reminded me of something, but I couldn't quite remember what. When I did finally remember, I sat quietly for several minutes wondering what to make of it.

My reverie was interrupted by my cell phone. I looked at the screen. It was the producer of *Wake the Nation*, and I was in a quandary.

Secrets. This whole messy situation was about secrets. And I, as a public relations professional responsible for maintaining images and reputations, was supposed to keep secrets. I wasn't sure I could do that anymore.

Jill Cooksey does not fail.

This time, she might have to.

I took the call from the producer.

Sometime later, my mother and the Scotts stole quietly from Juliet's room just as I was hanging up with *Wake the Nation*.

"How is she?" I asked.

"With a good night's sleep, she'll be right as rain," chirped my mother with ferocious optimism. Dud and Shirley were somewhat less sanguine.

I knew they hadn't eaten since lunch, and it was now half-past eight. I suggested they go downstairs to one of the restaurants for dinner.

"I know the concierge, and I will make sure he takes excellent care of you," I gushed. "Afterwards, how about a nice walk through Times Square or a trip to the Empire State Building? The view at night is spectacular."

I gathered up my belongings and shoved them into my Behemoth Black Bag.

"Then tomorrow you can have breakfast at the best diner in town. I'll arrange a car for you. And you can do some sightseeing, maybe the Met or Central Park. Then we can meet for lunch at noon. By then it will all be over."

"What will be over?" asked my mother sharply.

My career.

"Juliet's appearance on *Wake the Nation*," I replied. "That will be the end of the launch, and life will go back to normal."

Dud and Shirley seemed comforted by the thought of a return to sanity, but my mother eyed me suspiciously.

As I ushered them from the suite, she hissed into my ear, "Why do I get the feeling you're trying to get rid of us?"

"Because I am," I whispered back.

I left the Virginians in Jean-Paul's capable hands. He was delighted to meet my mother, too delighted if you ask me. I had a sneaking suspicion that by the end of the evening he'd know every embarrassing story there was about me.

"It would be an honor if you would allow me to join you for dinner," he crooned. "I am so eager to hear all about your home and about Jill growing up."

Suspicion confirmed.

"Don't you dare tell him about the sixth-grade play," I hissed in my mother's ear. I'd played a Munchkin in *The Wizard of Oz*, and in the middle of the scene where Dorothy arrives in Munchkinland, Toto had trotted over and pooped on my shoe. As a result, sixth grade was a dark time in my life.

When I said goodnight to the party, Jean-Paul made a big show of kissing my hand and telling me he hoped we would spend time together soon. This display had my mother and Shirley Scott waggling their eyebrows at each other. I just rolled my eyes, gave my mother a kiss, and headed for the door. Without thinking, I descended the stairs to the Park Avenue entrance but was brought up short by the Amber shrine blocking the revolving doors. I could also hear shouting from outside. I hurried back up the stairs into the lobby and took a shorter set of stairs up to the cocktail terrace. From there I could see the front sidewalk.

The weather hadn't discouraged the mourners who had added even more items to the shrine, including a giant stuffed tiger. They had also been joined by protesters carrying signs that read "Justice for Amber" and "Juliet Scott is a murderer." I said a prayer of thanks that Juliet hadn't seen them earlier and added a plea that by this time tomorrow it would all be history. Then I headed for the side entrance.

The nor'easter had blown itself out leaving behind cool fall air that felt gloriously fresh on my face and in my lungs. I realized just how oppressive the atmosphere had been in the Buckworths' suite and took a moment just to breathe and relax. The next twelve hours were going to be busy, and I tried to prepare myself mentally to work against all the principles of my profession.

With one last deep breath, I stepped forward and raised one hand to hail a cab. With the other, I reached for my phone.

CHAPTER 28

At five thirty the next morning, I rapped firmly on all the bedroom doors in the Buckworths' suite.

"Rise and shine!" I called out. "It's *Wake the Nation* time."

One by one, Juliet, Hoss, Meredith, and Dustin appeared.

"Help yourself to the breakfast buffet," I suggested, gesturing to the fabulous spread I'd ordered the night before.

The Eshellon folks, however, were more interested in the hustle and bustle going on in their penthouse suite than in eggs and bacon.

Two women in jeans and *Wake the Nation* sweatshirts were moving the living room furniture around while a tall bearded man set up lights. A makeup artist with very big hair and bangs was arranging the tools of her trade over in the corner, and a male hairdresser was plugging in multiple curling irons next to her.

"What the Sam Hill is going on here?" demanded Hoss groggily.

"A slight change in plans," I replied with a smile. "I have arranged with the show's producer for Juliet to do her interview remotely. That way she won't have to face crowds and the press while going to and from the studios in Times Square.

"We'll have more control this way," I reasoned. "And the focus of the interview has shifted, as well. They'd like you to appear too, Hoss, and you, Dustin."

"Me?" Dustin croaked and paled behind his freckles.

"How has the focus shifted?" Meredith cut in.

"The Buckworth family is obviously being targeted by someone who wants to bring them down," I said. "The producers want to focus on how the family is holding up. Admittedly, it will be less about Fall Fantasy and more about the Buckworths and Eshellon, but with all that has happened this week, we couldn't expect to go on national television and sell perfume. This segment will give you a chance to show the world that the Buckworths are united. Your brand is at stake now, and I think this interview will cast a favorable light on the Buckworth family."

"But Juliet isn't family," whined Dustin.

"Shut your mouth, Dustin!" snapped Hoss. "Juliet is family, and you better get used to the idea."

I decided that the Buckworths were not morning people.

"Let's have some breakfast," I chirped pleasantly, hoping a rise in blood sugar would make the interview go more smoothly.

"So is Pamela okay with this strategy?" asked Meredith. Never kid a kidder, I thought wryly.

"Absolutely," I lied. I hadn't talked to Pamela since the day before and I wasn't planning on doing so until it was all over. With my smile firmly in place, I led the way to the buffet.

The Eshellon folks were just sitting down to eat when the doorbell rang. I went to answer it and found Kate and Hilda on the doorstep. I'd asked Kate to help me run the show this morning. After the Jackie Jordan fiasco, my confidence was shaken, and I knew I was going to need moral support while I threw my career away. I'd also managed to track down Hilda and invited her along for the ride. I followed a hunch, and sure enough, she was staying at the Waldorf.

"So glad you could both make it," I smiled. I was Little Suzy Sunshine that morning. "Please help yourself to breakfast."

The door was almost closed when a foot appeared between door and frame. It was Mike.

"Do I get to come in today?" he asked warily. After our conversation the previous night, who could blame him?

"I invited you, didn't I?" I replied as I opened the door wide to let him in. After a brief hesitation, he leaned in and brushed my cheek with his lips. He smelled terrific as usual, and I reminded myself that there was more to life than work. I would need to keep that in mind in the coming weeks of unemployment.

"Had breakfast?" I asked with a bit more warmth. "We've got enough food to feed an army."

Mike glanced at the buffet where chafing dishes were heaped with eggs, bacon, sausage, and potatoes.

"Last meal?" he asked with a crooked smile that made my heart skip.

"Something like that."

With a wink, Mike headed for the food, and I started to shut the door for the second time but was interrupted by the arrival of Branch with a beautiful young Indian woman.

"Padma Singh, *Wake the Nation* correspondent," she introduced herself confidently and thrust her hand out. I shook it.

"Friend of yours?" I asked Branch.

"We just met in the elevator, but I'd like to be friends." He shot her a brilliant white smile. "Do I smell breakfast?"

I directed Branch toward the buffet and led Padma into the living room to assess the work of her crew.

The grips had arranged a sofa and armchair and placed the suite's large potted plants attractively around them. The humongous cameraman, who introduced himself as Larry, had set up two cameras, one focused on the interviewer's chair and the other on the interviewees' sofa. Several large lights on stands gave that part of the room an artificial glow and an abnormally warm temperature. Everything seemed to Padma's liking, so I left her with her crew and went back to my own.

Everyone was ranged around the suite's enormous dining room table, and it was the Waverly conference room all over again with the addition of Mike and Kate who were the only people with appetites. The others were picking at their food and stealing glances at each other.

"I've tasted everything this morning, folks," I announced reassuringly. "Nothing's poisoned."

Mike choked on his eggs, and Kate came close to spraying orange juice out her nose.

"I hadn't thought of that," said Mike once he regained his breath. He surveyed his plate critically.

To further make my point, I grabbed a fork, dug into the chafing dish of eggs, and took a big bite.

"Yum!" I exclaimed. Then I doubled over, clutched my stomach, and moaned.

Juliet screamed, everyone else gasped, and Mike jumped out of his chair.

"Just kidding!" I laughed as I stood up straight and grabbed a piece of crispy bacon. "Really folks, the breakfast is delicious."

Everyone glared at me, but soon they were munching away.

As soon as Juliet finished eating, I sent her off with Angie the makeup artist and Nick the hairstylist to get beautified.

"You're next Hoss, and then Dustin," I directed.

"I have to wear makeup?" Dustin was horrified.

"Everyone has to wear makeup on television," interjected Padma smoothly. She stood next to me at the head of the table, and although she was petite, she commanded the room. "I'm Padma Singh, and I will be interviewing you today. Now first things first, I hope you will all oblige me by taking out your cell phones and silencing them. It would look like amateur hour if a phone went off while we were on the air."

Padma waited while everyone took out their phones and dutifully muted them.

"You certainly wouldn't want my phone going off. It plays *The Yellow Rose of Texas*," said Hilda as she extricated a Swarovski crystal-encrusted flip phone from her purse. Hilda kicked it old school.

When all the phones were silenced, Padma continued.

"Now I want you to know there's nothing to be nervous about. This has been a trying week for all of you, and I'm interested in hearing your side of the story. We'll talk briefly about the tragic passing of Amber O'Neil, but then we'll move on to how you've been targeted yourselves this week and why you think it might be happening. Now, which one of you is Meredith Hopkins?"

"That would be me," said Meredith as she set down her coffee cup.

"Jill was telling me that Fall Fantasy was your brainchild," said Padma.

"Well," replied Meredith as she shifted in her seat, "we're really a team at Eshellon."

"Don't be modest," put in Hoss. "The whole idea of seasonal fragrances was yours."

"I think it would be a great idea if you were part of the interview," coaxed Padma. "The events of this week must have had quite an effect on the launch of your new product, and I think it would be good to hear the perspective of the creator. What do you say?"

Reluctantly, Meredith said yes. I beamed a smile her way.

"I knew we could shine some light on Fall Fantasy," I said once Padma had walked away.

"Nicely done, Jill," said Hoss. "You may save this product launch yet."

"From your mouth to God's ear," I replied.

The interview was scheduled for the first segment of the eight o'clock hour, and by seven forty-five Juliet, Hoss, Dustin, and Meredith were in makeup, miked up, and seated on the set. The grips had swapped out the sofa in favor of two love seats, one for Juliet and Hoss and one for Meredith and Dustin.

I was passing out bottled water when Padma came rushing over.

"Guess what?" she exclaimed. "Branch Matheson has agreed to be part of the segment as well. I think he'll add another dimension to the story. Dustin and Meredith, would you mind making room? Thanks." She flitted back across the room where Angie was airbrushing foundation onto Branch's face.

"I don't think I like this, Jill," began Hoss.

Meredith threw up her hands.

"Yeah, how are we going to put Eshellon and Fall Fantasy in a good light if all anybody wants to talk about is the murder of that…"

"Tramp?" interjected Dustin.

"She wasn't a tramp," said Juliet hotly.

"Did she or did she not attack you a week ago at our launch event?" countered Meredith.

"That doesn't make her a tramp," argued Juliet. "She was unhappy and disappointed!"

I glanced over to where Mike, Kate, and Hilda were seated in a row of armchairs that we had arranged for the spectators. Yep, they were hanging on every word. We weren't even rolling and the show had begun.

Just then Branch came strolling over, and his presence put the kibosh on the argument over Amber's virtue. One of the production assistants brought him a wireless mic and tried to help him put it on.

"I'm an old pro at this, sweetheart," he smirked and took it from her. Soon he was squeezed between Meredith and Dustin, and it was almost time to go live.

I'd persuaded the producer to let me contribute some interview questions, which I'd written on note cards. I wandered over to my bag to retrieve them only to find them in the hands of Hilda Griffith.

"I believe those belong to me," I snapped.

"I just found them here on the floor," she said sweetly while handing over the cards. "They must've fallen out of your bag."

"Cut the crap, Hilda," I hissed in a low voice. "I know who you are, and I know what you write."

In the blink of an eye, her butter-wouldn't-melt-in-her-mouth expression was gone, replaced by a frank gaze and a jaded smirk.

"I know a little something about you too, Jill Cooksey," she murmured pointing at my question cards. "Good luck with the interview."

And with a wink, she turned on her heel and went to sit back down. Not for the first time I wondered if all people from Texas were crazy. I also wondered if I hadn't overplayed my hand.

I gave my note cards to Padma who was now miked up. She went to sit in the armchair on the set and quickly reviewed the questions. Larry took his place behind one of the cameras. The blond production assistant took up position behind the second camera, while the small brunette donned a headset and stood between the two cameras to act as the floor director.

"We're on in sixty seconds," she called out.

"Thirty seconds"

"In five, four, three..."

She gave Padma the cue, and the last interview of my career began.

CHAPTER 29

"The murder of starlet Amber O'Neil shocked the nation and left countless fans in mourning," began Padma addressing the camera. "But no group of people has been more affected by the tragedy than O'Neil's costars Juliet Scott and Branch Matheson and the CEO of Eshellon cosmetics, Hoss Buckworth, who is joined today by his son Dustin Buckworth and Meredith Hopkins, the creator of their newest fragrance, Fall Fantasy, which has become an unlikely center of the investigation. Branch, I'd like to begin with you. Having dated Amber for close to a year as well as working with her, you perhaps knew her better than anyone. How are you holding up?"

"It's been very hard," said Branch. "I'm just taking it day by day."

"What would you like the world to know about Amber?"

"I'd like them to know that she was a fun-loving girl with a zest for life. She had a big heart."

"She broke yours, didn't she?"

The question took him by surprise.

"We ended our relationship mutually, but we remained good friends up until her death."

"Didn't she leave you for Hoss Buckworth?"

"That's…no…we left each other. What does this have to…"

"Then why did you feel the need to go digging around in her past?"

"I don't know what you mean, and I'm pretty sure I'm offended by that question."

"Ian O'Neil, the former guardian of Topaz O'Leary, also known as Amber O'Neil, has reported to police that you were the only person he ever told about Amber's past as a stripper. You went to see him about a year ago, right after Amber dumped you."

"He…I…I was angry. Look, this is no one's business but mine."

"Then why did you tell Hilda Griffith of the *Dallas Sentinel*? Surely if this was something you wanted to be kept private, you wouldn't have told an investigative journalist."

Branch glared at Hilda. I looked over at her and saw three people who should have been out sightseeing sitting behind her. Mama made a little wave.

"I was hurt," continued Branch. "I wanted her to come back."

"You thought that if Hoss Buckworth found out about Amber's unsavory past, he might dump her, and you could catch her on the rebound. Is that it?"

Branch nodded and buried his face in his hands.

"Only Hilda Griffith was not interested in having her byline attached to a story worthier of the tabloids," finished Padma.

"Oh, she was interested," trumpeted Branch snapping back to attention. "She's very protective of Hoss Buckworth. I saw the story she wrote when Shelley Buckworth died. I knew I had the right person."

"So why didn't she publish it?"

"She didn't need to. Hoss broke it off with Amber."

"But Amber didn't come running back to you, did she? That must have made you angry."

"Furious," he replied and then considered what he'd just said. "Hey, wait a minute, I didn't kill Amber!"

"No one said you did. I'm trying to uncover how a complex woman like Amber impacted the people in her life."

Padma turned to Hoss. He looked scared.

"Hoss, did you know Amber had been a stripper when you dumped her?"

"Uh, no, I didn't. Amber and I spent some time together, but we were never serious. Then I met Juliet, and that was all she wrote."

"Do you think the person who murdered Amber was the same person who tampered with the perfume that almost killed street performer Frank Ferguson yesterday?"

"Yes, I do. I believe someone has a grudge against me or Eshellon cosmetics."

"Do you think it could be the same person who kidnapped your son ten years ago and held him for ransom?"

"Uh, no…that is…it could be."

"So you believe the kidnapper and the murderer could be one and the same, but didn't your son Dustin in fact orchestrate his own kidnapping?"

Stunned silence. No one moved, especially Dustin.

"That was a cry for help." Hoss laid his hand on his son's knee. "Dustin had lost his mother, and I was grieving her too."

Dustin wheeled on Meredith.

"You told him?"

"I didn't."

Hoss shot Meredith a look, but she couldn't meet his gaze. Padma rolled on.

"So you don't believe that Dustin killed Amber O'Neil?"

"Of course not!" bellowed Hoss.

"Even though he was in New York the night she died?"

"No, he wasn't. He was in Dallas." Hoss turned imploring eyes on Dustin. "You were in Dallas."

"A photo appeared in last Friday's *New York Gazette* of Dustin Buckworth at a club called Rasta in the East Village," said Padma. "You were here visiting your business partner Daniel Winston with whom you own the popular surfboard company Buckboards, were you not?"

"You have a surfboard company?" croaked Hoss.

Padma kept going.

"You used the money collected during your faked kidnapping to fund the venture, true or false?"

A deer in the headlights, Dustin could only nod.

Hoss opened and closed his mouth several times, but no sounds came out.

"Now back to the night Amber was murdered," continued Padma. "Cell phone video of the altercation between Amber O'Neil and Juliet Scott was leaked to the *New York Gazette*. That video message has been traced by authorities to a cell phone registered to Dustin Buckworth. Do you have any comment, Dustin?"

Dustin had no comment. I wasn't sure he could draw breath to speak.

Now it was Meredith's turn to be outraged.

"You tried to sabotage Fall Fantasy! Dustin, how could you?"

"Because I hate you, you stinking cow!" Evidently, he could.

"But Dustin, you can't mean that?"

"Why not? Because you're my mother? My lover? Well, you're neither!"

"Saints preserve us!" whispered Shirley Scott. But Dustin was just getting started.

"You never could replace my mother, and you're not my

lover. You thought you could play on both teams. Father and son, right?'

Juliet, who had been watching the exchange like a rapt spectator, snapped into participant mode.

"You slept with Meredith?" she rounded on Hoss. "When?"

That had Dud Scott jumping to his feet, but his wife and my mother had the good sense to pull him back into his seat.

"The night of the launch. We'd been fighting. I was going to tell you." Hoss tried to take her hand.

"Don't touch me!"

"Baby, I was stinking drunk! I don't even remember doing it. She helped me to bed, and then we woke up together. I was not in my right mind!"

"Were you in your right mind when you slept with her after Mom died?" spat Dustin.

This was news to me!

"I don't have to explain that to you, Dustin. You don't know what it's like to lose a wife."

"I know what it's like to lose the person you love the most to someone else!" cried Dustin, his eyes glued to Juliet's face.

"So do I!" Branch yelled and looked squarely at Hoss.

Meredith was looking directly at me, eyes wide with horror at the morning show interview that had morphed into a trashy afternoon talk show. The only thing missing was a paternity test.

I shrugged my shoulders helplessly at Meredith.

"We're on the air," I mouthed silently.

Dustin, who had been practically silent for days, had been loosed, and he had a lot to say. While Dustin exorcised his demons, my phone began to vibrate in my pocket. I pulled it out and almost dropped it when I saw the caller ID. It was Tanya! I pressed talk while I hastily walked to the other side of the suite.

"Hello?" I asked.

"Jill! Jill, is that you?"

It was Tanya all right.

"Where the devil have you been?" I whispered furiously.

"Jill, I'm in so much trouble."

"No kidding! Where are you?"

"I'm not saying, not yet. Jill, the police are looking for me. My picture is in the papers. Even here."

I hadn't seen the morning papers. Donato must have stepped up the search for Tanya. But why was she calling me? She hated my guts.

"I tried to call Pamela, but she didn't pick up."

Pamela probably didn't want to get involved. And Tanya was supposed to be her friend.

"Jill, I didn't know I was doing anything wrong."

Tanya was near hysterics. I would have to tread carefully.

"Of course you didn't, Tanya. Now what did you do?"

I looked over at the interview. Dustin seemed to have finished his tirade because Meredith was talking about Fall Fantasy, probably trying in vain to save the interview. When it was all over, I knew Padma Singh was going to be eviscerated.

Back on the phone, Tanya was weeping.

"Tanya, tell me what happened. You know I'll understand."

"I stole her shoe," Tanya whispered. "And now everyone thinks I murdered Amber O'Neil."

"No one thinks that, Tanya," I lied. Personally, I thought murder called for more effort than Tanya wanted to expend, but the police didn't know her the way I did. I kept that to myself.

"Why, Tanya?" I prompted. She was crying quietly now, and I was afraid she would hang up. I looked back at the interview. Still going.

"I thought it was just a perverted fan with a foot fetish," she finally replied. "I didn't know it was a murderer."

"Who?" I said a little too loudly. In unison, the spectators looked over their shoulders at me. I smiled to reassure them.

"That's fine, Aunt Myrtle," I said. Everyone turned back around except my mother who looked at me suspiciously. I hadn't talked to Aunt Myrtle in two years, and she knew it.

"Huh?" muttered a confused Tanya.

"Nothing Tanya," I whispered. "To whom did you give the shoe?"

"I don't know!" Punctuated by sobs, sniffles, and hiccups, Tanya explained that she had received a text message offering twenty-five thousand dollars for a shoe worn by Juliet Scott at the Fall Fantasy launch. It was signed Julietfan01, but the number was blocked.

How odd. How could Julietfan01 know that Tanya would be in a position to steal Juliet's shoe?

The next day, Julietfan01 had texted her again with instructions. She was to put the shoe in a paper sack and leave it in a boxwood hedge at the entrance to Conservatory Garden after the launch. The twenty-five thousand dollars would be waiting for her there in another sack. All she had to do was swap sacks.

The day after that, Julietfan01 had sent the last text message: "We're counting on you."

We? Creepy. Kind of like Big Brother.

"The money was there in the bushes, just like they said. I promise I didn't know what would happen." Fresh sobs filled my ear.

While Tanya cried and the Buckworths argued, I scanned the suite and soon found what I was looking for. In plain view on the dining room table was Dustin's phone along with several others left behind when Padma asked everyone to silence them.

"Tanya," I whispered. "You still there?"

"Yes," she whimpered.

"It's going to be all right. If you still have the messages, you can show them to the police. You still have them, right?"

"Yeah! Do you think they'll believe me?"

"Absolutely," I replied, trying to sound upbeat while maintaining a whisper. "Now I need you to do something for me." I had to make it very clear. Tanya and directions were like oil and water. "I need you to hang up now, but keep your phone on and sit tight. I will call you again in a few minutes."

I slipped my own phone into my pocket and sidled casually over to the dining room table. I pretended to pour myself a cup of coffee but turned my back on the interview to hide my actions. A glance over my shoulder told me I needn't have worried. Dustin was holding forth again. I snatched up his phone, grateful yet again that he had no patience with passcodes, and opened his sent text messages. Dustin was a prolific texter, and I had to scroll back pretty far to get to the text messages sent by Julietfan01 over a week ago. Finally, I found one, then another. But where was the third? Frantically, I searched for text number three, the last one sent to Tanya, but it wasn't there.

What had the final message said? "We're counting on you." Goosebumps prickled my arms as I realized that Dustin hadn't acted alone. "We" was not a figure of speech. But who was Dustin working with? Who was the second murderer?

I slid a napkin over Dustin's phone to hide it and turned to survey the room. Juliet, Hoss, Meredith, Branch, and Dustin—they were currently at each other's throats on national television. I couldn't see how any of them could be partners in crime.

Yet calmly watching the proceedings from a gilt chair was a person that I could easily imagine working with Dustin to take out Amber O'Neil, someone who had known about her sordid past. I turned back to the table. There, next to a coffee cup, was a sparkly flip phone covered in crystals forming the flag of the

Lone Star State. So close to the truth, I was shaking, and my hands were sweaty. I could barely hold on to the crystal-encrusted phone much less operate it. I said a silent prayer that the phone would be unlocked and another prayer of thanks when it was. It was harder to scroll through text messages on a flip phone, and with slippery fingers and thumbs, it seemed to take forever. But at long last, I was looking at the third text message. I had all the evidence I needed.

Before I could stop myself, I was leaping across the room toward the set, phones in hand. I was almost there when I tripped over an ottoman, went flying, and landed at the feet of Meredith, Branch, and Dustin. Padma Singh, interrupted in mid-question, was frozen with her mouth open. Everyone else looked at me like I was crazy. I didn't care. I pointed a phone at the heir to the Buckworth fortune.

"You murdered Amber O'Neil!" I cried.

In fumbling with Hilda's phone, I must have unmuted it because at that moment *The Yellow Rose of Texas* filled the room. I pointed accusingly at her too.

"And so did you!"

CHAPTER 30

"Jill, are you out of your mind?" cried Hoss as he leaped to his feet. He sat back down when he saw that Mama, Dud, and Shirley had all drawn their weapons on Dustin and Hilda. At the sight of her mother wielding a Glock, Juliet slumped over in a dead faint that distracted Hoss for the moment.

"This is absurd!" shouted Hilda Griffith from the peanut gallery.

"You just stay cool, or I'll have to pull out the cuffs," ordered Shirley.

"We're on national television," hissed Meredith who had gone white around the mouth.

I didn't care. I hauled myself to my feet with as much dignity as I could muster considering my skirt was torn, my stockings were in shreds, and everyone in the room had seen my underwear.

"The two of you are in cahoots and I can prove it," I proclaimed. "I just got off the phone with Tanya who was instructed via text messages to steal Juliet's shoe in exchange for twenty-five thousand dollars. Those text messages came from your phones."

"Why would I want Juliet's shoe? And why on earth would I send a message like that from my own phone?" sputtered Hilda. "How stupid do you think I am?"

"Yeah!" chimed in Dustin. My mother moved in closer with her gun, and he shut up. I rounded on Hilda.

"You wanted to save Hoss from the women you saw as gold diggers. In fact, you wanted him for yourself. So you enlisted Dustin, knowing he was bitter over his father taking up with the woman he loved. You both hated Amber because you thought she was trashy, so you didn't care if she died. If you framed Juliet for the murder, then both women would be out of the picture, Dustin's inheritance would be secured, and you could move in on Hoss. Sending messages from your phones was your one mistake," I replied smugly. "All criminals make a mistake. That's how they get caught."

"There's no such thing as the perfect crime," announced my mother. "Criminal Justice 101."

"Mike, call Donato," I directed.

"Already done," said Mike as he pocketed his phone.

"Jill, this is preposterous," sputtered Hoss. Juliet had regained consciousness, and Hoss was no longer distracted.

"I know this is painful, Hoss," I assured him. "But I can prove it."

With a few clicks, I opened Dustin's sent messages folder.

"First message, 11:30 p.m., Monday, September 14."

I scrolled some more.

"Second message, 11:52 p.m., Tuesday, September 15."

Then I opened Hilda's phone.

"Third message, 7:30 p.m., Wednesday, September 16."

When I showed Hoss the messages, his face fell.

"It can't be true," he muttered.

Dustin was wild-eyed with panic.

"It's not true," he cried. "I was in bed asleep! How could I send a text message? What was I doing? Sleep texting?"

"I was at a DAR meeting!" shouted Hilda.

"Right!" I sneered at both of them. "And I suppose you have people who can verify your stories?"

"Yeah," they said in unison. "Meredith."

Hmm.

"Right motive, Jill. Wrong suspect." Hilda shook her head at me like a mother who didn't know what to do with an errant child.

"But you lured Amber to the alley behind the hotel using blackmail over her stripper past," I persisted. "You were the only person other than Branch who knew about Topaz O'Leary."

"No, Jill, I wasn't."

Slow. You're really slow, Jill.

Hilda might have shared her knowledge of Topaz with Meredith Hopkins. They were friends, after all, and both fiercely protective of Hoss Buckworth. Still, I couldn't be sure. Hilda and Dustin might have planned all along to try to frame Meredith for the murder. But if Meredith was being framed, why wasn't she protesting her innocence?

I looked around.

That was easy to explain. Meredith had vanished.

It took only a few seconds to determine that Meredith had left the penthouse. As there was only one elevator leading to it and Meredith was in it, we would have to wait to pursue her. Meanwhile, I called the concierge desk and apprised Jean-Paul of the situation. His response summed it up perfectly: *Merde.*

"The police are on their way," I told him. "Just try to keep her from leaving the hotel."

"What am I supposed to do? Tackle her?" he sneered. Was capturing murderers and preventing them from killing again beneath his dignity?

"Yes, tackle her!"

With a *humph*, he rang off.

It seemed like it took forever for the elevator to come, but Mike made good use of that time persuading the three Virginians to put their guns away.

When it finally came, we all piled on: Hoss, Juliet, Hilda, Dustin, Branch, Mike, Kate, me, Padma, the makeup artist, the hairdresser, the production assistants, and Larry the cameraman. When the alarm sounded from too much weight, we all looked at Larry who was the biggest person there.

"I'll take the stairs," he muttered.

He got off, but the alarm kept going. The makeup artist got off too, and the elevator doors closed.

When we got to the lobby, Meredith was nowhere in sight, but I saw Jean-Paul standing guard at one of the side entrances. I ran over to him.

"Any sign of her?"

"I saw her get off the elevator. She started to come this way, but then she spotted me and took off in the other direction. Philippe is guarding the other side entrance, and I put Marcel on the Lexington Avenue entrance."

There was no way Meredith was going out the front entrance on Park Avenue because the Amber shrine was still covering it. With any luck, she was still in the hotel.

"Let's split up, everyone. If you see her, take her down."

I saw my mother reach for her gun.

"Don't kill her!" I clarified. "Just tackle her and start yelling for help."

Mike headed for the service areas of the hotel as he was familiar with them. I sent the Virginians to the Peacock Alley restaurant because I didn't think they could do too much harm there. Hoss and Juliet went to check out the bar, big surprise. The rest of us fanned out.

I headed for the other side entrance to check with Philippe, a desk clerk with concierge aspirations. He hadn't seen Meredith. Next, I made my way toward the Lexington Avenue entrance passing the wedding salon and the beauty salon.

The wedding salon was where brides sat down with a Waldorf special events coordinator to spend their parents' retirement funds on weddings fit for royalty. The salon was small, and a glance showed me Meredith wasn't hiding among the models of wedding cakes and the sample place settings and flower arrangements.

Next door, the beauty salon was large with a reception desk, four stylist stations, a row of sinks, two manicure stations, two pedicure chairs, and a row of hairdryers. The back wall was lined with storage closets with louvered doors. The place was empty except for a woman in a pink smock sitting under a dryer, not surprising for early on a Saturday morning. I started to ask her if she had seen anyone, but the big hairdryer was like a sensory deprivation tank.

I looked behind the reception desk. No Meredith. I walked over to the first storage closet and opened the door. It was full of towels and smocks but no psycho-killers. The next closet was locked, and I looked around for a key but didn't see one. I was headed for the next closet when I heard a bump from inside. I tried the handle again but the lock was strong.

"Let me handle this," said my mom out of nowhere. I jumped four feet.

"Jesus, Mama!" I cried.

"Don't blaspheme," she said and shot the lock off.

A small part of my brain registered alarm that my mother had just discharged a firearm in a hotel and that she was probably going to jail, but the majority of my brain was occupied with the beautician who was bound and gagged on the floor of the closet.

My mother dropped to her knees to untie the woman, but I

gently nudged her aside. Okay not so gently, but my adrenaline was raging.

"Put your gun away!" I ordered.

She did so, glaring at me in a way that let me know I'd be baking my own birthday cakes from now on. Gun holstered, she bodychecked me and took over rescuing the stylist.

I didn't care because just then I remembered the lady under the dryer. I turned to question her, but she was gone.

Was she scared off by the gunshot, or was she a murderer? All of the above.

I took off and exited the salon just in time to see a bit of pink smock rounding the corner and headed for the main part of the lobby. Abandoning my high heels for bare feet, I headed off in hot pursuit. I raced past the reception desks and concierge desk, saw Meredith make a quick turn at the iconic bronze clock at the lobby's center, and followed suit. Out of the corner of my eye, I saw Mike and members of the Posse converging as well.

Meredith led us out of the main lobby into the elegant, feminine foyer by the stairs leading to the Park Avenue entrance. She was cornered, standing in the center of the mosaic floor looking wildly about her for an avenue of escape. Mike, my mother, the Posse, Hector, and I blocked the way back to the main lobby. Hoss, Juliet, Hilda, Dustin, Vinny, and Antoinette blocked the stairs on either side of the foyer that led up to the cocktail terrace. The only way out was the front entrance, and it was barricaded by the Amber shrine and protestors.

"Give up, Meredith!" I ordered.

Her response was to spit in my general direction and bolt down the stairs to the Park Avenue entrance. She took the revolving door going about thirty miles per hour with all of us hard on her heels. With that much speed, she managed to dislodge enough of the shrine to make it out.

When I squeezed through a couple of seconds later, the first thing I saw was fire. A lot of fire. Then I felt it on my bare feet and jumped about three yards.

Meredith had overturned several candles, proving once again that flames and stuffed animals don't mix. In a chain reaction worthy of a Hollywood action film, fluffy critters were spontaneously combusting right, left, and center. Most of the mourners were looking on aghast at the carnage, and the protestors had momentarily ceased their calls for justice, distracted by the dancing flames and flying sparks.

I scanned the crowd for Meredith and spotted her slowly making her way through the masses but meeting little resistance as all attention was on the conflagration. She was headed for the street and probably a taxi.

I wrenched a megaphone out of a protestor's hand.

"Hey, that's mine," he whined. I ignored him.

"Do you want justice for Amber?" I cried through the megaphone.

"Yeah!" replied the protestors and the mourners who were starting to feel indignant over the desecration of their shrine.

"Amber's murderer is getting away!" I pointed at Meredith. "Stop her!"

It took only a moment for the crowd to focus and get organized. Amid shouts and screams, I watched as Meredith was lifted high in the air and, borne on the arms of Amber's most devoted fans, was forcibly crowd surfed back toward the hotel to be deposited with a thud at my feet.

Her clothes were in shreds, some of her hair was gone, and she was babbling incoherently. In retrospect, it might not have been the best decision to loose an enraged mob on her, but it all worked out okay in the end.

"Here's your murderer," I announced triumphantly to Detective Donato who had arrived during the melee. For some reason, he didn't look as pleased as I'd expected.

CHAPTER 31

Our moment of triumph was short-lived as the fire department arrived to deal with the flames. Most of the stuffed kitties had burned themselves out, but they still had to evacuate the entire hotel as a precaution. In the hustle and bustle, I caught a glimpse of a deathly pale Jean-Paul wringing his hands. I had a feeling he wouldn't be asking me out again anytime soon.

A couple of hours later, we were back in the Buckworths' suite. The police were still taking statements from all of us, including Tanya by phone, and trying to make sense of it all, and so were we. Hilda helped to fill in the missing pieces.

"About a year ago, when Hoss was still dating Amber," began Hilda, "Branch came to me with the Amber-Topaz story."

"But how did you find out about Topaz?" Kate asked Branch.

He explained that after Amber had broken his heart, he had been consumed with finding out why.

A billion dollars, that's why, I thought but kept it to myself.

Amber had always refused to talk about her past except to

say that she came from New York. He found a matchbook from O'Leary's Pub at her house one day and asked her about it, but she claimed to have no idea where it had come from. After they broke up, the matchbook and O'Leary's Pub had stuck in his mind. On a break from shooting his mountain man movie, Branch had flown to New York to do a little digging.

When he found out she'd been a stripper, he thought he could use her past to break up her relationship with Hoss and get her back. He wanted to leak the info to the Dallas papers, and in doing research, he stumbled across investigative reporter Hilda Griffith. After reading the obituary she wrote for Shelley Buckworth, Branch thought she would be sympathetic and interested.

Hilda took up the story from there.

"I wouldn't have run the story," she insisted, and I tended to believe her. Hilda's stuff was about corruption and betrayal of the public trust, not tabloid fodder like people taking their clothes off for money. But she had passed the information on to Meredith.

"I was starting to have suspicions about her," said Hilda. "And I sort of wanted to see what she would do with it. Of course, right afterwards Juliet came along and Amber was history, so Meredith didn't have to do anything with the knowledge except sit on it."

With the arrival of Juliet, Meredith's focus had shifted. Discovering Dustin's obsession with the actress, she had zeroed in on him.

"Meredith came to me and told me that she knew I was hurting," said Dustin while he stared at his shoes. "She also told me that she knew I'd faked the kidnapping but that she completely understood. She said that she cared."

"But we always knew about the kidnapping," said Hoss. "It was a cry for help. We didn't involve the authorities."

"She said no one else knew," explained Dustin, "and that she would keep my secret. We began, er, a relationship. Then I told her about Buckboards."

"And you've been running this surfboard company for how long?" asked Hoss.

"Three years," admitted Dustin.

"Didn't you ever wonder what had happened to the ransom money?" I asked Hoss.

"It didn't matter to me," he said with a shrug. "It was only fifty thousand dollars."

Only fifty thousand dollars? Unbelievable.

Eventually, Dustin's feelings for Meredith had started to cool, but now she knew all his secrets. He didn't want to hurt her by ending the affair, and he really didn't want her pissed off and running to his father. So the affair continued, and Meredith continued to feed Dustin's anger over Juliet and his dad.

"Did she ever let anything slip about her plan to frame Juliet for Amber's murder?" asked my mother. "Does anything jump out at you in retrospect?"

"No," Dustin shook his head. "She did at one point suggest breaking Dad and Juliet up by making it look like Juliet and I were having an affair. At first, she suggested it as a joke. Then she kept bringing it up, but I couldn't do something like that."

But you could fake your own kidnapping and take the money, I thought but, as usual, kept quiet.

"I guess she figured out she could break them up by making it look like she'd had an affair with Hoss," I said instead. After more questioning by Donato, Hoss had revealed that he had no recollection of the night Amber was murdered. He'd believed Meredith when she told him they'd slept together, and her naked presence in his bed the next morning had been pretty convincing. In reality, nothing might have happened between them, especially as Meredith had left in the middle of the night to meet Amber. That realization had done much to repair relations with Juliet who was now seated next to him holding his hand.

"Why was Amber in town?" Mike asked while furiously scribbling in a notepad. "I can't believe it was a coincidence."

"Amber told me she was coming into town," said Branch. "She hinted that there were going to be some changes at Eshellon. She was elated when I last spoke to her."

"So that's why you've been hanging around," said Mama.

"Partially. That's why I initially showed up at Waverly Communications the day after the funeral," he clarified. "But when I saw Hilda there, I stuck around."

"So maybe Meredith lured her into town with the promise that she would replace Juliet at the last minute," I suggested.

"That would explain her showing up in a rage," said Mike. "She was probably pissed off when it didn't happen. Do you think that was part of Meredith's plan?"

It was hard to say. Meredith had seemed genuinely surprised when Amber showed up at the launch. I didn't think we would get all the answers to our questions unless Meredith coughed up to the police.

I had a thought.

"Dustin, why were you spying on the launch?"

He turned beet red, and I figured he'd been there to spy on Juliet and torture himself further. I put him out of his misery.

"I mean, why did you leak the video to the media?"

He relaxed a little, fading from magenta to bubble gum pink.

"I was just so pissed off at everybody, especially Meredith."

"You hated her because she knew your secrets, because you felt trapped in the relationship?" prompted Shirley. I was seeing a whole new side of my nearest and dearest.

"Because she murdered my mother," he said simply.

Stunned silence prevailed, broken at last by Hoss.

"You can't know that, Dustin," he said quietly.

"No, he can't," said Hilda with iron in her voice. "Padma, or whatever your name is, what was the last question on those cards?"

Anupa reached for the note cards she had left on the coffee table and rifled through them.

"Why didn't you agree to an autopsy after your wife died unexpectedly?" she said.

"I didn't write that question," I cried.

"No, I did," said Hilda. She turned to Hoss.

"Why didn't you have an autopsy on Shelley after she died? She was supposed to live!" Hilda's voice shook just a little, and Hoss's eyes filled with tears.

"We couldn't put Shelley through an autopsy. Her little body had been through so much. We couldn't do it to her."

"Who's we?" Hilda asked softly. "Who helped you make that decision?"

"Meredith," he whispered and then put his head in his hands and cried like a baby. As much to distract us as to elaborate, Hilda explained how her suspicions had been aroused.

"Meredith seemed devastated by the loss of Shelley the way we all were. I have to hand it to her. She was subtle and very patient. She didn't rush in to fill the void that Shelley left behind."

Meredith started to contribute ideas for products very slowly—a shade of lipstick here, a packaging concept there.

"Then one day," said Hilda, "there she was calling the shots for the most part. It took years for her to get there, so no one noticed."

"Except you," I added.

She smiled wryly.

"Shelley was my best friend. Had she lived, Meredith never would have had much input into the product line. Then when I figured out she and Dustin were involved..."

"Meredith wanted a piece of the company," interjected

Mike. "The only way she could get that was by marrying a Buckworth."

Hilda nodded.

"As soon as I figured it out, I went to Dustin." The two of them had been working together to build a case ever since.

"At some point, Meredith must have figured out that you knew," I said. "That's why she tried to frame you by using your phones to contact Tanya."

"That or we were just the easiest targets," said Hilda.

Tanya had been an easy target, that was certain. Meredith couldn't have picked anyone more susceptible to her offer. Twenty-five thousand dollars could buy a lot of ugly outfits and expensive dinners. It could also buy one heck of a trip to someplace tropical. I couldn't wait for Tanya to get back to find out where she had fled. Wait a minute. Was I really looking forward to Tanya's return?

"What I don't get," said Mike bringing me back to reality, "is why Meredith targeted you, Jill. Was it a panicked move of desperation?"

I looked at everyone except Hoss and Mike.

"I don't think my attack had anything to do with this case," I said firmly. "I think it was just a thief who got scared off before he could steal anything. My landlady is pretty formidable." I mustered a laugh. Out of the corner of my eye, I saw Hoss's shoulders relax. I glanced over at Mike to see him staring at me thoughtfully. I looked at my mother and saw blatant disbelief. Curse my honest face!

"I think Meredith was desperate when she tried to poison Jackie Jordan," I rolled on smoothly. "It would be easy for someone who works around laboratories to order sodium cyanide without raising suspicions, and it was even easier for Meredith to swap out the bottles when I wasn't looking. But who would really believe that Juliet would try to kill someone on national television? It's too absurd. I think at that point Meredith was starting to lose it."

"And with a criminal so unbalanced on the loose, it's a good thing we were here," added my mother with a gentle pat of the firearm under her pant leg. That she still possessed the gun (and was not currently in the hoosegow) was down to the rescued hairstylist who had promised not to tell who fired the shot in the Waldorf.

"Why were you here?" I asked the Virginians. "You were supposed to be safely sightseeing this morning."

"We were watching *Wake the Nation*," said Dud. "But when they didn't mention Juliet, we thought something must be up."

"We came to investigate," said Shirley as she popped a breath mint into her mouth and then offered them around.

"Wait a minute," said Dustin. "We weren't on television?"

PR was not Dustin's area. It was a good thing he had surfboards to fall back on.

"Have you ever seen an interview last twenty minutes without ever going to a commercial break?" asked Anupa with a laugh.

"So none of it was on TV?" asked Hoss.

I shook my head. He let out a huge sigh that turned into a belly laugh.

"What a relief!"

"It was all Jill's idea," put in Kate loyally. She went on to explain how I'd called an emergency meeting with the Posse and Mike the night before after canceling the *Wake the Nation* appearance. Anupa had volunteered to play reporter Padma while Liz and Surya had volunteered to be crew. Mike got Vinny to get us cameras and lights and to be Larry the cameraman, and he in turn had included Antoinette who, as it turned out, was a real makeup artist. To reinforce our numbers and add even more believability, I had also called on Hector to play Nick the hairdresser.

"But why go to all that trouble?" asked Juliet.

"On national television," I explained, "no one was going to run away, even when confronted with some unpleasant secrets. I figured the only way to get the killer to reveal himself, or herself as it turned out, would be to reveal everything I'd learned, or at least guessed, so far."

And it had worked, I thought smugly. They had all vomited their private lives and feelings like guests on an afternoon talk show.

"So your name isn't Padma?" Dustin asked Anupa.

"It is when I'm giving fake phone numbers to men I don't want to date," she replied with a smile.

"Will you tell me your real name?" he persisted. "And will you attach your phone number to it?"

Murder. Mayhem. It didn't matter. The world would keep turning.

CHAPTER 32

Once the police were finished with all of us, Hoss ordered a feast for the ages, and we celebrated what we hoped was the end of this crazy chapter in our lives.

At some point in the evening, I found myself alone with Hoss, and a private conversation followed that ensured that Waverly Communications would retain the Eshellon account for many years to come. All is fair in love and public relations, and I had decided that I wasn't done with PR just yet. In fact, I was feeling pretty good about myself. From crazy talent bookers to crazed murderers, I had come up against some formidable foes and won...mostly.

Jill Cooksey had not failed.

It had been a wild ride, but I felt alive. I decided that I agreed with my mother. Anything else, anywhere else, would have me bored to tears.

By ten I was bushed, but the party was still raging. Despite Hoss's invitation to put us all up at the Waldorf that night, I just wanted to go home. I said my goodbyes, arranged to meet my mom for church and pedicures the next morning, and headed for the Buckworth limo that was waiting to drive me home.

As the chauffeur opened the door for me, I heard someone calling my name. Mike came rushing up jacket in hand.

"I'll see you home if that's okay." He gave me a warm look that sent my stomach on a roller-coaster ride.

I nodded and we climbed into the car.

The door had barely shut when I was being pulled into a crushing embrace and Mike's lips locked onto mine ferociously. Somewhere along the way, my mind registered the sound of the privacy barrier rising into place. It was several minutes before anyone spoke.

"Do you know how sexy you look when you're running barefoot after murderers?" Mike said when our lips were momentarily disentangled.

"And do you know," he continued, "just how scared I was that something was going to happen to you?"

My heart stopped for a moment. Unexpected emotional intimacy! Mike's eyes bored into mine, and I couldn't, wouldn't look away. He smoothed the hair away from my face and tucked it gently behind my ears. Then, taking my face in his hands, he kissed me again so softly that my entire body liquefied, but I didn't care. I never wanted to be solid again.

I was just shy of actually turning to vapor when I was brought unwillingly back to a solid state by a loud *ker-clunk*! The limo coasted to a stop accompanied by a symphony of horns as cars swerved to avoid us. I rolled one of the tinted windows down and peered out. We were broken down on the upper level of the Queensboro Bridge.

Soon the privacy barrier came down.

"Sorry, folks," said the driver. "She's dead. I called the company, and they're sending another car. Should be here in about thirty minutes."

I looked at Mike. He smiled back.

"Let me," he said and pulled out his phone.

Exactly five minutes later, the blare of *La Cucaracha*

heralded the arrival of our chariot. Soon we were snuggled together on the orange velour backseat. With Mike's arm around me, his soft breath in my ear, and the sweet scent of air freshener in my nose, all felt right with the world. Jorge hit the gas, and we rocketed into the night.

ACKNOWLEDGMENTS

This book wouldn't have been possible without the love and support of many people. I offer my heartfelt thanks to all of them. To Matthew for believing that I am the best writer in the world. To my parents for buying me all those books and telling me I could be anything. To Melissa without whose faith and constant cheerleading I would never have finished this journey. To Thamesey, who helped with the original research. To Christine and Samantha, the best beta readers ever. To my friends and family who liked, subscribed, and offered words of encouragement. To everyone who has had to hear about this book over the last twenty years, especially my Heavenly Father, who has probably heard about it the most. Many thanks and much love!

Psalms 37:5

ABOUT THE AUTHOR

Lesley St. James began her career in film and television before moving to public relations and then to education. A devoted, lifelong reader of mysteries, she always knew the kind of books she would write. When she's not writing or teaching writing, Lesley enjoys traveling, movies, and genealogy. She resides in Virginia with her husband, Matthew.

facebook.com/LesleyStJames

instagram.com/lesleyst.james

www.ingramcontent.com/pod-product-compliance
Lightning Source LLC
Chambersburg PA
CBHW021137110726
47900CB00002B/386